★

Lynn Woo and Bill Weir were sitting in the beached boat about to become engrossed in a discussion of the merits of restricting boat traffic in the back bays to protect the endangered manatee. Then they heard it. It was an eerie, bloodcurdling sound that to Lynn seemed like the wailing of an injured animal. It didn't stop—just kept repeating itself like a siren.

Lynn and Bill looked at each other for a couple of beats. Weir said, "My God, that's Fran."

They scrambled out of the beached boat and sprinted toward the sound. In a clearing they found Fran Weir standing with her hands on either side of her face, wailing that eerie sound they'd heard. She was looking up at a very dead Millard Savage, whose naked body was stretched and tied between two red mangrove trees, presumably to make it easier for the buzzards.

Lynn immediately reached for her cell phone to call Truck Kershaw. Bill immediately reached for his still-screaming wife and began leading her back to the boat. They almost made it before she stopped, leaned over and vomited raucously on the beaches of Turtle Bay.

★

That which is not good for the beehive cannot be good for the bees.
—Marcus Aurelius

BOCAMOON

FRANK FOSTER

WORLDWIDE®

TORONTO • NEW YORK • LONDON
AMSTERDAM • PARIS • SYDNEY • HAMBURG
STOCKHOLM • ATHENS • TOKYO • MILAN
MADRID • WARSAW • BUDAPEST • AUCKLAND

For Grumpy, who always wanted to write a book;
And for Frances, who would have devoured this one;
And for Patti, without whose love and encouragement this would never have happened.

BOCA MOON

A Worldwide Mystery/July 2010

First published by Hilliard & Harris.

ISBN-13: 978-0-373-26716-3

Printed in U.S.A.

Acknowledgments

I am blessed to have as dear friends and mentors Stuart Kaminsky and his wife, Enid Perll. Stuart, with over fifty novels published, was the 2006 recipient of the Mystery Writers of America's Grand Master award and Enid is his expert private editor. For a first-time novelist like me to receive personal instruction from a Grand Master (Agatha Christie won the first year and Stephen King is the 2007 winner) and his editor is like an apprentice golfer being able to hang with Tiger Woods. Thank you, dear people.

Another famous writer friend, Winston Groom (Mr. Forrest Gump himself) was kind enough to read the first draft of my first book (not this one) and carefully explain how dreadful it was. I am in Winston's debt for his candor and his insistence that I spend the years it took me to hopefully learn the craft of fiction writing. My original introduction to Winston was through my great friend Martha and I thank her for that and her constant support.

Without the computer technical help of my fine friend and former associate JBS, I simply could not have done this. This was an eyes-only, have-to-kill-you-if-you-tell, secret project for me because if no publisher had ultimately bitten, I could not have stood the embarrassment of failure. My only confidantes were my manuscript-reading immediate family and a precious few others. Among those were some great folks with the Lee County Sheriff's Department who I pray will be pleased with my technical accuracy, former covert CIA officer Chase Brandon and my dear friend Fred whose efforts to plug me into the New York publisher and literary agent scene are recognized here with great appreciation.

Author Note

The village of Boca Grande, and certain back bays, islands and towns surrounding Charlotte Harbor are real places in southwest Florida but are used fictionally in this book. I hope I have described them vividly and accurately.

With the exception of The Governor's Club in Tallahassee, everything in the pages that follow, including names, characters, business establishments and events, are purely the product of the author's imagination or are used fictitiously. Any resemblance to actual persons, living or dead, or to actual places or events is purely coincidental.

ONE

It was almost two weeks since the blackness paid her a visit. She'd been expecting it and this was the night. As it did every time, her last diver's light went out. All she could feel when she reached out her gloved fingers were the limestone walls of the cave. Couldn't even see enough to check her regulator to see how much air was left. But she didn't have to. She knew she was in danger herself; she'd looked for Dave too long. How could he have lost track of their guideline? Panic rose in her throat...

A loud ringing, a new twist to the dream. Then she got it: it was that new alarm clock. Got to get rid of it. As she peeled back the furriness of her nightmare-laden sleep, she realized it wasn't the alarm but the phone. Fumbling for the handset, she saw 6:02 a.m. on the digital clock. Although she usually slept nude, she was drenched in perspiration. Who could this be? Don't have anything to do today. Wanted to sleep in. But at least it sent her nocturnal visitor away. Until the next time.

"Lynn Woo," she mumbled into the handset.

"Lynn, it's Whit. Sorry to call this early, but—"

"Admiral, do you know what time—"

"Any chance you could come over here right away?"

Lynn sat up in bed. There was panic in the voice of Whitman Jenkins IV.

"Whit, what's up?" Lynn asked, using his nickname instead of calling him the usual "Admiral," and not knowing why.

Jenkins' voice tightened. "Just come as quickly as you can. Please?"

"On my way," Lynn said. She hung up, sprang out of bed, and looked in the mirror. No time to put her face on. Just a quick brush of her silky, black hair, then she went to let out her black Labrador retriever, Mullet.

Lynn rarely allowed Mullet to sleep in the room with her because while dreaming he would whap his tail on the floor, keeping Lynn awake. When Rolf was with her and insisted, Lynn made an exception. The dog was working that tail hard when Lynn opened the door to the laundry room—Mullet's room. After Lynn let him outside, she pulled on her usual island garb of shorts and a khaki, outdoorsy-looking shirt. She slipped into her sandals, then hit one more quick lick with the hair brush. No coffee, no nothing, just out to her Honda CR-V, holding the door open for Mullet.

Looking out on the Gulf of Mexico, she saw only blackness, heard only the gentle surf. But that was illusory, because fifty feet above her, the tops of the casuarinas were bowing like ballerinas with each gust from the strong east wind. The bayside water would be sloppy today; she was glad she didn't have to take any tourists shelling, or any divers diving.

As she drove, she stewed about the phone call. She didn't need another crisis, but Jenkins' call sounded like one. She just wanted to enjoy her new island life. The admiral's voice. There was something in it she'd never, ever heard in all these years: fear.

TWO

WHITMAN JENKINS WAS a widower. He and his daughter Muffy, and her husband Millard Savage, had taken a cottage at the southwest Florida resort village of Boca Grande for a month. Islanders, new and old, called it "Boca." The real Boca, they would say, not that urban mess over on the state's east coast named after a rodent.

The village of Boca Grande was on narrow, five mile long, Gasparilla Island—named after the pirate José Gaspar. Until 1957 when a bridge was built, it was only accessible by ferry or train. Originally a fishing village, it was discovered by wealthy industrialists with their private rail cars when a phosphate mining company built a railroad to take advantage of the natural port afforded by seventy-foot-deep Boca Grande Pass. The rich folks built walled, gulf-front estates, a magnificent lodge, and made "Boca" their chic winter retreat.

This month—March—was nearing the end of the social season and was well before Boca Grande's famous tarpon fishing season, but a good choice when one was fed up with cold weather in northern climes.

It was 6:15 a.m. and still dark when Lynn Woo pulled up to Jenkins' rental cottage at the Boca Grande Lodge and parked between two coconut palms, their fronds billowing toward the west. She left Mullet in the CR-V staring at her through the open window and whimpering softly. She walked by a hibiscus hedge, close enough to notice shiny globules of dew on the pink flowers picking up the streetlight reflection.

The two-bedroom, two-bath cottages were blue clapboard like the lodge, all with screened front porches. The admiral's hand was on the inside of the screen door a split second before Lynn reached the step.

"Thanks for coming," he said tightly.

In a moment Lynn was standing in the living room looking at a red-eyed Muffy Savage and her father, a drawn, grave-looking Whitman Jenkins.

The admiral was a little lumpy without being stocky. Accentuated by tortoise-shell horn-rimmed spectacles, his round, weathered, outdoorsman's face frequently erupted into a crinkly, infectious grin. A distinguished, snappy-looking gray-haired man in his mid-sixties, his civilian garb usually included a trademark bow tie and preppy things like seersucker and khaki. This morning he wore a pair of fishing shorts and a Guy Harvey T-shirt with a leaping tarpon on the front.

"It's Millard," said Jenkins before Lynn could speak. It came out *Milluhd* in his accent. Jenkins was born and reared in Montgomery, Alabama and now lived in Birmingham. "He's missing. We rented a seventeen Mako for the month. Millard left in it late yesterday afternoon. He was going to the back bays to take pictures on the mangrove islands in the low evening light. Wanted to stay after dark to try for some shots of wildlife. Dreamed of maybe even lucking into a panther." Jenkins looked at the floor as he spoke rapidly in a military monotone familiar to Lynn from years ago.

"He must have spent the night out there," Lynn said with a shrug as she spread her hands.

"No. He's never done that. Hates camping out."

"He probably just got lost, anchored up, and when the sun comes up good, he'll come trucking right on in here," Lynn said with forced cheer.

The admiral looked straight at Lynn. "He's almost as good with a boat and navigation as he is with a camera. You know that, you've been with us enough," he said dryly.

Now Lynn was concerned. She had spent some time with Millard Savage in the five or so years Savage and Muffy had been married and liked him. Savage worked in Whit Jenkins' food companies, and was an expert naturalist photographer and fervent environmentalist. Lynn admired Millard's talent and his dedication to preserving the world around him. This was not sounding good.

"How about cell or VHF?" Lynn asked.

Jenkins jammed his hands in the pockets of his fishing shorts, looked at the floor again, and shook his head. "'The customer you are trying to reach is out of the area,' or some such message. No answer on the radio, either—tried him on my handheld."

"You call the authorities?"

"Muffy didn't miss him until just before I called you," he said, looking back up at Lynn. The gloom in Jenkins' voice was palpable.

The cottage was old Florida style with white wicker furniture, pine floors with a palm-tree-pattern rug. The walls were adorned with seascape prints and one small Jane Carlson watercolor of the quaint old Fenton's Marina on the island. Lynn picked up the phone on the white wicker desk next to the window.

It was now after 6:30 a.m. and Lee County Sheriff's Deputy Luther "Truck" Kershaw had toweled his six foot six, 290-pound ebony body after his shower. He was pulling on his green-and-white uniform when his phone rang.

"Kershaw," he said after two rings.

"You on or off?" the phone voice asked.

"On or off what? You talking the can, my wife, duty…?" Truck Kershaw responded to the voice, which he recognized as Lynn Woo's.

"Duty."

"Just pulling my uni on. Seven o'clock shift."

"How about starting it here?"

"Where's here, and what's up?"

"Missing person. The real deal. Cabin 6 at the Lodge. Can you come right away?"

After the deputy's affirmative reply, Lynn replaced the receiver and announced, "The law's on the way."

"Sounds like somebody you know," Muffy said, uttering her first sound since Lynn had arrived.

Lynn went to her and the two women embraced for a moment before Lynn gave Muffy the most confident but nurturing look she could muster. "His name is Truck Kershaw. The sheriff's deputy here on the island. One of the best law officers I've ever seen. And he's a good friend of mine. He saved my life once when I got into a little…difficulty."

"His name's Truck?"

Lynn smiled. "High school football nickname. You'll see. Biggest man, black or white, I've ever seen."

"That means he's black."

"Problem?"

"Of course not. I don't care if he's purple, you know that. Want some coffee?"

"Black's fine. No pun intended."

That got a wry smile from Muffy, despite her distress. "How about you, Daddy?" she asked Jenkins, and after he declined, retreated to the small kitchen which adjoined the living room of the cottage.

The coffee on, she came back into the living room, her arms folded across her chest as if she were chilled. She came to Lynn and turned her unmade face to her, brown eyes moving from side to side, welling with moisture. "Lynn, I'm scared," she said, her small, thin lips curling as her composure sagged.

Lynn held her again. "We're going to find him and he's going to be all right. That's the way most of these things end."

WHEN TRUCK KERSHAW ARRIVED he accepted a mug of black coffee from Muffy Savage. It seemed large in her hand, but in Truck's it seemed to shrink to demitasse size. They all sat. Truck took the wicker love seat in a sprawl that caused his two hundred ninety pounds to preclude sharing it with anyone.

Truck Kershaw was fond of saying with his growling, gravelly voice, "I don't have a weight problem, I have a *height* problem." But his girth was deceiving because it was mostly granite-hard, and did nothing to hamper his agility. His complexion was almost coal black and he wore a pencil-thin mustache and kept his hair very short. His brown eyes were usually doleful, but perceptive and vigilant.

Truck Kershaw initially followed the same drill as Lynn: Could he have camped out? You try his cell phone? VHF?

After he got the same answers from the admiral as Lynn, he rolled out his own questions.

Q: What time did he leave?

A: Just at dark.

Q: Anyone else know he was going?

A: No.

Q: What was the condition of the rental boat?

A: Excellent—been running great.

Q: Fuel?

A: Topped it off yesterday afternoon.

Truck scratched his head and continued in his gravelly voice. "Has he been troubled by anything lately? Seem depressed?"

Muffy bristled. "Certainly not."

Truck pressed on with no acknowledgement of Muffy's testy response. "What I'm supposed to do is file a missing persons report, then wait another—whatever the hell it is—twenty-four hours. Now, if he'd gone out in the gulf, that'd be easy. We scramble the Coast Guard, alert ships, that stuff. But there was an incoming tide all night, so unless he went somewhere on his own and sort of forgot to tell you, he's got to be in the back bays somewhere."

Lynn leaned toward Truck Kershaw and said quietly, "Truck, I don't think these folks want to wait twenty-four hours."

"Already figured that. Tell you what. Let's you and me get in your skiff. It draws less water than the sheriff boat. See what we can turn up."

Lynn stood. "Meet you at the dock?"

Jenkins followed the two out the door to the sidewalk. Lynn lingered after Truck pulled away in his patrol car and she locked eyes with her former commanding officer. Lynn had never seen the admiral look this way, even in their toughest situations when they worked together in Naval Intelligence.

"That's my little girl's husband out there," Jenkins said, motioning his head in the direction of the back bays of Charlotte Harbor.

"We'll find him, Admiral," Lynn said with as much resolve as she could muster.

Whitman Jenkins could only manage a tight-lipped, appreciative nod.

THREE

BY HALF PAST SEVEN, Lynn and Truck Kershaw were bumping through a Charlotte Harbor chop at about thirty miles per hour in Lynn's twenty-foot boat, the *Boca Broke*. It was so named because it was the latest and greatest in flats skiffs, and put a major hole in Lynn's bank account. The *Boca Broke* was a teal green Lake 'n' Bay model with the boat name in gold letters and a beautiful flying osprey painted beside it. Under the boat name in small letters was *Capt. Lynn Woo,* her phone number, and the words *Back Bay Nature Tours, Shelling, Diving.*

Lynn was at the helm, Truck beside her, and Mullet in his customary place just behind the casting platform, possibly the driest place on the boat in the chop. Each wave they hit sent a shower of spray cascading over the rain gear they'd donned when they noticed the whitecaps.

"So what do you think?" yelled Truck over the outboard engine noise.

"I think I'm a lot more worried than I let on back there," Lynn yelled back.

"How come you call him Admiral?"

"Because he is one. Retired. My commanding officer many moons ago."

Lynn Woo had been furious when she found out the Navy SEALS did not accept women. She did the next best thing and became a Navy diver, a "hard hat," going to great depths in a dive suit. It was after she worked her way up to second in command of a salvage ship that Whitman Jenkins, then a captain, recruited her to work for him in Naval Intelligence.

Like many of Chinese ethnicity, Lynn was small. Her features did nothing to belie her heritage, but with her milky skin and silky hair, she was somewhere between pretty and drop-dead beautiful, mainly because of an interesting double curl in her upper lip which was accentuated when she smiled. Her 110-pound body was all woman but she was best avoided by anyone looking to inflict physical punishment.

"So what's up with his son-in-law?" asked Truck.

"Good guy," Lynn said. "Works for the admiral. Very capable. That's why I'm worried."

"What kind of work?"

"In charge of OSHA and environmental stuff for the admiral's food companies. Ever eat any Whitman's peanut butter?"

"Hell, yes, man."

"Why do you always call me 'man'?" she asked, giving him a mock scowl.

"Probably because I call just about everybody that. You know. It's a black thing. You probably got some Chinese thing you say but I wouldn't know 'cause I don't speak no Chinese."

Lynn knew the grammar, usually impeccable, was just for effect. A huge wave crashed across the bow, drenching them both. She had forgotten to put the hood up on her rain jacket. So much for the hair, she thought.

"What makes you think I speak any Chinese? I'm a second-generation American, you know." She asked it in her odd combination of a New York twang and a Tallahassee drawl as she licked the salt off her lips.

Ignoring the question, he said, "The other reason I can call you 'man' is I've seen what you can do to one about my size. I remember that Ft. Myers police diver who gave you that half-empty tank—"

"Don't bring that up," she said. "Look, back to the peanut-butter company. It was started by Whitman Jenkins, Jr. Get it? Whitman's peanut butter? The admiral is Whitman the fourth. Lately I understand he's been buying up other food companies."

"He must be rich."

"Better off than you and I, mister," said Lynn, grinning.

"Sounds like ya'll are pretty close, man."

"Yeah. We went through some stuff together I can't talk about." She cut a glance at Truck. "Of course, you and I went through some stuff I don't want to talk about."

"Yes, we did, Cap'n Lynn, yes, we did."

Charlotte Harbor was bordered by a vast, pristine estuary comprised of hundreds of islands of red mangrove and buttonwood trees which form countless small bays, creeks, and bights. The islands were home to pelicans, egrets, raccoons, the occasional frigate bird, and, it seemed to Lynn, perhaps 100 billion singing, swarming mosquitoes. Without local knowledge it was easy to run aground, get lost and have to spend the night out there, or both.

They were heading east into the teeth of the chop, but now Lynn turned north into the entrance to Bull Bay and welcomed the opportunity to hug a lee shoreline with smoother water. She realized that the search was now on, and felt apprehension and dread. This was not what she had in mind. She was trying to reduce stress in her life, not take more on.

She began piloting her skiff along the shorelines in Bull Bay, Turtle Bay, Whidden's Creek, and along Cayo Pelau where most of the old Calusa Indian burial mounds were. They ran the mangrove island shorelines for over two hours. After that they went to the east through the chop around Cape Haze, and north along the windward shoreline for a while. They even came back and explored some of the small creeks in Turtle Bay. They saw nothing but normal back-bay fishing activity.

Lynn's stomach felt like someone had reached through some hole in her abdomen and re-arranged it. It was pushing eleven o'clock. How could she face the admiral? And Muffy? She was getting low on fuel, but she and Truck rode another thirty minutes in some places they had forgotten about.

Nothing.

FOUR

LYNN ARRIVED BACK AT the cottage alone. Whitman Jenkins was sitting behind the white wicker desk. He took one look at Lynn's expression and slumped forward in despair, looking at the floor.

"No good, huh?" he said.

Lynn shook her head. "Burned a tank of fuel riding every shoreline I know. Rode twice in the places where I know there are Indian mounds. Truck Kershaw's organizing a full search with sheriff's personnel for first thing in the morning."

Muffy Savage had slipped into the room, listening. "First thing in the morning. Why not right now?" She was agitated.

Lynn explained that it would take that long to organize it. When Muffy became more upset, Lynn agreed to go out looking again and take her along.

"Can we grab a bite to eat first?" Lynn asked, patting her abdomen. "No breakfast and it's past noon." She did not say that she was hung over from last night's dinner wine, and she declined to *think* about the double vodkas which preceded it.

Muffy beckoned her into the kitchen and sat her down at the little breakfast table. "We've got a ton of leftover shrimp salad."

"Sounds wonderful," Lynn said.

"How about you, Daddy?" she called to Jenkins, who was still in the living room.

"Just a little bit, darlin'," he called back.

Muffy spooned shrimp salad onto three paper plates and popped a couple of slices of her homemade bread into the toaster.

They sat at the small table. "He's out there somewhere,

Lynn," Muffy said. "I just know he is." Then she looked down and her shoulders started to move as the sobs came. She was sitting between Lynn and her father and both put a hand on an arm in comfort.

"What would I do as a widow?" she sobbed. "It took me long enough to find Millard. He didn't want children, and if he's gone I'll have nobody."

Lynn said nothing as she cut a quick glance at Jenkins. She looked at Muffy Savage, who was a small, forty-one-year-old woman with delicate features, including a small mouth and soft brown eyes. Her appearance had the potential for an Audrey Hepburn look, but her aquiline nose dashed that. Still semi-cute and perky, she was a very talented commercial artist.

"Millard wasn't the greatest. Not handsome like Daddy..." She was talking about him like he was dead, Lynn noted. "But I love him and want him back." She said all that in a kind of monotone while looking at a scrap of shrimp she was absently pushing around her plate with her fork. "You've got Rolf," Muffy said to Lynn, still playing with the piece of shrimp, "I forget his last name—"

"Berglund."

"Right. I still want to meet him."

"I want you to. You'll love him. He's an artist like you—"

"I'm not really an artist."

"Don't you do all the art stuff and ads for—?"

"Yes, but Rolf's a real artist."

"Well, I guess people do pay lots of bucks for his water-colors."

"You love him?" She was still looking at her plate.

Lynn opened her mouth but nothing came out.

"So when's the wedding?"

Whitman Jenkins put a gentle hand on his daughter's arm and said, "Now, don't get nosey, honey."

Lynn felt herself tighten. She'd had enough pressure for one day without someone forcing her to face a question she often asked herself without coming up with an answer. She'd lost her father to murder, her college sweetheart to an acting career, and her husband to the tragedy in the cave. She had not overcome the guilt in her life, but she *had* overcome her phobia of losing yet another man—Rolf—and admitted to herself and to him that she was in love with him. But she couldn't seem to move past that point. She forced a smile as she wiped her mouth with the paper napkin Muffy had provided. "I'm still working on that one. Let's go find Millard."

FIVE

IT WAS A NIGHT WHEN the blackness did not come. Instead, Lynn was diving in sun-brightened, blue-green, shallow water. The Florida Keys for lobster. Her mesh dive bag must be getting full of lobsters, it felt so heavy. Way too heavy. She swam to the boat, heaved the bag up on the deck of her flats skiff, climbed aboard and opened it. In horror, she stared down into the bag at Millard Savage's severed head.

"IT'S A MARVELOUS NIGHT FOR a moon dance..." Van Morrison sang from Lynn's new clock radio, waking her from the shadowy depths of her rabid nightmare about Millard Savage. She sat up in bed to clear her head. That dream. That *nightmare*. It was a warm March morning in Southwest Florida, but thinking about the nightmare made her shiver.

The authorities' search for Millard Savage was three days old now and had turned up nothing. Lynn had searched that first day with Muffy Savage after their lunch, and again with Muffy and her father the next day. Lynn introduced Muffy to Rolf Berglund, and Rolf was occupying Muffy in his art studio to try to take her mind off her crisis. They hit it off well, and it was helping, but not much.

Meanwhile, Lynn had to carry on with her back-bay nature tour and diving business. Such as it was. She just wasn't getting as many trips as she needed to make things work for her financially. True, she was a double dipper with her Navy pension, but buying the gulf-front cottage, modest as it was, and her boat, elaborate as it was, had hit her hard. Lynn had gotten some money from selling her Chinese restaurant in Tallahassee after she lost Dave in the cave dive, but her imbecilic stockbroker had managed to shrink that pile. Meanwhile, the resort of Boca Grande was frightfully expensive. The local joke was that the billionaires were running off the millionaires. Well, she was a long way from being a millionaire, and knew that would never happen. Sure, Rolf was always buying things for her and he paid for everything they did together, but all that did was make her uncomfortable. She liked to pull her own wagon.

So she was glad to have a client today. It was a couple from Ohio in their sixties, Bill and Fran Weir, and, during their back bay cruise, they were looking forward to one of Lynn's famous shore lunches of chow mein, won-tons, and tea. Lynn always asked permission to bring Mullet along, but, to her surprise, the Weirs said they preferred to go without the Lab. Lynn was dressed in her customary khaki "uniform," but today had the time to use make-up, lipstick, and grab her floppy wide-billed hat to defend herself against the March sun.

They got lucky in Turtle Bay. Lynn found two manatees swimming near the surface. The Weirs were thrilled, particularly when Lynn was able to pole her skiff close enough for the couple to entice the huge vegetarian sea cows with some of the lettuce she had brought just in case. The manatees' brown noses seemed to wiggle their whiskers as they lazily floated to the surface to take the lettuce directly from the hands of Lynn's customers. It was a rarity, but it happened. One of those special days, Lynn thought.

Afterwards, she went to her favorite shore lunch place in Turtle Bay. It was an anomaly: a short stretch of sandy beaches on a mangrove shoreline. She positioned them as far away as possible from the mosquito infested mangroves. Lynn beached the *Boca Broke* and Fran Weir promptly announced that she had to "go to the little girl's room," adding that if they would stay right there, she'd be back in a jiffy.

Lynn and Bill Weir were sitting in the beached boat about to become engrossed in a discussion of the merits of restricting boat traffic in the back bays to protect the endangered manatee. Then they heard it. It was an eerie, blood-curdling sound which to Lynn seemed like the wailing of an injured animal. It didn't stop, just kept repeating itself like a siren.

Lynn and Bill Weir looked at each other for a couple of beats. Weir said, "My God, that's Fran."

They scrambled out of the beached boat and sprinted toward the sound. In a clearing they found Fran Weir standing with her hands on either side of her face, wailing that eerie sound they'd heard. She was looking up at a very dead Millard Savage whose naked body was stretched and tied between two red mangrove trees, presumably to make it easier for the buzzards. They had made good progress already as evidenced by the fact that Millard Savage no longer had eyeballs.

Lynn immediately reached for her cell phone to call Truck Kershaw. Bill Weir immediately reached for his still-screaming wife and began leading her back to the boat. They almost made it before she stopped, leaned over, and vomited raucously on the beaches of Turtle Bay.

SIX

ROLF BERGLUND'S ELABORATE beachfront house was a quarter mile down the shore from Lynn's considerably more modest cottage. A nationally known watercolorist, Rolf made plenty of money selling his work, but didn't need it. He was already a wealthy widower, having sold his environmental consulting business for a handsome sum.

"No, no, you want to float the color, so make your paint juicy," Rolf said to Muffy Savage in the midst of giving her a watercolor lesson.

"You told me that before. I'm so sorry," Muffy said as she dropped her brush arm to her side in despair.

Rolf gave her a sympathetic look. "Don't apologize. You're just learning. Anyway, you do have a few other things on your mind."

Muffy stared at her palette. "My mind? My God, I feel like I'm losing it, like I'm in a dream where nothing's real. My husband's missing, maybe dead, and here I am swabbing watercolors on this press paper."

Rolf looked at the floor, silent.

"Oh, Rolf, I'm sorry. You've been so sweet to me, and the painting lessons have helped so much. I probably would have been in the loony house by now without you."

While the two were getting on famously, Rolf would later tell Lynn that he thought Muffy asked too many questions about his relationship with Lynn. She seemed fixated on what a perfect couple they made. Rolf did not take the conversation further. After Lynn recently realized she was in love with Rolf and acknowledged it, things had nonetheless stayed in their previous mode of sometimes spending the night together, sometimes not, and no discussion of plans to do anything more serious.

Rolf was short like Lynn. When they made love she sometimes told him they fit well together. Funny, she had never asked him his age. She was forty-six and figured him for maybe ten years past that. He wasn't so handsome, more like distinguished, with cobalt eyes which were tucked under a prominent, high forehead, which, in turn, was tucked under plenty of graying hair which was swept straight back with no part. He had strong, tanned hands, with what she thought was just the right amount of male hair. She very much liked the way those hands moved over her body in their intimate times.

Rolf usually painted in shorts, sandals, and a tropical shirt, all covered by a painting apron which was Technicolor after much use. He took it off when he heard Lynn at the door. Lynn didn't have to utter a word. Rolf and Muffy took one look at her and knew Millard Savage was dead.

Muffy was fairly composed; said she'd been expecting it. At least until she found out her husband had not had a boating accident, but been murdered. Then she was hysterical. Lynn tried to leave the goriness out of her report. She didn't want to replay the scene in her mind anyway. It had been a long time since Lynn had seen anything like that. She hadn't missed it.

The three of them piled in Lynn's SUV and drove to the cottage to find Whitman Jenkins. Under the circumstances, Lynn took the most direct route instead of her usual slight detour so she could drive down the charming island landmark, Banyan Street, lined with trees of the same name. Jenkins was at the cottage and, like Muffy, took one look at Lynn and knew.

"He's dead, isn't he? Where'd they find him?"

When Muffy went into her bedroom, Lynn told Jenkins what she knew.

"What do you think? Who's responsible?" Jenkins asked.

"Too early, Admiral."

Jenkins just looked at the floor and shook his head in despair. Then Lynn suggested she try to get Truck Kershaw to convince his superiors in Ft. Myers to excuse Muffy from identifying the body.

"They ought to let you do it, Admiral. He's your son-in-law," Lynn said.

Jenkins nodded. He had his military game face back on now. "Lynn, after this many days I figured he had to be dead. Been thinking about it, and I'm going to suggest to Muffy that we take the body back to Birmingham, have the funeral forthwith, and then come back down here and finish our month's rental. Muffy grew up in Montgomery, you know, and still doesn't know many people in Birmingham. I think she'd be better off doing her mourning down here. I know I will. You and Rolf have been so nice to her..." His composure began to falter.

Lynn put her hand on Jenkins' arm. "And we'll continue to be. Your plan sounds like a good one. Hope you can convince Muffy."

The game face was back. Steely. "One thing, though."

"What?" Lynn dropped her hand.

"I'm counting on you to make sure your big sheriff friend and his people find the son-of-a-bitch who did this."

"He will," she said, although she knew Truck Kershaw was not in the Criminal Investigation Division. "And if he has any trouble, I know a couple of ex–Naval Intelligence folks who just might help him out."

Jenkins said nothing, but the intensity of his nod, and the look he gave Lynn, was all the reply she needed.

SEVEN

LYNN LEFT THE JENKINS COTTAGE, climbed in the CR-V, and drove toward her house. Mullet was in the front seat beside her, his tail pounding on the passenger-side window as he drooled on the center console while facing Lynn in a quest for attention. Lynn absently petted him as she drove.

As she moved her hands over the dog's head, she realized she had become accustomed to Mullet only having one ear. Sometimes she would look at his one ear alertly perked and it would all come back and make her sad again. It happened during a twilight golf outing, she and Mullet riding in the golf cart with Rolf, her with a vodka on ice, watching him play several holes to try out a new driver. Mullet loved it, leaving the cart at will and romping wantonly, perhaps pretending that he was about to be commanded to retrieve a shot bird. Rolf had asked her to watch his next golf shot. "Tell me if my backswing is past parallel," he had said. She hadn't noticed Mullet so near the lake. She could still hear his frantic yelping as he sprinted away from the alligator. It was maybe a nine-footer; most Florida lakes housed at least one. Mullet's left ear must have been an hors d'oeuvre to the gator. They never even looked for it, just used a golf towel as a compress and rushed him to the vet.

Lynn engaged Mullet in the usual one-sided conversation. She asked the dog why all this was happening. Why the simple life she had come to Boca Grande to pursue couldn't be hers. Having put that question to Mullet, she immediately felt guilty for making her thoughts all about herself. After all, it was her long-time friend's son-in-law who, despite the assurances she had given to Muffy Savage, had been brutally murdered.

Lynn knew she had to go the distance on this; it was for the admiral.

Thailand, 1985. The admiral, then a lieutenant commander, had assigned her to the embassy in Bangkok, but she was, of course, a spook. He needed a female, Asian-looking officer who could dive. Lynn could still smell the putrid, acrid aroma of the opium in the tent where she went for the drop. Lynn was a double agent, posing as a turned American covert agent. She was passing bogus secrets in exchange for drugs, which the other side figured she could turn into large amounts of cash. The heroin was in plastic bags, neatly arranged in a briefcase, and Lynn's "secrets" were in a similar case. The swap was made and Lynn left the tent. That's when everything went terribly wrong.

The Thai "police" apprehended her, took the heroin, and kidnapped Lynn. She was put in a solitary-confinement hole. She saw no light except when a little bread and water was brought every other day. Her only company was her own excrement and the rats. She counted the days. They reached eleven when, approaching delirium, she was pulled out by Jenkins himself, who dragged Lynn through a pile of freshly dispatched Thai "police" bodies, threw her in the back seat of a waiting car, and sped away with her. Lynn never did find out how Whitman Jenkins pulled it off.

Yes, she had to make sure Truck Kershaw and the sheriff's department found Millard Savage's killer. She just hoped detective Lieutenant Stan Symanski, the source of her only rough spot since she'd arrived in Boca Grande, wasn't assigned to the case.

Lynn reached her cottage and parked under the shed beside her golf cart she often used to get to the marina and her boat. She let Mullet out, then opened the door to her house. She grabbed her portable phone, sank into her favorite porch chair, and dialed. While waiting for the connection to be made she looked out on the Gulf of Mexico. It was now March eighteenth and a cold front was muscling through. It caused a roiled, gray sky, the color of granite and a stark counterpoint of foamy, rolling whitecaps. After three rings, Lynn heard an answer.

"Kershaw," the voice said.

"You still at the crime scene?" asked Lynn.

"That's a roger."

"Can I come back over there?"

"That's a negative."

"Why?" asked Lynn.

"Because your buddy's here running the show."

"Symanski?"

"Stan the Man himself."

Lynn groaned. Through Truck, she had met Symanski, a detective with the Criminal Investigation Division (CID) of the Lee County Sheriff's Department. He had stiffed her on her fee for some contract diving she did for the department. Offered some flimsy excuse about an administrative snafu.

"Can you talk?" she asked Truck.

"For a minute. Hang on while I walk a little ways away and pretend I'm talking to the wife." There was a ten-beat pause. "Okay, here's what's up. The victim was likely already dead before he was strung up. Somebody beat the shit out of him with a blunt object. Haven't found it."

"What else?"

"Not much, Cap'n Lynn. The rope he was tied with is generic. Just a standard 3/8" mooring line. And there was no other physical evidence. You could plainly see where the footprints had been smoothed out."

"How about the Mako?"

"Ain't seen hide nor hair. Probably sunk in the middle of the harbor or maybe the gulf."

"How about signs of beached boats?"

"Cap'n Lynn. What part of 'no other physical evidence' didn't you understand? Stan the Man ain't exactly talking big on this one."

Lynn just grunted at that.

"So what's next?" Lynn asked.

"ID the body. Your buddy, the admiral, got hold of me and

I got Symanski's permission to let the victim's wife off the hook."

"That's good news."

"Yeah, but there's always bad to go with it."

"What?"

"Symanski wants to talk to the family."

Lynn groaned. Not surprising. And necessary. "When?"

"This afternoon at the cottage. Want to come?"

Lynn thought for a moment. "He's the last person I want to see, but I probably should."

EIGHT

SITTING IN THE living room of the admiral's cottage with Lt. Stan Symanski was not Lynn's idea of having a nice day. Their greeting was quick and terse, consisting of a curt nod.

Symanski was viewed as the ace detective for the Criminal Investigation Division (CID) of the Lee County Sheriff's Department. Originally from the Paterson, New Jersey, police department, Symanski was a small, wiry man with a constant five o'clock shadow over angular features. He had two quirks: one was peppering his speech with the vocalized pause "basically" with a frequency which was distracting. The other was that he always wore a white necktie, having two of them, a primary and a back-up. He said he figured white went with anything. Throughout his day, he constantly adjusted the knot on said white necktie, making his ties two-tone white, as the knot portion would, over time, become semi-soiled from all the fingering.

They sat in a circle on the white wicker furniture with green-and-yellow palm-tree-pattern cushions, Whitman Jenkins in khaki flats fishing shorts and shirt, and Muffy Savage in flowered island shorts and a cool lavender, sleeveless blouse. Truck Kershaw again monopolized the love seat with his sprawling two hundred ninety pounds.

After taking a gulp from the mug of coffee Muffy provided, pulling the back of his coat down so it didn't ride up on his neck when he sat, then adjusting the knot on his white tie, Symanski began. "Now, Mr. Jenkins," he said, "let's start with you."

"*Admiral* Jenkins, Lieutenant," said Lynn, not looking at the detective.

"Oh?" said Symanski, with what passed for a smile. "Navy

man, eh? I was Coast Guard myself. Okay, Admiral, I understand you're basically down for some fishing and diving?"

"That's right."

"And you've rented this cottage, let's see, for how long?"

"A month."

"Long time."

"Well, it was to be sort of a working vacation, a getaway for all three of us, and a way to duck the cold in Birmingham."

"Birmingham?"

"Alabama. Where we live. Where my companies are headquartered."

Lynn wondered if Symanski had ever heard of Birmingham, Alabama. Or if he had, if he thought anything went on there other than race riots featuring police commissioner Bull Conner.

"Can't say as I've ever been there," said Symanski. "Steel town, right?"

"That used to be the big industry, but the economy there is considerably more diverse now."

Jenkins' answer was delivered pleasantly, but Lynn thought she detected a hint of impatience. The admiral was sitting in his preferred place behind the white wicker desk. The place where the senior officer would sit, holding court, in charge. Over the years it had become rote to him. He leaned back in his chair, eyes fixed on Symanski with a cold, this-better-be-good-mister stare.

Symanski continued. "I understand the deceased—Mr. Savage—was your employee as well as your son-in-law."

"That's right."

"Which came first?"

"Millard married my daughter and I invited him to join the company."

"Was he a good employee?"

"He was a wonderful employee." Jenkins was now cradling his chin with his hand, his index finger across his lips, moving his finger aside when he spoke.

"Basically what kind of company do you have and what did Mr. Savage do for you?"

"We're in food manufacturing and processing. Perhaps you've had some Whitman's peanut butter—"

"Practically raised my kids on it."

"—yes, well, that was our flagship line. Then after we sold the company I left and began acquiring other food companies. We're in various brands of jellies, syrups, spoonable oils, and some specialty teas. Everything's headquartered in Birmingham, but we have plants all over the country."

"Why did you basically leave the company after you sold out? Doesn't the management usually stay on?" Symanski asked.

Lynn was now certain that irritation was percolating inside Whitman Jenkins.

"I didn't gee haw with the company that acquired us—Federal Foods. I wanted to start making acquisitions and they didn't, so I left and started doing it on my own account. Lieutenant, what can this possibly have to do with my son-in-law's murder?"

"Just background, Admiral. I appreciate your patience. You didn't say what Mr. Savage did for you."

"He was our chief compliance officer for environmental matters and for OSHA compliance."

"OSHA?"

"Occupational safety and health. Government agency. A nightmare."

"So you say you had no problems with the deceased as an employee?"

"No, that's *not* what I said. I said he was a wonderful employee. And a terrific son-in-law, I might add."

Symanski went to his coffee mug again. Lynn noticed it was white with a blue hand-painted leaping tarpon on it. Symanski again adjusted the knot on his white necktie. Truck Kershaw, after some squawky static, turned down the volume on his epaulet-mounted radio then laboriously re-arranged his girth on the love seat.

"Admiral Jenkins," Symanski began again, "tell me about

Mr. Savage's behavior, say, a couple of weeks prior to his death. Did he seem worried about anything?"

Jenkins moved his index finger from his lips again. "Not at all. The only thing he seemed worried about was getting all his camera equipment together for this trip. He was very excited about it—taking pictures of the backcountry here, the wildlife, the birds, the habitat."

"Did he have any conflicts or disagreements with anybody at the company?"

"No. Millard got along with everybody. He was the boss' son-in-law but everybody respected him."

"Did he have any conflicts with you?"

Whitman Jenkins did not answer. He and Symanski began a protracted stare down. To occupy herself during this stalemate, Lynn did some staring of her own—at a five-inch-long green lizard which had attached itself to the window pane directly behind Muffy. The creature was sitting there, alternating between flashing its red tongue and performing its strange push-up-like maneuver. It reminded Lynn of a miniature, green Jack Lalane.

"Well, Admiral?" Symanski said.

"I shouldn't have to answer such a question, but no, he had no conflicts with me. We got along famously," Jenkins said tightly.

Symanski turned to Muffy Savage and said, "How about with you, ma'am. Basically, how would you describe your relationship with your husband?"

Muffy opened her mouth, widened her eyes and just stared at Whitman Jenkins, silently begging her father to rescue her from this unthinkable breach of propriety.

Jenkins spoke, his voice laced with irritation, "Lieutenant, my daughter had a happy, loving marriage with no conflicts."

Symanski said nothing in reply as he studied the notes on his pad for a moment. That's when Lynn noticed it. The humming. It was almost under Symanski's breath, but not quite, and very warbly with excess vibrato. Lynn couldn't make out the tune, but thought it was *Sweet Adeline* or something of that genre.

Damned if Symanski wasn't a hummer. Muffy Savage, now recovered from the detective's blunt question, noticed it, too.

"Do you sing, Lieutenant?" she asked.

He looked up quickly, surprised, suddenly uncomfortable, then seemed to brighten as he nodded. "Matter of fact, I do. Barbershop quartet. Been at it for years."

"What was that one you were just humming?" she asked.

He flushed. "Was I? Sorry. I don't even know, maybe *Sweet Adeline* or something."

Lynn silently complimented herself.

"I'm in the church choir," Muffy said, suddenly sitting erect with almost child-like pride. "Contralto."

Symanski made an effort at a smile which didn't really come off, only telegraphing an obvious desire to get out of the hole he had fallen into. He flipped the page in his book and, looking back and forth between Jenkins and Muffy, said, "Now, getting back to this, when did you people last see the deceased?"

Jenkins nodded gently toward Muffy. Taking his cue, she looked down at her clasped hands and said quietly, "The afternoon before Millard went missing, a shrimp boat had come into the dock at Boatmen's Marina and was selling fresh ones right off the boat. Millard and I bought five pounds about three o'clock and came back here. He spent his time getting his camera equipment ready, and I fixed shrimp salad....."

Symanski abruptly looked at Jenkins. "Where were you, sir?"

"I was here, mostly on the phone. We're working on a large acquisition. A manufacturer of salad dressings and spoonable oils. Can't say which one, obviously."

Symanski turned back to Muffy, signaling her to continue.

"Anyway," she said, "the three of us had an early dinner so Millard could get away before dark."

"Tell me again where he said he was going and why," said Symanski.

"He's...he was...an amateur wildlife photographer. A good one, too. One of his pictures of flying Canada geese made the cover of *Field and Stream* once. He was excited about photographing the Indian mounds on the mangrove islands, and he had some new infrared equipment for shooting wildlife after dark. He even dreamed of seeing and photographing a Florida panther. They're almost extinct, you know."

"Yes, I know," said Symanski. "So what time did he leave?"

"As I said, just before dark, maybe forty-five minutes before," said Muffy.

"And what did you do then?"

Muffy shrugged. "Cleaned up the kitchen, finished a book I was reading, watched part of the news and went to bed."

"How about you, sir?" Symanski asked, turning to Jenkins.

"Read some production reports from Birmingham and watched the news with Muffy. We turned in at the same time. A very sedate evening, to say the least," Jenkins replied.

"Neither of you got up during the night?"

"Lieutenant, I'm sixty-six years old. I can assure you that I got up during the night," said Jenkins.

"But that was it, just nature calls?"

Jenkins nodded.

"How about you, ma'am, did you get up?"

"No."

"When did you notice that your husband was missing?"

"Just before six when I woke up."

At that Symanski nodded and began looking down at his notes and biting the end of his ball point pen.

"More coffee, Lieutenant?" Muffy asked.

It took him a couple of beats to disengage his deep thought, look up, take the pen out of his mouth, and say, "No. No, thanks, Mrs. Savage."

"They say too much of it's not good for your vocal cords," she said.

He gave her a quizzical look. "I hadn't heard that, but I'll look into it." Then he went to the knot of his tie again before starting a new tack. "Admiral, what can you basically tell me about the boat?"

"Great little boat. Seventeen Mako with an 85 horse on it. We rented it for the month from Boatmen's Marina. Ran perfectly."

"When was it fueled last?"

"We already went through this with the deputy here. She was topped off that afternoon at Boatmen's when Millard and Muffy went to buy the shrimp. That's how they got to the marina."

Symanski looked at Muffy Savage. She nodded her affirmation and then looked back down at her clasped hands.

"Where was the boat docked?"

"The Lodge has a dock at the end of this street. Covered slips under a waterfront cottage," answered Jenkins.

"Anybody staying in that cottage?"

"No. The Lodge told us there wasn't. Said otherwise we'd be cautioned to keep the noise down."

"Was your son-in-law good at the helm of a boat?" asked Symanski.

Jenkins let his chair come down on all four legs and rearranged a clear glass tarpon replica paperweight on the desk before answering. "Yes, and an excellent navigator. He could make a GPS play a tune if he wanted to."

Symanski studied his pad again. More of the absent-minded humming came. Lynn didn't recognize this one.

The humming stopped as he said, "Who did Mr. Savage know here on Boca Grande?"

Jenkins and his daughter both shook their heads.

"Muffy? Nobody but Lynn, right?" said Jenkins.

She nodded.

"Had he met anybody while he was here?"

Muffy shook her head. "Just waiters, lodge staff. People like that. We'd only been here a couple of days."

Symanski reached beside him for a large manila envelope.

"Mrs. Savage, I wonder if you would examine your husband's personal effects here and tell me if anything looks out of the ordinary or if anything is missing."

Muffy took the envelope, hands shaking slightly. She looked at a wallet, the credit cards and money that were in it, two rings, his Rolex watch. As she lingered over the engraved, wood-handled pocket knife she had given him birthday before last, her lower lip began to tremble. "There's nothing missing that I know of. It's all here."

"Thank you, Mrs. Savage," Symanski said. "That's all I have for now, but I need to know how to contact you. What's your schedule? I think the body will basically be released to you tomorrow."

Lynn wondered how a dead body is *basically* released.

Jenkins spoke up. "The funeral home will fly Millard to Birmingham as soon as they...get him ready. We'll go up for the services and probably come back down the next day, do our mourning down here. I'll give you my business card so you can reach us while we're gone."

Symanski began to rise to fetch the card.

"Just a moment, Lieutenant. Sit down," said Whitman Jenkins.

NINE

JENKINS' VOICE AND its stern, commanding tone made Symanski sit right back down. Rear Admiral (Ret.) W. Whitman Jenkins IV remained sitting in the white wicker chair behind the matching desk. All of him that was visible above the desk was his smart, khaki fishing shirt with epaulets topped by his close-cropped, white hair, grizzled but distinguished countenance, and black horn-rimmed glasses like Cary Grant's. That movie-like imagery and two other things made Lt. Stan Symanski sit right back down. One was Jenkins' small, brown, marble-like eyes boring into Symanski's, and the other was that voice. It was different. The *admiral* was now in charge.

Jenkins looked at his daughter and said, "Martha, honey, why don't you go out on the porch for a few minutes." Jenkins sometimes used Muffy's formal given name when around strangers. She silently complied.

When the porch door closed, Jenkins looked back at Symanski and said, "I have a few questions of my own."

"That's not the usual procedure, but I'll do what I can," Symanski said.

"Start with a summary of the medical examiner's work."

It was less a question than an order, delivered with a tone that signaled that Jenkins was accustomed to compliance and deference, and expected concise facts, delivered with brevity.

Symanski hesitated a moment, then began, "Blunt force trauma was the cause of death. We suspect your son-in-law was basically beaten to death with a common claw hammer like you'd use to frame a house with. Of course, you were at the morgue and saw what the buzzards did."

"Right. Any physical evidence or clues on the body? Hair samples, that sort of thing?"

Symanski's lip curled in a wry smile. "Admiral, I thought you commanded ships, have you been reading up on forensics?"

"I was in Naval Intelligence. We ran into some violent death here and there." The voice was gruff and the brown marbles ground into Symanski who seemed to be struggling to maintain contact with them.

"Admiral, I'll be frank with you. We've got very little to go on here. The physical evidence is almost nil. Unfortunately, that's all I can tell you right now." Lynn thought Symanski squirmed.

Years ago Lynn had been in Symanski's place more than once. Lynn felt the familiar vacant sensation in her gut, the off-center gyro of inadequacy which she had too often experienced while trying to meet Jenkins' expectations. She thought Symanski must be feeling the same thing.

"That's all you can tell me right now," Jenkins parroted Symanski's last statement, except with a chilling edge on his voice. "Well, mister, I'm going to tell *you* something right now. Or maybe I should *sing* it to you." Lynn noticed that Jenkins emphasized *mister,* just like the old days. Just like Symanski was an ensign. He also saw the detective bristle at the reference to his singing.

Jenkins pointed his right index finger straight at Symanski. "You find the animal that did this to my little girl's husband, and you do it quickly. Don't make me have to make a big contribution to your sheriff's election campaign fund so he knows who I am when I call. Have I made myself clear?"

Symanski performed a wrenching tug on the knot of his white tie before replying, "We'll do our best no matter what you do, Admiral. Is that all?"

Jenkins rose from his chair, which signaled everyone else to stand. Then he came around the desk and performed what Lynn recalled to be a classic Whit Jenkins maneuver. He gave Symanski his business card then stuck out his hand and gave him a warm handshake while resting his left hand on Symanski's shoulder. He looked the lieutenant intensely in the eye and said quietly, with some drama, "I have a good feeling about you. I have confidence in you. I'm counting on you to come through for me, mister."

Lynn had seen Jenkins work this carrot-and-stick charm many times, pulling out the lush and cozy velvet glove after the iron fist had already struck. It was almost always effective. Symanski wasn't immune to it, replying, "We'll get him, Admiral. We'll get him."

TEN

LYNN'S TRIP TO TALLAHASSEE came just at the right time: when Whitman Jenkins and Muffy Savage took Millard's body to Birmingham for the funeral. Lynn wanted to cancel her trip and go to the funeral, but the admiral and Muffy wouldn't hear of it. Lynn figured she'd get back to Boca Grande about when they did. She wanted to comfort them in their mourning and she wanted to stay in close touch with Truck Kershaw.

On her way off the island, midmorning, in her white Honda CR-V, she and Mullet pulled into a parking space under Rolf Berglund's house and climbed the stairs to the main level. Rolf's front door was of etched art glass depicting the well known Lamar Sparkman painting of an osprey, its wings elegantly splayed, gliding over Boca Grande Pass with a small sea trout in its talons. The two artists were friends and Rolf had the glass done with Sparkman's permission.

Like most on the island, the house was unlocked, and Lynn turned the knob with one hand and put the other on the etched, flying osprey, then pushed her way into the entry hall, Mullet at her knee.

"Woman in the hall," she called. It struck her that the greeting, a throwback to dormitory days, was ironic since she was on her way to Tallahassee where she'd gone to college.

"Come on in, babe, I'm totally naked," Rolf called back from his studio. It came out *nekkid.* Rolf Berglund had grown up in Columbus, Georgia.

Lynn moved into the living room. Rolf emerged from his studio in his blue painting smock under which he was fully clothed in khaki shorts, yellow tropical shirt, and sandals. His salt-and-pepper swept-back hair had a touch of paint in it. Rolf had a habit of scratching his head as he contemplated his next brush strokes.

"You lying bastard," Lynn said. "Getting me all excited, hoping you'd be wearing nothing but your smock."

He smiled. "Yeah, I'm just a big tease. But I guess I'd better be careful. Most of the times I've played hard to get, I've ended up being successful at it."

The night before, they had dined at Squid Row with Whit Jenkins and Muffy Savage, a somber occasion on the eve of their trip to Birmingham. Lynn's head was still pounding from the double vodkas on ice followed by the wine with dinner. She kept telling herself that getting on the outside of a little alcohol fended off her recurring, nocturnal visitor—the replay of Dave's death in the cave. When the nightmares happened anyway, she told herself it made them less frequent. She and Rolf had made love later and spent the night at Lynn's house. So despite the sexual repartee, their embrace this following morning was more warm and cuddly than urgent or passionate.

"Well, I'm delivering your house guest," Lynn announced with a large grin.

Rolf looked down at Mullet. The one-eared black lab was looking up at Rolf with a globule of drool about to leave his mouth on the way to the custom heart pine floor. The dog's tail was wagging vigorously, each wag narrowly missing a Herend porcelain dolphin on the coffee table.

"Why don't you send Mullet to Tallahassee and *you* be my house guest?" he said with a smirk and one eyebrow slightly elevated.

She laughed. "I would, but Mullet doesn't drive a stick shift."

"Your SUV has automatic."

"I know, but it made a good joke."

"I'm going to miss you, kid," he said.

She folded herself into his arms. "I'll miss you." Then she slid her hands inside the painting smock. But not inside anything else. They just held each other.

When they disengaged she said, "Can you help me while I'm gone?"

"What?" he asked while leaning to pet Mullet, his sub-agenda being to keep the dog's tail from putting his coffee table treasures in harm's way. Lynn knew that the minute she left, germ-freak Rolf would immediately wash his hands in warm, soapy water to rid himself of "dog germs." *They eat everything from lizards to other dogs' poop,* he often said.

"Stay in close touch with Truck Kershaw. See what you can find out."

"I'll do my best but I won't have much time. This commission work is stacking up on me."

"Maybe I should commission you. Then I might get a little more attention."

Rolf folded his arms across his chest and pursed his lips in an expression of mock reproach.

"Just do what you can," Lynn said. "And maybe you can check on Muffy. I'm not worried about the admiral, but Muffy seems about to come unglued."

He nodded.

"I'll be calling you every night, even though I'll only be gone two or three."

"Don't forget," he said.

Lynn's eyes twinkled as her mouth turned up at one corner. "I'll have to check on Mullet anyway."

ELEVEN

LYNN DROVE FROM Rolf's house and took her usual detour down lovely Banyan Street, named for the gnarly-trunked, tropical beauties that lined it. The last hurricane had wounded the trees severely, but Lynn always drove that way and tried to silently nurture the stately banyans back to good health. She turned north on Gasparilla Island and drove across the causeway to the mainland. She turned onto state road 776 which she took to I-75 and eventually I-10. In six hours she was in Tallahassee. On the familiar street corner near downtown and the state capitol, she found her usual bikini-clad flower vendor. Lynn told the girl once again she didn't have to dress like that to sell flowers, bought the red roses, and continued to her next stop.

Another in a series of late-March cold fronts was pushing through, causing a leaden sky and a freshening breeze. The Spanish moss hanging from the stately live oaks surrounding the cemetery swayed in response. She kneeled and gently placed her father's favorite red roses on his grave. As she stared down at them, her vision began to blur and spin into an image of her father in intensive care with what seemed like miles of plastic tubes in him. When she first saw him she didn't know he was already brain-dead from the gunshot wound.

Lynn's grandparents were born in mainland China, Lynn and her own parents in New York. She worked in the family Chinese restaurant on the lower east side as everything from waitress to wok girl to hostess. She decided on a career in the business and chose Florida State University's renowned hospitality industry school.

It was at Florida State that she met Sammy Osceola, a full-blooded Seminole Indian. They were not lovers but best friends, and it was Sammy who got the tomboy Lynn involved in the outdoors—camping, bow hunting, fishing, and diving. Lynn especially liked diving and she and Sammy became prolific cave divers in the many springs connected to the Wakulla River south of Tallahassee. Lynn worked briefly for Marriott before yielding to her passion for diving. When the SEALS wouldn't budge on their no-females rule, she became a Navy "hard hat" diver, going to great depths in a full suit. She became second in command of a salvage ship before moving over to Naval Intelligence with Admiral Whitman Jenkins.

When she retired from the service, she opened her own Chinese restaurant in Tallahassee and her parents worked for her. When Dave died in the cave accident, she sold the business. It was a quick decision in response to the guilt. Her parents began working for a competitor and that's when the drug-crazed gunman shot her father late one night for the contents of the cash register. She told herself that if she hadn't sold, they'd still be working for her and perhaps she could have prevented what happened. Her guilt multiplied like rabbits. Her evening count of vodkas on ice increased. Her doctor had prescribed the antidepressant Zoloft which she took sporadically. She knew she wasn't supposed to mix it with much alcohol but it didn't seem to make a difference.

Lynn was in Tallahassee for a public forum the state government was holding about the endangered manatee. Environmentalists believed that the very survival of the sea cows was threatened by power boats being able to run full speed in some of the backcountry waters where Lynn conducted her tours. Their proposal was to limit such boat traffic to kayaks, canoes, or electric trolling motors. If such a measure passed, Lynn's struggling new business would be crippled. Lynn was conflicted about the issue because she had seen a few manatees with prop scars on their backs, but had never heard of one actually dying from it. Although she was an ardent conservationist, she didn't want to have to give up on her new business. It was a conundrum.

TWELVE

AFTER THE CEMETERY VISIT, Lynn checked into the Cabot Lodge on the Thomasville Road, rested, showered, and changed before heading to the Governor's Club to meet Sammy Osceola for dinner. In deference to her friend, who would probably have just come from the capitol in a business suit, Lynn actually wore a dress. In fact, it was a straight beige skirt with a white blouse and a short navy blazer. She even put on heels and a necklace which matched some dangly silver earrings, and spent some extra time on her hair. She always had to be careful putting on lipstick because of the distinctive curl on her upper lip which men always seemed to be fascinated by.

Sammy Osceola was waiting for her in the lobby of the club. Wearing a wide grin, Lynn bounded across the lobby with her side of their standard greeting, "How's my favorite injun?"

Sammy Osceola, the full-blooded Seminole, stood, hugged her warmly, and came back with, "Damned if it's not Madame Butterfly herself."

"When are you going to learn that I'm Chinese, not Japanese?" she asked with a grin.

"When I think of something more clever than Madame Butterfly. How are you, Lynn?"

"If I was any better, I couldn't stand it," Lynn answered with a grin. Her father taught her to always say something like that even if the opposite were true. *Never let them see you down,* he had said. Her grin dissolved as she added, "That's not totally right. We had some trouble on the island. I'll tell you about it."

Osceola, the club member, led Lynn into the grill room and to their table. The Governor's Club was a private city club a few blocks from the capitol which, along with a popular watering hole a few doors away, served as the unofficial venue for the transaction of a major portion of the "people's" business in Florida's state government. Lynn had been right. Sammy was dressed in a khaki suit with a white dress shirt which was so perfectly starched it could have been on a cathedral altar. It was complemented by a blue-and-gold British regimental tie.

When he wasn't at the capitol lobbying, Sammy wore plenty of Seminole garb, including the bright, multi-colored jackets for which the Florida tribes were known. If Lynn had brought a stranger to the meeting they might not have known Sammy Osceola was an Indian. Sure, his hair was dark and his complexion ruddy, but his features were refined and almost patrician, with a slimmer nose than one would expect. His speech was standard North Florida-South Georgia in syntax and dialect. There was, however, one concession Sammy made to his heritage, even when in business attire. He swept his hair back into a short ponytail, perhaps three inches long, and knotted it with a piece of colorful, beaded rawhide.

"The usual?" Sammy said when they were seated. When Lynn nodded, he told the waiter, "An Absolut on ice for the lady, and bring a bottle of the Selby pinot noir. We'll both have it with dinner."

"Could you make it a double?" Lynn said. "Traffic on I-10 was a mess."

Sammy nodded his assent to the waiter, then turned to Lynn. "So, what's up? You mentioned something about trouble in Boca Grande?"

"A murder, Sammy. Son-in-law of my old commanding officer. You've heard me talk about Admiral Jenkins."

As Lynn told the story, Sammy listened intently and interrupted occasionally with pertinent questions. In the middle of it the waiter came with the drinks. The pinot noir's vintage suited Sammy. No stranger to ritual, he performed some on the wine, swirling it in his glass, taking a mouthful, caressing it with his palate, and nodding his approval to the waiter.

"You sure it's safe to come down there and go out in the back bays with you next week?"

"Sometimes I wonder if anybody's safe anymore, but the *Boca Broke's* leaving the dock at the appointed hour and I hope you're on it."

He nodded and gave Lynn a thumbs-up sign.

After college, Sammy Osceola had gone on to law school, practiced privately for several years, then had become the head of inter-tribal affairs for the Seminole Tribe and their chief lobbyist. He was instrumental in creating and maintaining the blessing of the Tribe for the university's use of the sports nickname of "Seminoles." More importantly, he was instrumental in waging the fight to get Seminole gaming approved, the Tribe's major source of income. The two friends were out of touch for many years, but renewed their relationship when Lynn came back to Tallahassee after the Navy. Sammy had never lost his love of the outdoors and diving, and he introduced Lynn to Boca Grande where they met for diving and backcountry exploring and fishing. Sammy even orchestrated an attractive, off-market transaction when she bought her cottage after he learned from a lobbying client that it was available.

"So how's Rolf?" Sammy asked.

"Oh, fine, great. Yeah, he's good."

"How are *you* and Rolf? Any plans?"

"You mean like marriage? Nope, no plans yet."

"By the way," said Sammy, "I'll be bringing my daughter down with me this time. She'll be on spring break."

Lynn finished a pull on the vodka, swallowed, and said, "Johnnie. How is she? Last time I saw her was, what, four years ago when that manta ray jumped in the boat with us?"

"She's twenty-one now. A senior here at the university." Sammy grinned and added, "Anyway, she's in her fourth year, put it that way. Lynn, I don't know what I'm going to do with that girl. She's wild as a panther, nuts over Indian history and lore. Thinks she's a Seminole warrior and, unfortunately, tries to prove it sometimes, including drinking too much. I've been called in the middle of the night more than once."

"Oh, she'll outgrow it."

"The sooner the better. I'm getting too old for this shit."

The waiter returned for their dinner order, Lynn choosing grouper piccata and Sammy sautéed pompano.

"So what's happening with our legislature?" Lynn asked.

"Oh, the usual wheeling and dealing, give and take. Especially the take."

Lynn finished her vodka with a murmured chuckle.

"Big thing I'm worried about is some rumbling about a proposal to allow real-estate development on some of the estuarial mangrove islands—like in Charlotte Harbor where you do your tours. Even the ones that have Calusa Indian burial mounds on them. That would be an ecological and historical disaster."

Lynn dabbed at her mouth with her napkin then put it in her lap, spread her hands in the air, and looked out into space as she said, "Ah, the beautiful, pristine back bays. The herons, the ospreys, the mangroves...the scrapers, the bulldozers."

"I'm afraid some of them are actually talking about it. What I mainly want to do when I come down next week is go out and take some pictures of some of the sensitive sites."

THIRTEEN

LYNN'S FIRST BACK-BAY tour charter after returning from Tallahassee was a single, elderly gentlemen from Tampa named Clyde. Lynn had forgotten his last name, but it wasn't important because clients and guides were always on a first-name basis anyway. It was midday, an unusual time to be leaving on a tour, but Clyde wanted to watch the sun set over the mangrove islands from Turtle Bay. She checked her watch. Ten till two.

"You get stood up, Cap'n Lynn?" said a familiar voice from behind her.

Lynn was standing in her skiff, folding and stowing some new mooring lines she had bought. She recognized the voice. "Truck, what's up? Sounds like you're ready to get out of that uni and go AWOL on the water somewhere."

"You readin' my mind, man," Truck Kershaw said, slowly shaking his head in a longing sort of way.

"I'd be a willing accomplice except for one thing. Millard Savage. What's the latest?"

Truck looked to either side, then stepped about three dock planks closer to Lynn before answering. "Whoever did it's been watching too many of those TV shows."

"What kind of shows?" asked Lynn.

"The ones about forensics, crime scene investigations, stuff like that. The perp or perps didn't leave us jack shit to go on. Talking zip for physical evidence. No prints anywhere, no footprints, couldn't find any stray hairs or anything else on the body that might give up some DNA. And no murder weapon left at the crime scene."

"Ever find the boat?"

Just then a loitering tourist in bright red Bermuda shorts, a

Boatmen's Marina T-shirt, and tube socks with sneakers sauntered up, arms folded, and stood admiring Lynn's skiff. Truck drew himself up to his full six foot six and glared down at him for a few moments, saying nothing. Sufficiently intimidated, the man shrank away.

Truck resumed the conversation. "Found it day before yesterday. They tried to put her on the bottom, but those older Makos won't totally sink because of all the flotation they put in the gunwales. She washed up over near Matlacha. The semi-good news is the weapon was in a hatch. A simple ball peen hammer, just like we figured. A few traces of the victim's blood type, but no prints, and the salt water killed any DNA we could have recovered from the handle."

"So what do you think?"

"I think Symanski doesn't know whether to shit or wind his watch."

Lynn continued to fiddle with the mooring lines without looking up. "You have a plan? Or does Symanski?" Lynn asked.

"Stan the Man hasn't told me to do anything yet, but the only thing I can think of is to start asking around in the commercial fishing crowd. There's still plenty of illegal netting going on in the backcountry. Maybe Savage stepped on somebody's toes when he was out there taking his pictures that night."

"Not a bad theory considering that Millard was a passionate conservationist. He wasn't shy, either. I can see him confronting some outlaw netter. You know those guys—they'd as soon cut your nuts off as look at you." She looked up at him with a smirk. "Not that I have any."

That got a chuckle from Truck. "There's a couple of those guys owe me a favor. I cut 'em some slack not long ago. Maybe I'll see what I can turn up."

FOURTEEN

CLYDE, THE CHARTER CLIENT, walked across the dock toward Lynn with a limp. "Arthritis in the knee." He gave Lynn an engaging smile. "Only time it doesn't hurt is when I'm on a boat."

Clyde, in his mid-seventies, had a lanky, low-body-fat frame and a shock of white hair which gave him a distinguished look. His outdoorsy wardrobe looked as if he had just emerged from an Orvis outfitter's store.

They pulled away from the dock at about two-thirty into one of those dream March days in Boca Grande. Sunny, about seventy-five degrees, and a light breeze out of the southeast. Lynn and Clyde got on well enough, but he was rather quiet. He had a fancy new Canon digital camera with a huge lens and a thick book on Florida waterfowl. She asked him to send her some choice prints of what she suspected would be marvelous pictures he took of some bald eagles, osprey nests, and an island swarming with frigate birds.

BY THE END OF THE TRIP, a sea breeze had developed out of the west, and to avoid running home into the teeth of it, Lynn took a backcountry route around the north side of an island named Cayo Pelau. She saw a commercial fisherman illegally laying gill nets on a prime snook-fishing flat. Lynn slowed to an idle and approached the man. She recognized him—it was Aubrey Lowe.

This was not the first time Lynn had seen Aubrey Lowe breaking the law. Although Lowe was fishing for mullet, because he was using a gill net, his by-catch usually included prized game fish like snook and redfish, which lost their lives in the process. Which is why a ban on gill netting was passed by Florida's voters. Commercial fishermen like Aubrey Lowe could still fish for mullet but they were now supposed to use a cast net. Less productive, but it avoided the mindless slaughter of a precious resource.

Lynn had had enough. As she idled up to Aubrey Lowe, she reached under her console, pulled out her cell phone, and held it in the air. As she continued drifting toward Lowe, she yelled across the water, "Aubrey, damn it, if you don't pull that gill net in right now and start using your cast net, I'm calling the marine patrol."

Aubrey Lowe was a direct descendent of the Padilla family, which started fishing the waters around Boca Grande for their living over a hundred years ago. Lowe was unique in that his mother was a descendant of the Miccosukee Indian tribe prevalent in the Florida Everglades. A hulk of a man, he was square-jawed, and in a strange twist for a commercial fisherman, clean-shaven. He wore the bottoms to a heavy-duty yellow rain slicker, a white T-shirt underneath, and a grimy, gray-green cap. Lynn had quickly updated Clyde on what was happening and he stood beside Lynn in a similar defiant posture. The two boats were now almost gunwale to gunwale.

Aubrey Lowe looked at the two for a few moments without saying anything. Then he took a few steps on his mullet boat to a storage compartment and pulled out something of his own with his right hand. It was a .357 Magnum pistol and he pointed it right at Lynn's head. He held out his left hand as he said, "Toss me that cell phone, pretty lady."

Lynn immediately did as she was told. Lowe caught the phone, then switched the gun to his left hand and the phone to his right. He reared back and pegged the cell phone as far as he could throw it, over Lynn's head and into the middle of Bull Bay. Then he switched the Magnum back to his right hand.

"Okay, pretty lady, you got five seconds to get that fancy little boat up on a plane and out of here. You call anybody when you get to the dock and Ol' Nellie here and me's gonna come calling." He patted the gun barrel with his left hand.

At the first sight of the gun, Lynn felt her gut tighten as though her intestines had tangled like a backlash on a fishing reel. She swallowed and noticed saliva had taken leave of her throat. She watched her cell phone sail over her head and land in the water before turning back to Aubrey Lowe and the gun barrel. In that moment, she was convinced Lowe would not shoot them, but she concluded that there was nothing to be gained by doing or saying anything else. She slipped the outboard in gear and idled away, all the while making intense eye contact with Aubrey Lowe. When she reached deeper water, she pushed the throttle forward and headed for home.

Clyde had stood beside her in silence the entire time and still did as they idled into Lynn's slip at Boatmen's Marina. In the windless confines of the marina's docks, Lynn smelled something and one glance told her that Clyde had befouled his expensive Orvis shorts.

FIFTEEN

LYNN BID HER GOODBYES to an embarrassed Clyde, apologizing for the terror they had experienced in the back bay and promising a free day to make up for it. Mumbling something about it not being necessary, Clyde made a hasty departure.

Lynn quickly washed down the *Boca Broke* and walked to the parking lot. Behind the wheel of her CR-V, she involuntarily shivered as she recalled looking at the small dark hole at the end of Aubrey Lowe's .357 Magnum. She never figured anything like that would be a part of her new island life.

She drove straight to Truck Kershaw's house on Damficare Street, which ran parallel to streets named Damfino and Damfiwill. Truck's sheriff's cruiser was in the driveway. The deputy was still in his uniform when he answered the door, but in his stocking feet.

"Want a beer?" Truck asked.

"Can't. Got to get home and let Mullet out. Got a second?"

Truck Kershaw's house was among the most modest on the now tony resort island. It was frame, yellow, and had two bedrooms, one for Truck and his bank-branch-manager wife, Darla, and one for their twelve-year-old son. It was only fifteen hundred square feet, but they were still struggling with it because of Lee County's predatory ad valorem tax policies. Truck was among the last of the working folks still living on the island instead of commuting each day over the causeway.

Truck had grown up off island, over between Port Charlotte and Punta Gorda. His mother was one of the first black female police officers in the state, working for the Englewood department. When Truck was just a teenager, he lost her. She was shot in the face by a drug mule she had stopped on a routine traffic violation. He still felt guilty over his wayward behavior as an adolescent, which had included some drug activity, and he had dedicated his law-enforcement career to her memory.

They sat in the living room, a bright, airy venue, made so by new white Berber carpet and pastel furniture and draperies. This included Truck's chair, which was the largest recliner Lynn had ever seen. It was solid white Naugahyde with brown trim and was aimed right at the large-screen television across the room. Lynn sat on the couch which was covered with a burlap-looking off-white material. Her eye swept the coffee table and picked up the Flip Pallot pictorial book on salt-water fly-fishing she had given Truck for Christmas.

"Darla's not here?"

"Grocery shopping," Truck answered as he worked the lever on the side of his recliner and angled his gargantuan figure backwards, still maintaining eye contact with Lynn.

"What's the book on Aubrey Lowe?" Lynn asked.

Truck looked at the ceiling, which wasn't difficult in his reclining position. "Aubrey Lowe," he said. "Commercial fisherman. Pretty tough customer. Marine patrol's caught him more than once for illegal gill netting. Last time he was prosecuted but got off on some technicality about the construction of his net. Don't think he has a record, but I could check. Why?"

Lynn told Truck what happened on the water that afternoon. "Guess I was thinking maybe Millard Savage ran into Aubrey Lowe at the wrong time. Millard was a conservationist, an activist really. In fact, he could be a pain in the ass when he wanted to be. Wasn't the type to be scared off or back down. What do you think?"

Truck went for the lever again and abruptly brought himself down to a regular sitting position before he answered. "I think we know that Savage was killed with a hammer, not a handgun. But I also think Aubrey is a pretty mean motherfucker."

Lynn smiled. "Some folks say that about you."

Truck cut a knowing glance at Lynn as he said in one of his growls, "I can exert influence on people when the situation calls for it. I'll tell Symanski about this and we'll check ol' Aubrey out."

SIXTEEN

IT WAS AFTER DARK when Lynn got home and let Mullet out. The evening was clear and she looked out at the calm gulf and saw the lights of three shrimp boats on the horizon. She picked up her phone and heard the stutter dial tone indicating a message. Sammy Osceola had arrived on the island for his photography of the Indian mounds. He'd called after checking into the Lodge. Wanted to meet for drinks at Boatmen's Marina. Said if he didn't see Lynn by seven, he'd know she wasn't coming.

Lynn looked at her watch and figured she could make it. Usually Sammy stayed with Lynn, or lately sometimes with Rolf, but since his daughter Johnnie Osceola was coming, he'd opted for the Lodge.

Sammy was at the bar nursing a Ketel One vodka on the rocks. He was dressed in khaki outdoor garb. Lynn slipped up behind him and, in a low grunt, said, "Injun drink firewater."

Osceola spun around and, grinning, said, "Hey, Madame Butterfly. Man, it's good firewater, too. I-75 was a pain in the ass." They exchanged a short hug and Sammy added, "What kind you want?"

As she climbed on the stool next to her friend, Lynn said, "Same old thing, I guess. Absolut. Lynn's a dull girl."

Sammy shrugged. "Butterfly just know what she like."

"Has your daughter arrived yet?"

Osceola's face took on a grave look. "No. Johnnie was supposed to be here by now, but..." He shook his head. "Lynn, there's no telling where she is."

"What do you mean?"

Osceola looked hard at his vodka for a few long moments before he spoke. "She'll just stop at a bar and start drinking.

You haven't seen her in several years. She's not that glamorous or anything, but she just has a kind of magnetism. Takes men whenever she wants. Women, too, for that matter. But she'd just as soon beat the shit out of them. The men, I mean. And does. Particularly if they come on too strong and she just doesn't like them."

"Has she been in any kind of trouble?"

"Sure. She's a college coed but thinks she's an old timey Indian. Studies all the lore. Talks to the old guys, the 'warriors,' never the women. Seems like she's trying to recapture the past. Keeps reminding me that our Seminole Tribe was never conquered by the white man. You know about it. No peace treaty ever signed? Never any surrender? It was my namesake, Chief Osceola—his name was Billy Powell before that—who sat down with the government officials over the treaty the white man drew up and took out his knife and stabbed it. 'That's my signature,' he said and walked out. Anyway, I've tried everything to convince Johnnie it's the twenty-first century, that the white man's running the show and that there are many wonderful things for us to have, but..."

"What about the trouble?"

"Assault charge on some guy in a bar, carrying a concealed weapon. Stuff like that. I pulled all the right levers and got her off."

They were sitting side by side at the Boatmen's Marina bar. The bar was of cedar, but finished so it looked like teak with a high-gloss urethane finish. The walls were of rustic pecky cypress, stained to match the teak shade of the bar. Fishing and boating stuff was everywhere—nets, buoys, anchors, lures and plugs, and rods wired to the wall. There was also local art, including a Rolf Berglund watercolor of the exterior of the marina. The centerpiece of the bar was a mount of a giant tarpon. It was said that the fish was one of the few landed in Boca Grande Pass which exceeded two hundred pounds.

The place was bustling with a mix of fishing guides, tourists and islanders, and Jimmy Buffet was heard over the sound system singing about his cheeseburger in paradise, a song about nearby Cabbage Key. Lynn sensed someone behind them. Before she could turn she heard a familiar voice.

"This a private party?"

A man flashing a pearly grin was standing behind and between Lynn and Sammy Osceola. He was mid-forties, going perhaps six-two and with a pro linebacker's build. His curly hair was prematurely gray and long enough in the back to protrude prominently from underneath a cap. A full but close-cropped almost-white beard covered his square jaw. That and his tan made his lively brown eyes appear to peek over the top of his beard. He was dressed in khakis and a white shirt with a leaping tarpon logo over his heart, with his name under it.

"Sammy Osceola, meet Capt. Jack Espinosa," Lynn said as she turned.

"Jack," Sammy said and shook the man's hand.

"Bar open?" Jack Espinosa said with a grin.

"Have at it," Lynn answered with a wave in the direction of the mounted tarpon.

"Dewar's rocks," Espinosa called to the bartender.

Lynn eyed the man who had joined them. She didn't know Jack Espinosa that well. He was a fly-fishing guide and they had worked together a few times when she had needed another boat for a tour, or where he had needed another boat for fishing. She'd taken his extra anglers a few times even though she was far from expert at being a fishing guide. Espinosa had grown up in Tampa with a 97-mile-per-hour fastball for which the Pittsburgh Pirates paid him a nice bonus. He almost made it to the show before his arm gave out, then used his skills as a consummate outdoorsman to make a living: fishing guide at Boca Grande and other places, running duck trips on Lake Kissimmee. Occasionally he would attempt something more mainstream, like trying to promote the development of a residential subdivision using someone else's money.

But it was something else in his background which everyone always talked about. Jack Espinosa was a convicted felon. He had always been adept at trapping alligators, both when it was legal and when it was not. What he served time for was somehow obtaining his fishing clients' drivers licenses and social security information and using them to fraudulently apply for gator trapping permits, then harvesting the extra gators and selling the skins.

"Listen, if ya'll are having a romantic evening or something, I can just slide down the bar here and wait for the women to start hanging off me," said Espinosa, flashing his pearly molars like a strobe light.

"No, stay," said Lynn. "Sammy's an old friend. He just got on the island. He's waiting for his daughter."

"Heard you had a rough trip the other day," Espinosa said to Lynn. "Well, I guess I heard it *and* read it in the paper. Pretty gory, huh?"

Lynn mentally whipped out her goriness scale and measured the horror of finding Millard Savage's body against the terror of staring at Aubrey Lowe's gun barrel. Realizing that Espinosa could not know about today's incident, she replied, "It was worse than it sounded in the paper."

"So what happened? The paper said somebody beat the guy up?"

"That's about all they know," Lynn said.

"No clues? Who do they think did it?" Espinosa asked.

"I don't think they have any clues, and I don't think they have a clue as to who did it, either."

"Well, you were there—what did you see?"

Lynn answered, went on to explain her relationship with the family, and finished with a request to change the subject. The whole conversation weighed on her. She realized that Symanski and Truck Kershaw did not, in fact, seem to have any clues regarding Millard Savage's murder. She thought again about the afternoon encounter with Aubrey Lowe, something she hadn't told Sammy or Espinosa about. She was supposed to take Sammy to the back bays starting tomorrow, but wondered if she should get Espinosa to take him the first day so she could stay close to the murder investigation, particularly to run down the Aubrey Lowe thing. She owed it to the admiral. Sammy would understand.

"You got a trip tomorrow?" Lynn asked Espinosa.

"Nope. But it's okay because I probably won't be guiding that much longer anyway. Got too much else working."

"Yeah? Like what?"

Espinosa nodded deferentially at Osceola. "Sorry to bore you with this, pardner." Then turning to Lynn, said, "I got some real-estate development deals cooking that, if they come together, I won't piss on the few hundred bucks a day I get for guiding. Hell, I'll be hiring you to take me on the water."

"Sounds great, Jack. You talking about around here somewhere? And, by the way, where are you going to get the money?"

"I'm working on the money part, and I can't say too much about where, except it's someplace that's never been considered for residential development before."

Lynn wondered if Espinosa might be angling for the development of some of the mangrove backcountry if the state legislature approved it as Sammy Osceola feared. She looked at Sammy and wondered if he was thinking the same thing.

Looking back at Espinosa, Lynn said, "Well, until you get rich, how about helping me out tomorrow."

Then Lynn turned to Osceola and said, "Would you mind going with Jack tomorrow? There's something else I really need to do. Jack knows the back bays as well or better than I do, and we'll still have dinner tomorrow night with Rolf. Johnnie, too, if she shows up. What do you say?"

"I say I'll do whatever. I'll go with this fellow tomorrow, no problem."

"We'll leave at eight," Espinosa said. "But I have to be back at three."

Osceola thought a moment and said, "Tell you what. Let's leave at ten, then when you bring me back I'll rent a small boat and go back out. I want to take some pictures around sunset."

"What are you going to take pictures of?" Espinosa asked.

"There's a move afoot in the legislature to approve real-estate development on some of the backcountry mangrove islands. Pictures of how pristine they are will help me fight it." Osceola's answer was delivered in a measured tone, but its edge was unmistakable. So was the intensity of his eye contact with Espinosa.

"Fight it. Gonna write a letter?" Espinosa asked.

Sammy shook his head. "Going right to the horse's mouth. I'm a lobbyist. I'm doing it for a living, but if I weren't, I'd definitely write a letter."

Sammy Osceola and Jack Espinosa looked hard at each other for a few moments, each appearing to try to divine something from their exchange.

When Espinosa agreed to take care of Osceola the following day, Lynn turned to Sammy. "Remember, dinner at Squid Row tomorrow night with Rolf. I'll make the reservation for eight o'clock. And Sammy. Be careful out there taking those pictures. The last guy who did that…"

She didn't finish.

SEVENTEEN

ROLF BERGLUND'S HOUSE was right on the gulf, and like all Boca Grande structures built after 1978, was built on pilings. Its first level was on the second floor with the ground level as parking. The Gulf of Mexico had washed under the house more than once during hurricanes, and had risen high on the pilings during the killer storms.

The place was magazine material. The floors were exquisite old pine from Hardee County, as were some of the walls. Expensive wallpaper covered the rest. Rolf had many fine things. They were collected over the years with his late wife, the most remarkable of which was a massive twelve-foot, eight-panel, black-lacquered Cormandel screen from China. Rolf had excellent taste and appreciated his surroundings.

Lynn was sitting in the breakfast room which was a windowed, cupola-shaped annex off the kitchen. It was angled out from the kitchen to take advantage of Rolf's view of the gulf. She was in her jogging gear after doing her morning three miles.

She looked at the breakfast table Rolf had prepared. She saw a sectioned pink grapefruit in a Vietri bowl which was made for the purpose, a matching plate of eggs Benedict with small nasturtiums as garnish, and a crystal flute filled with bubbling champagne. Freshly picked sea grape leaves served as place mats and fresh gardenias were floating in water in the center of the table.

Rolf. He was all man, but he had some wonderful moves to go with it. He was easily the most complex, yet most sensitive man she had ever known. He was a walking dichotomy. He was an accomplished fly-fisherman, had been on the wrestling team at Georgia Tech, and had an impressive collection of vintage shotguns. Yet, he was an artist, collected and knew fine wines, loved opera and cooking, and could just as easily be found watching *Antiques Roadshow* on television as sports.

Rolf was a regular Howard Hughes, Jr. Never touched a door with anything but his elbow. Detested shaking hands, always immediately thereafter looking for a bathroom to furiously wash his. Lynn thought she saw him hyperventilate once when he couldn't find his little pocket bottle of Purell hand sanitizer. "Are you sick?" he would ask anyone who dared to cough.

He had been an aggressive businessman before selling his company. But one reason he sold was his rising disgust with the activities of the very group which were his prime customers: real-estate developers. He finally concluded they were having a rapacious effect on the environment and decided to withdraw from participating in the industry.

Their relationship had grown in bursting fashion like a spring flower, but now had stabilized, and Lynn wasn't sure just how. The concept that one must love to be loved was operational in her relationship with Rolf, but Lynn knew she had the better of the bargain. Rolf's love usually seemed unconditional, and his capacity for it exceeded hers. Lynn, often lugubrious and distant, and still wallowing in guilt, was the brooding recalcitrant, but she told herself she did her best. She treasured him, wanted to please him, wanted him to be proud of her. Above all, she needed him.

Rolf swept into the room like Cary Grant might have in a forties movie. He had showered and wore off-white linen shorts, a navy island shirt with yellow palm trees on it, and slip-on loafers. He came up behind her, putting his arms around her, and kissed her ear, whispering, "How was the run?" Lynn could feel her goose bumps emerging.

"Can't you tell by the smell?" she said. "One of us is inappropriately dressed, and me thinks 'tis I."

He stayed behind her and switched to the other ear. "You smell fantastic to me."

"Are you saying you like sweaty, stinky, Chinese-American women?" she said.

"Mmm, something like that," he said.

She craned her neck and flashed him a smile. "Then you're weird."

He left her, then came around and sat across the table from her. "Well, we both know that," he said brightly. "Hungry?"

She looked at the table. "You shouldn't have," she said.

But she knew why he had. Last night after she left Sammy Osceola at the Boatmen's Marina bar, she had phoned him. She told him about begging off with Sammy Osceola so she could check on the murder investigation. He told her about one of his commission clients giving him some fresh stone crabs and asked her to come over right away so they could dig in. She told him it sounded great but she needed to stop by and check on the admiral and Muffy. Rolf said something about that old man being more important than he was and something else about the time he had put in with Muffy, and wasn't that enough, and their quarrel was on. Lynn ended up at her own house eating a frozen chicken dinner while she watched a show on the History Channel about the Medici of Florence.

When Lynn had left for her jog that morning, she found the note taped to her door. It was on white notepaper with a big *Rolf Berglund* pre-printed at the top in black ink. In his bold hand, he had written with a black felt pen: *I'm really sorry, my love. Breakfast after your run, my house?*

What had she done to deserve such a sweet man? Lynn only sipped at the champagne, but dove in hard on the eggs Benedict. Afterwards they had coffee on Rolf's porch as they watched the whitecaps caused by the northwest breeze which would make boaters venturing offshore that day uncomfortable. They engaged in one of their rousing Scrabble games, Rolf winning on the last draw with the word "quip" using the triple-word-score square. Rolf then claimed the preservation of his "undefeated" record when in fact Lynn usually won at least half the time, maybe more. It was a marvelous morning, Lynn thought. But she still wished she had a charter that day. Or the next, or the next, for that matter.

EIGHTEEN

THE DAY WAS A BUST. Lynn regretted palming Sammy Osceola off on Jack Espinosa because the day's activity on Millard Savage's murder consisted only of talking by phone to Truck Kershaw, who was waiting for word on Aubrey Lowe from the Florida Department of Law Enforcement in Tallahassee, and of stopping by to visit with the admiral and Muffy. While there, she told them of her encounter with Aubrey Lowe. The rest of the day Lynn filled with doing a better job of cleaning her boat than she had after coming in from confronting Aubrey Lowe.

By seven p.m. she had showered and dressed for the evening in cream-colored pants with an untucked green-and-yellow-flowered blouse. She selected her grandmother's jade necklace and earrings. The ensemble was elegantly casual and perfectly suitable for coastal, resorty Florida. An exception to that was the high season at Boca Grande when the regulars staying at the Lodge would be at a Squid Row table next to a sometimes shorts-clad Lynn, wearing their yacht-club-crested navy blazers, bright-colored long pants, Gucci loafers and no socks.

Lynn took her golf cart to Rolf's in time for a drink prior to meeting Sammy Osceola for dinner. Rolf looked smashing in his slacks with a tropical shirt with leaping tarpon all over and Allen Edmonds casual loafers. He had a David Benoit CD rippling jazz piano throughout the house. They had agreed on a truce: in Rolf's house he could play his jazz which Lynn detested. Doody-doody music, she called it, which made him furious. In her house it was her music. Although she was not yet born when they became famous, Lynn was a Beatles devotee, Paul McCartney, in particular. James Taylor was her close second. One thing they did share a taste for was classical music, and Rolf was trying to get Lynn interested in opera.

They sat on Rolf's porch in ringside seats for the spectacular show, which was in progress. The dreamsicle orange sun had just melted into the horizon like a silver globule of mercury. They both swore to each other they had seen the legendary "green flash" at the moment the sun disappeared. Then the clouds became like Rolf's palette. Against the wide sky, orange and pink streaked through the few wispy clouds, making a garish, cotton-candy mosaic of color.

They sipped chardonnay while taking it all in. Lynn watched the spectacular sky, but her peripheral vision picked up Rolf regularly glancing over at her. It sent a ripple of sexual excitement through her.

"Thanks for forgiving me," he said when she looked over to face him.

"Thanks for asking me to," she replied.

"I was an asshole," he said.

"We covered that this morning," she said. "And, as I recall, I convinced you that you weren't."

"You still think I'm not?"

"I still think you're a wonderful man and I still love you very much, how about that?" Then, before he could answer, she looked at her watch and added, "Hey, we need to meet Sammy."

They stood to leave facing each other but Rolf stopped her by putting his hands on her shoulders, then let them slip down to her waist and around it in a seamless motion which resulted in their lips being clamped in a deep, wet kiss. Lynn felt her breathing become short and gently explosive. She experienced the accompanying light-headed spell of arousal as she felt the space between their torsos become occupied by something which wasn't there moments earlier.

"We've got to meet Sammy," she said between short, hard breaths.

"Let's be fashionably late," he said, also breathing hard.

"Wouldn't be fashionable," she said, eyes closed but exploring with her mouth.

"Aren't Indians always late, or is it the Chinese?" he said.

Lynn started unbuttoning Rolf's shirt. "Indians," she breathed.

"Now you're talking," he whispered.

"Have to be a quickie," she whispered back.

LYNN AND ROLF WAITED at their table at Squid Row, polishing off most of a bottle of Steele chardonnay while intermittently glancing at the clock on the wall near the kitchen door. Any worry they'd had about keeping Sammy Osceola waiting had dissolved as he had turned those tables on them.

When they weren't looking at the clock, Rolf sat with his hands under his chin giving Lynn a goo-goo kind of gaze. "You have a particular glow just now, miss," he said.

She smiled demurely at him. That surprised her until she realized that demure was what she was feeling. "I wonder why…" she said.

When they hit the forty-five-minute mark with no Sammy, Lynn had long since stopped feeling demure. Just plain worried was what she was. "I'm going to call him," she said, and left the table for the restaurant's phone.

Lynn dialed the Lodge. No answer in Sammy's room. She dialed her own voicemail on her home line. No message. Back to the table.

At the one-hour mark, they ordered dinner. By ten o'clock they were waiting for their pecan pie and Lynn tried the Lodge and her voicemail again. Nothing. She was worried—this was not like Sammy.

She found Jack Espinosa's number and got him.

"Jack, any idea where Sammy is?"

"No, am I supposed to have one?"

"You took him today?"

"Did I take him? He had his camera smoking. You should have seen these two eagles—"

"When did you get back?"

"Around three. Hey, you didn't tell me he's an Indian. Nice guy. We—"

"Did he have his daughter with him?"

"No, and he seemed a little fried that she hadn't showed."

"What happened after you got back?"

"Took him to Fenton's Marina and got him set up with a boat rental so he could take his pictures like he was talking about last night. What's with the interrogation?"

"You see him after that?"

"Nope."

"Listen, do you have Madeline Albury's home number?" Lynn asked.

"Now I get it. He was meeting you for dinner and he stood you up. Hang on, let me see if I can find Maddy's number."

Lynn waited. The phone at Squid Row was at the end of the bar and she watched a fishing guide she knew, and woman she didn't, slide off their bar stools and break into an impromptu, undulating exhibition of something like the Watusi, even though no music was playing.

Espinosa came back on the line.

"Okay, here's the number," he said.

"Got it."

"Good luck."

"Yeah."

Lynn reached Madeline Albury at home and learned that Sammy did not turn the boat in. "It's okay, he's got until tomorrow afternoon before he'll owe any more money," Madeline said.

"What'd he rent?"

"Eighteen Whaler, I think."

Lynn's fingers were unsteady as she dialed the Lodge and learned there were no Boston Whalers at the dock. They shook slightly as she made her next call. It was to Truck Kershaw.

NINETEEN

IT WAS JUST PAST NINE the next morning when a loud knock on the door and Mullet's accompanying bark woke Lynn from an after-breakfast doze while sitting on her living room couch. She was trying to cure a combination of her late-night dealing with Sammy Osceola's disappearance and the quantity of wine consumed while she and Rolf had waited for Sammy. The couch was an old, overstuffed, slip-covered piece that her grandparents used to own. The current slip-cover was ecru, but it was adorned with colorful pillows, some of which her grandmother needle pointed, some of which were placed there by Rolf. It was her favorite nap place because she could arrange the pillows to support her head as she dozed, sitting up with the television on low volume.

She and Truck had ridden the back bays in Lynn's skiff until two a.m., flashing high powered searchlights in every direction, finding nothing.

The knocking continued. Lynn was alert when she threw open the front door to find the sun trying to stream through her doorway. But the light was partially eclipsed by the hulk of Truck Kershaw. Mullet's tail whapped Lynn on her knee as the black lab offered his greeting to the large, familiar visitor. One look at Truck told Lynn it was bad news.

"Come on in," Lynn said.

When they had gotten as far as the living room couch, Lynn stopped and said, "Tell me."

Truck began with a large sigh. "They found him. Sorry, Cap'n Lynn, he's dead. Hate to have to tell you this, but his rental boat was found floating twenty miles offshore. His body was floating, too. It was tied to the boat with a fifteen-foot mooring line."

"You sure it's Sammy?"

Truck nodded. "His wallet was on him, that was the only way."

"What do you mean?"

"Well..."

"What?"

"The sharks kind of had their way with him. Ft. Myers will confirm the ID with dental records. Lynn, I'm sorry."

Lynn sagged onto the couch. Her vision went mushy and the room began to oscillate. She was only vaguely aware of Truck Kershaw's hand on her shoulder. She sat forward and held her head in her hands.

The image that popped into her head was from her college years, the first time Sammy Osceola had invited Lynn to Boca Grande. They were wade fishing for snook at Captiva pass. Lynn hooked a whopper fish which threatened to strip all the line from the spool of her spinning reel. She had no choice but to wade after the blistering run of the trophy snook. The deep hole surprised Lynn. She gulped some bay water, got into trouble. She would never forget feeling Sammy's strong hand on her arm, pulling her to a higher part of the bay bottom and safety.

Guilt washed over Lynn. Why didn't she take Sammy out yesterday like she was supposed to? They could have stayed as long as Sammy wanted and he wouldn't have had to rent a boat. She could have been with him the whole time and could have protected him. She knew her guilt over Dave's death and her father's was a serious issue in her life, and now this. It occurred to her that she was doomed to a life of heavy-drinking, pill-popping melancholy, and wondered why somebody like Rolf would even want to be around her, much less get married.

Sammy. The pain of the loss began to spread through her, but she told herself to shut it out and focus on doing her part to help track down what was perhaps now a two-time Boca Grande murderer. She owed it to the admiral. She owed it to herself.

She looked up to see Truck Kershaw sitting in a rattan chair across from her, methodically scratching Mullet under his chin. Between them was the coffee table, the oldest piece in the house, a seaman's trunk which Lynn's grandfather won from a Japanese sailor in a wager. Truck was looking at her, waiting.

"Sure sorry, Cap'n Lynn," he said, almost in a whisper.

Lynn gave him a doleful look, then gathered herself in a posture-straightening movement, indulged herself in a long sigh, and said, "Thanks, Truck. We need to get busy."

"What do you mean we need to get busy?"

Lynn was now sitting on the edge of the sofa, hands on her knees, looking intently at Truck. "Two people close to me have been slaughtered. I'm going to try to help you and Symanski."

"That's assuming Symanski officially lets me work on the cases. You *know* I'm not in CID. Of course, out here on this island I have a lot of freedom, so I'll do what I can."

"What did you find out about Aubrey Lowe?" Lynn asked.

Truck shook his head. "Nothing more than I told you when you stopped by my house night before last. Just a badass netter who pretty much does what he wants. Remember I said he beat the rap on the illegal netting arrest? But your theory about Millard Savage getting in his way makes sense. Aubrey Lowe should be what Symanski would call 'a person of interest.' Problem is Symanski got no interest."

"For God's sake, why?"

Truck shook his head again. "Beats the shit out of me. Says there could be a dozen of those guys sneaking around the back-country any given night. I don't agree with him, but he didn't seem to want to hear it."

"Look, Aubrey Lowe can't be ignored," Lynn said. "I think I'm going to follow him a couple of nights and see what he might be up to besides illegal netting."

"Cuidado, Senora," said Truck.

"Thanks," Lynn said. "Or *gracias,* I guess." Then simply, *"Symanski,"* spitting it out as though uttering a vile profanity.

Lynn stood and walked to the open French doors leading to

her porch. She stood with her back to Truck who was still sitting in the cottage's small living room. The weather was starting to deteriorate and the sky had turned to slate. Lynn watched a frigate bird conduct its laconic yet stately glide high above the gulf's surface.

"By the way," Truck said. "He's on his way over here to talk to you about your friend."

Lynn spun around to face Truck. "You're kidding," she said, and quickly sat down across from him again.

She told him about Jack Espinosa joining her and Sammy Osceola at the Boatmen's Marina bar. She included Espinosa's repeated questioning of Sammy about his photography expedition, his boasting about his real-estate development deal, and Lynn's own musing about the mangrove islands being Espinosa's possible site if the legislature approved it despite Sammy's vigorous lobbying.

"In addition to that," Lynn said, "Espinosa was one of the last people to see Sammy alive. I think we should go see him."

"I can't go officially. But if you go, maybe I'll tag along."

"After Symanski leaves?"

"You got it, man."

"Am I obligated to tell Symanski about Jack Espinosa?"

"Up to you, man. Why?"

"I want to talk to Espinosa first."

TWENTY

SYMANSKI, WITH HIS white necktie and ample supply of the word "basically," arrived and interviewed Lynn who gave him Madeline Albury's name as the person who rented Sammy his Boston Whaler. Lynn answered questions about her friendship with Sammy, but said nothing about Jack Espinosa or Aubrey Lowe.

Lynn thought about that and wondered why she was being cagey with Symanski. She knew the answer: Millard, Sammy, and her lack of confidence that Symanski could find their killers. But self-doubt began to rise in her like the reflux of overspiced gumbo. Should she have come clean with Symanski? In fact, was she obstructing justice, making her guilty of a crime? She ruminated about it, then convinced herself that she just wanted to have the first shot at Jack Espinosa, and that Aubrey Lowe was of no interest to Symanski anyway. Besides, she could tell Symanski about Espinosa anytime after talking to him.

Symanski was wrapping up but then seemed to have an afterthought. To Lynn it seemed planned. "What do you basically know about Osceola's family?" Symanski asked.

"Divorced. Has a college-aged daughter. In fact, she was supposed to be down here with him," Lynn answered.

"So where is she?"

"Good question. Sammy was telling me that she's kind of wild, maybe has a little drinking problem."

"I need to find her. Need to talk to her," said Symanski.

"What help could she be?" asked Lynn.

They were sitting in the living room, Lynn on the couch and Truck and Symanski in the two rattan chairs opposite. Mullet had been sleeping next to Lynn, but now unceremoniously rose, stretched, and ambled into the kitchen. The dog had ignored Symanski.

"Maybe she did it," said Symanski.

"Are you kidding? She wasn't even here," Lynn said.

"You just said you didn't know *where* she was. She could have been here and killed him. Most murders are committed by people who have a close relationship with the victim. And it sure wouldn't be the first time a father was basically killed by a daughter."

Lynn wondered how it was possible to *basically kill* someone. "So did Johnnie Osceola kill Millard Savage, too?"

Symanski flipped his note pad closed, stuck it in his coat pocket, then stood. "Maybe she became a copycat so she could kill her old man. Look, I don't know who killed either one of them, or if the two crimes are even connected. But the only way I'll find out is to talk to people and ask questions. Let me know if you hear from the girl."

Now Truck spoke for the first time. "Is CID going to want me to help on this, Lieutenant?"

"For the moment just keep your eyes open out here for suspicious persons or activity, which you're supposed to be doing anyway. I'll be in touch."

Lynn walked Symanski to the door. They neither spoke nor shook hands as he left. Back on her sofa, Lynn said, "That was uplifting."

"Charming man," Truck said.

"You know he sings barbershop?" Lynn asked.

"Unfortunately. I was at the interview with your admiral buddy, remember?" Then Truck launched an impromptu mimic of Symanski's humming.

"Ever heard him perform?"

"Haven't been that unlucky yet."

Lynn's lip curled in amusement. "You know where Jack Espinosa lives?" she asked.

"Nope. You?"

She picked up her phone and dialed the ship's store at

Boatmen's Marina. Donna told her that Espinosa's boat was in its slip, indicating no charter that day. She gave Lynn Espinosa's address.

"Ready?" Lynn said to Truck.

"I'll have to follow you."

Just then the brass dolphin door knocker on Lynn's front door sounded again, followed by Mullet's bark. Lynn and Truck looked at each other for a couple of beats. Then Truck rolled his eyes. "I'll bet it's Stan the Man. Sometimes I wonder if he thinks he's Columbo. He's probably going to say 'Capt. Lynn, just one more thing.'"

Lynn went to the door and opened it. On the steps stood Miss Johnnie Osceola.

TWENTY-ONE

SAMMY OSCEOLA'S DAUGHTER *looked* like an Indian. Her hair was straight and shiny black. It was parted in the middle and drawn low on either side of her head into braided pigtails tied with blue beaded rawhide. Her cheekbones were classically high, and her eyes, which seemed the color of onyx, were circumspect yet assertive. Her bare lips were thin, her thick eyebrows naturally arched. She wore a baby blue flats fishing shirt and khaki quick-dry flats shorts, and she was barefoot.

Four years ago, Lynn and her dad had rented a boat and taken a gangly seventeen-year-old high-school girl on the water who had not yet fulfilled her destiny of becoming a late bloomer. Now the grown woman standing before her was almost six feet tall. She was still slim, but now she was not slim everywhere. She looked athletic. Lynn saw her as handsomely attractive rather than beautiful, but recognized that she exuded a feral sensuality.

"You going to invite me in, Lynn? It is okay if I call you Lynn now, isn't it?" she said.

"Please come in, Johnnie. I guess it's been…what, four years? A real difference."

"You mean in the way I look? Yeah, I guess so. Kind of grew up, didn't I?" Johnnie said, stepping into Lynn's living room.

Johnnie Osceola looked down at Lynn who didn't know whether to hug or shake hands. She did neither. Mullet checked her out and immediately approved.

"I just got here," she said, petting Mullet while still looking at Lynn. As she petted, she suddenly looked down at Mullet. "What happened to your dog's ear?" she asked, leaving her mouth open after she said it.

"Got a little too close to a gator," Lynn said.

Johnnie made a little sad face and said she was sorry, then moved on. "My dad's room at the Lodge didn't answer so I figured I'd catch up with you both here. I'm ready to go."

Lynn looked at Truck then back at Johnnie. "Go where?" she asked.

"On your boat, what else? That's why I came down here."

Lynn stepped closer to Johnnie. She picked up a scent she recognized coming from her breath and her pores which told her that Johnnie's alcohol consumption the previous evening had been heavy. She took Johnnie by the shoulders, steered her gently to the couch, and then sat in the chair across from her.

"Johnnie..." she began.

Johnnie's eyes seemed larger. They were moving rapidly. "Something's wrong...what?"

"It's your dad, Johnnie."

She went to the edge of Lynn's sofa. "What? Tell me."

"I'm afraid he's gone."

"Gone? You mean..." She opened her mouth twice, but nothing came out either time. The third time something did. "You mean...dead?"

Lynn nodded. Then she saw Johnnie Osceola's dark eyes fill with water. An instant later a switch seemed to get thrown. She suddenly sat more erect, and gathered herself as she flicked the tears away, and her face grew stern. She got up and walked to the French doors leading to Lynn's porch, stepped out and stood looking at the gulf. Lynn followed. Truck stayed in the living room.

The March winds were now blowing in sheets of mist from the northwest in advance of a cold front. The breeze was stiff, creating whitecaps on the Gulf of Mexico. A wind chime Rolf had given Lynn tinkled. She hated wind chimes, but left it hanging and pretended to like it. Johnnie stood with her arms folded, Lynn beside her.

"What happened? Heart attack?" she asked, still looking at the water. Her voice was so quiet Lynn could barely hear it over the building surf.

"Johnnie, he was murdered."

She spun around, black eyes blazing. "What?"

"He went with another guide yesterday because I had something come up. Then he rented a Whaler to take some late-day pictures of the Indian mounds in the back bays. He never came back. His body was found offshore, tied to the Whaler."

Johnnie turned back toward the gulf and stared at it, arms folded. The breeze freshened slightly and caused just one wisp of her shiny black hair to escape its swept-back restraint, and it oscillated in the wind like a writhing, unattended garden hose.

"Who?" she said, quietly again, still staring at the whitecaps.

"Who what?" Lynn said.

She turned to face her, arms still folded. Johnnie's black eyes were cold, hard, and flat as a manhole cover. "Who did it?" she said with more volume and a gray flint edge on her voice. "Who killed my father?"

Lynn figured Sammy's daughter would show up, but she didn't figure on this. She figured on long, comforting hugs to a sobbing bereaved girl. Instead, her imagination flashed on a vision of this full-grown Seminole Indian woman with a real tomahawk in one hand, somebody's scalp in the other, and her flats fishing shirt splattered with blood. Maybe she was remembering what Sammy said about Johnnie spending so much time with the old Indians who remembered the "warrior stuff" their ancestors had told them.

"Johnnie, nobody knows who did this. Anyway, you just found out your father's dead, don't you want to...you know... be sad first? Do some mourning?"

"I'll have plenty of time for that."

"Look, Johnnie, you probably don't know that your dad's murder was not the first on this island lately." It was Lynn's turn to pause and look out at the gulf. After a moment she turned back to her and said, "Your dad is the second friend I've lost in as many weeks."

"No, I didn't know about that, and I don't want to know about it. I only want to know who killed my father."

"Well, the sheriff's trying to find out and so am I."

"That means you have some ideas."

Lynn looked back at the beach. The tide had been ebbing for several hours. The wind brought them the distinct scent of the open sea and the pleasantly sodden aromas which come with low tide. The shellers were out in force. She watched the derriere of a middle aged woman in a two-piece, yellow-flowered bathing suit with a short unbuttoned rain jacket as she bent over to pick up a shell. She heard her yell with delight to her companion that she had found the perfect olive. It occurred to her that the woman had certainly not found the perfect bathing suit. At least not for her. Don't be catty, Lynn told herself.

"Let's go inside," Lynn said.

Lynn formally introduced Johnnie to Truck Kershaw.

"Are you going to find my father's killer?" she asked.

"I'm not in the Criminal Investigation Division, miss. Sometimes I help when they ask me," Truck said.

"Sit down again, Johnnie. We need to talk," Lynn said, motioning to the couch.

"About what?" she said as she sat.

"About things like arrangements for your father, contacting your mother, what you're going to do. About your own grieving process. That's important, you know."

"My mother lives in Colorado now. I'll call her and she'll handle everything. As for me, I'm staying right here until we find my father's murderer. Except for going to Tallahassee for the funeral."

"What do mean, until we find the murderer?" Lynn asked.

She didn't answer. Just gave her a flat, cold, black-eyed stare.

Lynn's first thought was to invite Johnnie to stay at her cottage with her. Then she considered the young woman's determination to hang around until her father's murder was solved, and she came up with a different plan. "I suggest you use your dad's room at the Lodge," Lynn said. "I'll take you over there and see if I can come and stay with you tonight. You can call your mother and other people who need to be notified. The deputy here and I have a little errand to run," Lynn said.

"What kind of errand?"

"We have to go see somebody."

"It's about the killings, isn't it? I'm going with you. I can make my phone calls on my cell phone," she said.

"Oh, no, you don't. You're going to the Lodge."

The look she gave Lynn wasn't defiance. Wasn't a pout. Not petulance either. It was a look of pure certitude.

She said, quietly, "You may as well take me, Lynn, because I'll follow you anyway."

TWENTY-TWO

TWENTY MINUTES AFTER Johnnie Osceola vowed to follow Lynn on her "errand," she was in the passenger seat of Lynn's CR-V heading off the island with Lynn while Truck followed. They had dropped Johnnie's car at the Lodge. They tried to get the key to her father's room but were given a key to another one as Symanski's team was sweeping Sammy's room for any evidence they might find. No longer barefoot, Johnnie was wearing tan-colored moccasins.

"So where are we going?" she asked.

"To see a man named Jack Espinosa," Lynn said, her eyes on the road.

"You think he did it?" she asked.

"I don't know."

"Then why are you going to see him?"

"Because I think he might know something."

"Why do you think so?"

Lynn told her of the conversation at the Boatmen's Marina bar with her father and Jack Espinosa which led to her suspicion that Espinosa might have a keen interest in real-estate development being allowed in the back-bay mangrove islands. She pointed out that if the ace lobbyist in Tallahassee who could cause such development to be prevented were to disappear, that could help Espinosa tremendously.

"So what are you going to ask him, Lynn?"

Lynn said nothing for a few moments then glanced over and saw her still looking at her, waiting for an answer. She was still trying to get used to the transformation of her friend's child into a hot-blooded woman now addressing her by her first name. It made her feel old. She looked back at the road.

"I'm not sure," she said.

Lynn crossed the causeway islands and noticed a small fleet of recreational boats fishing in the rain for pompano in Gasparilla Pass. She cleared the bridge and turned onto 776. By the time she reached San Casa and turned onto it, Johnnie had fallen silent. It was the first time she had stopped talking. The only sound was the momentary low whir of the windshield wipers which were operating on intermittent mode in the light rain. Lynn used the solitude to ponder her unwanted circumstances. She was nervous, apprehensive, and figured she was getting too old for this sort of thing. She wished she could stop by and talk to the admiral to get his take on all this. And his advice.

It was after she made the San Casa curve and was almost abreast of the high school that she heard it. It was a strange sound. At first Lynn thought it was a sneeze being suppressed. Then she looked at Johnnie and saw that it was a sob. The sound came again, followed by three more. She stared out her window, giving Lynn the back of her head.

"Johnnie, it's okay to let it out," Lynn said, gently.

She turned her head to face her. Tears were streaming. Just tears, not the kind of muddy melting of gook that some women display when bawling, because Johnnie wasn't wearing mascara or make-up. She didn't need it. Her handsomeness was raw, primal, and spoke for itself.

"What do you call this?" she almost screamed, pointing both index fingers at her face.

"I call it grief, and that's a beneficial thing," Lynn said, still using a nurturing tone.

"You don't know the half of it," she said, the last word melding with a fresh sob as she turned back to the window again.

They had come to the intersection of 775 and 776. Lynn suddenly pulled into the parking lot of the Wachovia branch, stopped and put the vehicle in park, leaving the engine idling. The dominant sound was now the intermittent whir of the wipers when they cycled on.

"Then why don't you tell me the half I don't know," she said.

She kept her back to Lynn. "I don't want to."

"Look, young lady," she said, making herself feel old again. "You'd better tell *me* what's on your mind before you have to tell a sheriff's detective named Symanski."

She said nothing, still giving Lynn her back.

"Let me spell it out for you, Johnnie, he thinks you're a suspect."

She spun her head around. "Me? No way!"

"Way," Lynn said.

"Well, I'm not worried about that," she said.

"And why not?"

The tears came again, accompanied by sobs. Lynn waited them out. It wasn't a short wait. When her crying was spent, she gathered herself, gulped air a couple of times and spoke.

"I won't be a suspect because I have a solid alibi. And..." her lower lip curled again "...that's what I'm upset about."

"Spit it out, Johnnie."

"I was supposed to be here with him yesterday. I could have protected him. I could have saved him. Instead, on the way down from Tallahassee, I stopped at Gainesville to see some friends at UF. We were just going to have a couple of beers, but it ended up being a couple of days of beers. There, that's it. I can tell you one thing—I'm never having another drink as long as I live."

Lynn had heard that before from certain people in her life. In fact, she probably needed to tell herself that. Johnnie started crying again. Lynn heard a tap on her window. Truck was standing there with a quizzical look. Lynn rolled the window down and said, "Sorry. Just talking for a minute. We're ready now."

TWENTY-THREE

JACK ESPINOSA LIVED in an Englewood subdivision called Wavecrest Isles. Contrary to what the name implied, it was about a mile from any kind of water. His tract house was yellow stucco with black shutters, maybe two thousand square feet, and parked in front was a three-year-old black Nissan Pathfinder sport utility vehicle.

Lynn hoped the presence of the vehicle indicated the presence of Espinosa, because she hadn't wanted to call first. Truck pulled the Crown Vic police interceptor with green sheriff's artwork all over it behind Lynn's SUV in the driveway. It was pushing eleven, the rain had stopped, and Espinosa's next-door neighbor was in his yard. He openly gawked upon seeing the sheriff's cruiser.

Lynn, Johnnie, and Truck assembled at the front door and Lynn rang the bell. Espinosa took his time answering and held the door open wearing navy fishing shorts and a white T-shirt with a Boatmen's Marina logo, no shoes. He was holding the doorknob with his right hand and a lit cigarette with his left. When he saw the three people on his doorstep he did a single take which was a simultaneous lifting of his head back and his eyebrows up.

"Good God, the world at my doorstep," he said, with a wheezy, cigarette-voiced laugh that emanated from the hole in his beard which was his mouth.

Lynn had seen plenty like Espinosa in the years she'd been coming to places like Boca Grande. They were the ones from somewhere else—sometimes cities in Florida, sometimes up north—who had embraced the island life and "gone native." Espinosa's type believed that going native had a certain cachet, particularly when contrasted to the rigors and inherent constraints of whatever lifestyle may have preceded it.

Visibly, going native meant never wearing long pants, never tucking in the obligatory loud shirt (fish or flower pattern), and never wearing a sport coat anywhere. Sandals were *de rigueur* as was some kind of whacky tropical hat or cap. A beard or mustache was common. Many who went native took up smoking after a long hiatus, and often had whiskey on their breath during the day. Living on a boat garnered bonus cachet points for someone going native.

Like their big-city counterparts, who wore loud sport coats with the racing form protruding from the inside pocket, the gone-native types were dreamers. They figured it would be a lot easier knocking down some kind of score in a coastal Florida environment with all those moneyed people and the growth. Lots of opportunities in real estate: maybe bring some product in from up north those yahoos in Florida didn't know about; maybe make a fortune bilking the tourists for rental boats or bikes. Just work a few hours a day and enjoy the tropics afterwards. They adopted an affected salty insouciance which they figured displayed the chic of a coastal Florida island person who had truly gone native.

The gone-native types would relish visits by their old friends and lord their new free-spirit lifestyle over them with glee. Never mind that the reason they left where they were was that they never quite fit in or measured up. "Got fed up with the rat race" was a common euphemism for what really happened.

"Mind if we come in?" Lynn said.

Espinosa stood aside and used the hand holding the cigarette to wave them all in like a gatekeeper at a Las Vegas floor show taking down the ropes for some high rollers.

Once inside Lynn said, "You know Truck."

"You mean Big-Un?" Espinosa said with a wheezy chuckle. "Yeah, I know Truck."

"And this is Johnnie Osceola," Lynn said.

Espinosa said his name and offered his hand to Johnnie. She offered nothing to Espinosa except a hard, flat stare from her onyx-colored eyes. Espinosa slowly dropped his hand and it immediately became apparent that he felt compelled to answer the insult.

"Looks more like Pocahontas to me," he said.

Lynn grimaced but let it go. Johnnie's lips got thinner and Lynn thought she thought saw her move toward Espinosa but nothing happened. Lynn blinked and tried to decide whether Johnnie's move was her imagination or a feint which was too quick for detection by the naked eye. Johnnie's flat, cold stare was now a raging glare.

Espinosa did not invite them to sit even though Lynn hinted by looking around the living room they were in. The television was on and tuned to Outdoor Life Network. A glance in the kitchen revealed a laptop on the table which appeared to be connected to the internet. The place looked more like a fishing lodge than a living room. There were mounts of area fish on the walls, and rods and tackle boxes stacked in a corner.

Espinosa took a drag on the smoke and turned his head to exhale. Then he looked at Lynn and said, "I guess you're going to tell me the reason for the state visit."

"Sammy Osceola," Lynn said.

Still looking at Lynn, Espinosa narrowed his eyes. "Last time I heard that name was last night when he stood you up for dinner. What about him?"

Lynn watched Espinosa's eyes carefully from the moment Sammy's name came out. There was no change in the pupils or the movement, things Lynn used to look for many years ago. This guy is good, she thought.

"He's dead, Jack," Lynn said. "He was murdered and you were one of the last people to see him alive."

Espinosa nodded at Johnnie while still looking at Lynn. "Guess this is his daughter?"

Lynn nodded.

Espinosa looked back at Johnnie, his active brown eyes peeking over his full salt-and-pepper beard. He didn't smile but showed her just a hint of his perfectly capped teeth. "Sorry I called you Pocahontas. And I'm sorry your daddy died," he said, then waved toward a huge wraparound sofa covered with rust-colored burlap material. "Why don't we sit down?"

They all did. "Sounds like you have some questions for me, and I can tell you I have some for you. Like how was he killed, where'd you find him, all that."

Espinosa said this while sinking into a recliner not unlike the one in Truck Kershaw's living room. He said it with a breezy casualness which was hard to quantify. Contrived? Genuine? After all, he had just been introduced to Sammy Osceola two days ago. But that didn't mean anything. Lynn wanted to find out more about the real-estate development deals. Were they imminent and did Espinosa luck into Sammy as an opportunity to eliminate the last obstacle to his success?

If Espinosa was a bona fide suspect, Lynn could see that he would be a formidable one. He was a good-looking, roguish, swashbuckler of a man. He exuded a jaunty, mercurial flair which was maddening yet endearing, intimidating yet charming. Truck had described it to Lynn more succinctly: "That man don't give a shit," he had said.

"Start with yesterday afternoon," Lynn said. "What time did you meet and where?"

Espinosa half shrugged. "We met late morning at Boatmen's. I took him around the backcountry, Turtle Bay mainly. I think I told you on the phone last night about the eagles we saw."

"What time did you quit?"

"Around three. Took him directly to Fenton's Marina to get his rental boat instead of dropping him at Boatmen's where his car was. It ain't but a hundred yards."

There was a pause.

"Hey," Espinosa said with a shrug as he spread his hands, "that's it. End of story. He was a nice guy to be with. I'm sorry he's gone."

"What did you do after you dropped him off?" Lynn said.

"Went back to Boatmen's and cleaned up my boat. Then I came back here. Been here ever since."

"Can you prove that?" Truck said.

"Shit, no," he said quickly with defiance. Then, turning to

Johnnie and in a softer tone, added, "S'cuse me, miss." Then he continued. "I live alone, I didn't go out with any of my lady friends and none of them came over here. I just watched the Magic game on the tube and surfed the net a little bit. Minded my own business. Hell, you know I was here because you called me."

Lynn spoke. "Yeah, that was for a few minutes around ten. Speaking of your business, I want to talk to you some more about those real-estate deals you mentioned at the bar the other night."

"Well, you can go ahead and talk to *me* about 'em. But I'm not going to talk to *you* about them."

"Why?"

Espinosa was originally from Tampa and his roots were Latin, but his speech was pure Florida Cracker. He leaned forward and grinned defiantly while looking Lynn right in the eye. "Because, Miz Woo, it ain't none of your damn business."

"It's going to be a lot of people's business if it's proved that you dropped Sammy off to get his rental boat, then followed him to the backcountry and killed him."

Espinosa hesitated for a moment, weighing this, then abruptly stood. "Lynn, I've always liked you. Everybody does. But as of this moment, you are no longer welcome in my house."

Lynn and Truck looked at each other, then Lynn looked back at Espinosa. "Jack, I've lost the son-in-law of my old friend and commanding officer, and my good friend from college. All in a week. I just can't worry about whether I insult you or not, I've got to get to the bottom of this!"

The still-standing Espinosa nodded at Truck while still addressing Lynn. "Is this an official visit?"

"No," Truck answered. "But there'll be one. You'll have the pleasure of meeting Lieutenant Stan Symanski. I may or may not be with him."

"Okay, Jack," Lynn said, "let's say you dropped him off and came home just like you said. You have any ideas on what might have happened? Did Sammy say anything that you think might be important?"

Espinosa sat back down. "We just talked birds and fishing. I think we both deliberately avoided the touchy subject of real-estate development on mangrove islands."

"You know Aubrey Lowe?" Lynn asked.

"The commercial fisherman? I see him out on the water every now and then. Why?"

"How well do you know him?"

"Hardly at all, why?"

Lynn looked at Truck and they exchanged an unspoken signal. Lynn stood. "Sorry to bother you, Jack. If you didn't like the questions I asked, just wait until Symanski shows up."

They left. Johnnie Osceola had not said a word, and walked out without even looking at Espinosa again. Back in the car, heading to Boca Grande, she remained silent, looking straight ahead.

Lynn broke the silence. "Well, what do you think?"

She kept looking straight ahead. "I think he's lying and I think he killed my father. I could have killed him in about three seconds but you had to do your questions thing."

TWENTY-FOUR

"I WANT YOU TO STOP THAT," Lynn said.

She and Johnnie Osceola were approaching the Boca Grande Lodge after driving from Jack Espinosa's house in silence.

"Stop what?" Johnnie asked.

"Stop talking about killing people in three seconds."

"Is that too long or too short?"

Lynn fumed at the insolence and shook her head in disbelief of her circumstances. Johnnie's father had been so gentle. Where had his daughter gotten her tenacity and her rage? Lynn had studied the Seminoles a little. She wondered if Sammy and Johnnie were actually direct descendants of Chief Osceola. Probably not, since many Seminoles took that name. But her imagination could easily place Johnnie back in 1835 stabbing the paper on which Andrew Jackson's proposed treaty was written, then stomping out of the room.

Chief Osceola and Coacoochee fought on after that incident, but in 1837 they met again under the flag of truce with Colonel Jesup of the U.S. Army, but Jesup arrested them instead. Coacoochee escaped but Chief Osceola fell ill and was taken to Fort Moultrie, South Carolina, where he died a year later. He was succeeded by Billy Bowlegs who fought on with the result that the Seminoles were the only Indian tribe which never relocated, never signed a treaty, and never surrendered. The term "unconquered" remained their mantra.

Lynn stopped in front of the main entrance to the Boca Grande Lodge to drop Johnnie off. She turned in her seat to face her. Lynn knew her face was red as she pointed her finger at the bridge of Johnnie's nose. "Look, young lady. I'm trying to help figure out these murders and be accommodating to you at the same time, and you're not making the last part easy. Just stop being a smart-ass and go in there to your room and behave yourself. Make those calls to your mother and get started on the funeral arrangements. Understand?"

She looked at her lap and said quietly, "Yes, Ms. Woo."

"So now it's Ms. Woo, huh?"

"When you talk to me like that, it is."

"Look, Johnnie, I'm going to try to get the decks cleared so I can come over and stay with you tonight."

"I want to be alone," she said. Then she gave Lynn a totally different look and added, "Unless you'd promise to sleep in the same bed with me."

"What?"

"I've never been with a Chinese girl before. And I think you're kind of hot."

Lynn stared in shock, then quickly recovered. "All right, you win. You stay alone. It bothers me, though, because you're a twenty-one-year-old girl and your father was just killed."

"You don't think I'm attractive?"

"Doesn't matter. I'm not into sex with women. Not that you shouldn't be—that's up to you—it's just that I'm not. Thanks, but no, thanks."

"I actually prefer men, if it makes you feel any better."

Lynn just stared at her, not believing this conversation. "Johnnie, I don't *care*. It's none of my damn business." Then she flicked her right hand in a motion that signaled Johnnie to get out of the car. She did, but only after giving Lynn a steely look.

After she closed the door, Lynn rolled down the window and called after her before driving away. "Let me know about those arrangements, okay?"

Johnnie looked over her shoulder and nodded.

TWENTY-FIVE

AFTER DROPPING JOHNNIE Osceola off in front of the main Lodge, Lynn drove another two blocks to Whitman Jenkins' cottage. Muffy Savage was sitting on the screened porch reading a Stuart Kaminsky novel. She let her in.

"Daddy's in there on the phone," she said, motioning to the living room of the cottage. Lynn looked through the window and saw Whitman Jenkins sitting at the wicker desk, papers in front of him and the receiver at his ear. Lynn looked back at Muffy Savage. She was wearing white shorts and a nearly sleeveless yellow top. The shorts were not short, but not Bermuda-length either. They displayed her supple, tanned legs.

"Why don't you sit a spell with me until they're finished," she said.

"They?" Lynn said.

"Oh. Guess I didn't tell you. Robert Tyre is in there with him. You know him?"

Lynn tried to keep her face impassive. She knew Robert Tyre, but was hoping never to have to see him again after their clashes when they were in Naval Intelligence together, both reporting to Rear Admiral Whitman Jenkins IV. Lynn remembered Robert Tyre as a slippery corner-cutter who put his personal agenda ahead of his country. Originally from Atlanta, Tyre claimed to be related to the golf legend Bobby Jones, whose full name was Robert Tyre Jones, *Tyre* being pronounced like what cars ride on. Lynn remembered that Tyre always insisted on being called Robert.

Before Lynn could "sit a spell" with Muffy, she looked through the window again and saw that the admiral had hung up. She also saw Robert Tyre moving in the room.

She smiled at Muffy. "Looks like your dad's off the phone."

Lynn knocked gently on the front door of the cottage and pushed it open.

"Lynn," Whitman Jenkins said grandly. "Glad you're here. You remember Robert, don't you?"

Robert Tyre was six foot five, lanky and raw boned with almost no body fat. Naturally blond, a small shock of his hair hung over his forehead. His full mustache was whiter than his salty colored hair and took the edge off his prominent, sharply curving nose. He was wearing what appeared to be hiking shorts with lots of pockets and a Corona beer T-shirt. On his feet were tube socks and jogging shoes. The entire getup was apparently his crude interpretation of a resortwear ensemble.

"Been a while, Robert. How are you?" Lynn said, extending her hand.

"Great until I found out about Millard. Yourself?" came the reply, accompanied by an unnecessarily vigorous handshake and a forced gregarious grin.

Robert Tyre was what Lynn called a "close talker." Despite his height, his face was somehow inches from Lynn's as he spoke. Every time Tyre said something Lynn was awash in a putrid gaseous flow of garlicky breath flimsily masked by some kind of peppermint mouthwash.

Lynn nodded solemnly in acknowledgement of the remark about Millard Savage while trying not to gag on the killer beam of Tyre's halitosis.

"So it's Capt. Lynn, the shelling guide now, eh?" Tyre said.

Robert Tyre was a bruiser of a man, physically and otherwise, who knew nothing of finesse and subtlety. This was true in his conversation, his clothes, and his professional life. The antithesis of the refined, polished golf legend whose relation he claimed.

Lynn didn't comment on Tyre's guide remark.

"So what are you up to these days, Robert?" Lynn asked, her question fueled by genuine curiosity.

Tyre picked up a thin, unlit cigar from the wicker desk and jammed it in his mouth before answering.

"I have what's called a boutique investment banking firm. We do mostly M and A work. Uh…that's mergers and acquisitions."

Lynn let the patronization pass, saying, "And what brings you to Boca Grande?"

Tyre took the little cigar out of his mouth before breaking out in a grin and tossing his head toward Whitman Jenkins. "The admiral and I are working together. I'm representing him. Helping him with his strategy of rolling up small food manufacturers. Uh…roll up means acquiring a lot of small companies which essentially do the same thing."

Jenkins laughed out loud and waved an arm toward Lynn. "For God's sake, Robert, this gal knows a thing or two about business."

Tyre seemed unfazed by the mild rebuke.

"Glad you came by, Lynn. How about a cold cerveza or something," Jenkins said.

"I just wanted to update you on a few things, but I'll come back when you're not busy," Lynn said.

"Don't be silly. Robert's here for a few days, we've plenty of time for business. Sit down. Have something cool to drink and let's talk."

Lynn cut a barely perceptible glance at Tyre. "I could easily come back later."

Jenkins put a hand on Lynn's shoulder. "Lynn, Robert and I are close associates. You can talk about any of my business in his presence."

After they sat and Lynn accepted and downed half a glass of Muffy's sweet tea, she told the two men about her encounter on the water with Aubrey Lowe, the murder of Sammy Osceola, the arrival of Johnnie Osceola, and the "interrogation" of Jack Espinosa. It was an eerie feeling for Lynn because many years ago the same three had discussed Naval Intelligence investigations in the same way.

"We've got two murders here," Lynn said. "It's unclear

whether they're related. Jack Espinosa has a motive for killing Sammy, but connecting him to Millard would be a stretch. In Millard's case a more likely suspect might be Aubrey Lowe if Millard stumbled on to his illegal netting that night. Of course, I suppose that could have happened in Sammy's case, too. So maybe Aubrey Lowe should be the prime suspect."

"What does our friend with the white necktie say?" asked Jenkins.

"Symanski has said nothing about Espinosa because I haven't told him about the conversation at the Boatmen's bar with Sammy. As far as Aubrey Lowe is concerned, Symanski's not impressed. Says there are a bunch of those guys running around the back bays every night fishing illegally."

"Well, it sounds like you're doing all the right things," Jenkins said.

"Any ideas?" Lynn said.

"Let me think about it. Why don't you and Rolf join us for dinner here at the Lodge tonight and we can talk about it some more."

"Sounds great, Admiral, but I'm going in my skiff to the back bays tonight."

"How the hell are you going to see anything back up in there at night?"

"I'll only be looking for one thing. Aubrey Lowe."

TWENTY-SIX

OVER FORTY-EIGHT hours later, Lynn was into the second night of her surveillance of Aubrey Lowe. She found out that Lowe kept his mullet boat on a residential canal behind his house in Grove City, and, with running lights off, she was able to follow him easily in her skiff.

Lynn had tried again to tend to Johnnie Osceola. Johnnie continued to refuse all company, and insisted that she needed no help with her father's arrangements.

The first night of Lynn's surveillance of Lowe had been uneventful, yielding only the observation of Lowe using a perfectly legal cast net for mullet fishing. This second night was different as, under a bright half moon, Lynn watched Lowe haul out his illegal gill nets. Lynn pondered the difference between the two nights, wondering if it had something to do with the schedules of the Marine Patrol. Maybe Lowe knew them.

Lynn was in Turtle Bay, not far from where her charter clients had discovered Millard Savage's body. The only occasional sound was the back bay mullet as they made their inexplicable soaring leaps only to fall back to the water's surface with a resounding splash. On the shore, perhaps a quarter mile away from the Millard Savage crime scene, she thought she saw a flicker of light. She peered intently to see if it appeared again. It did.

She was about six hundred yards from the shore, and with running lights still off, she engaged her electric trolling motor and moved toward where she had seen the lights. There it was again. A light which seemed muted like it was behind or underneath something. Like a wall. But there were no walls on this desolate, uninhabited mangrove island which helped form Turtle Bay.

Using the trolling motor, she edged closer. She saw the light again but only intermittently. As she pulled within fifty yards of the shoreline, she thought her eye picked up a silhouette outlined by the moonlight. A shape. Then she saw that it was several shapes. As she got closer, her eye scored four mullet boats similar to Aubrey Lowe's and all beached on the shore.

With her electric motor, Lynn edged closer. The light shone with more frequency and seemed brighter. She beached her boat beside the four mullet boats, quietly fetched a mooring line, and hopped out. She tied the line to a branch of a mangrove tree, moving quickly as the mosquitoes fiercely attacked her.

Since mosquitoes congregated around mangroves, Lynn sought open ground as she crept inland on the island in the general direction of where she had last seen the light. Then she heard voices, perhaps 150 yards away, but could not make out any words.

She crept closer and, as she did, she used the moonlight to carefully pick her path, avoiding the brush and going for the clear areas. After every third step or so she looked down to confirm her route. In a small clearing, she looked down at where she was stepping, and saw the too-neatly arranged sea grape leaves. Something about the leaves was all wrong. But that signal didn't travel through her brain to her leg fast enough. She stepped on the sea grape leaves. A mistake.

Lynn fell helplessly into darkness. The four-by-eight-foot pit was about ten feet deep, and at its bottom the moonlight was sparse. As she fell she put her hands out to brace herself and they raked the side of the pit all the way down. After landing on one foot, she lurched and hit hard on the side of the pit with her shoulder. Her landing was accompanied by a splash as there was perhaps two feet of water at the bottom of the pit. Burlap had supported the sea grape leaves, thereby perfecting the trap which was like one might set for an animal. The burlap was now partially wrapped around her feet, and the sea grape leaves fluttered down on top of her.

Excruciating pain seized Lynn's leg. She reached for it, and as she did, thought she felt something. Sensed something. She realized she was not alone in the pit. As her eyes adjusted to her darker surroundings, she squinted. What she saw made her shrink to one end of the rectangular pit in terror.

TWENTY-SEVEN

THE SIX-FOOT ALLIGATOR Lynn was looking at was very much alive and making noises which sent Lynn's terror level to the red line. Hugging the wall of the pit furthest from the gator, she looked skyward. It was impossible to climb out. She ran her hands over the walls of the pit and felt only relative smoothness and nothing on which to get a foothold. The gator was definitely annoyed at the arrival of its unannounced visitor.

Lynn stared at the gator. She figured she had to do something fast. But what? In the next few seconds, which seemed like forever, Lynn racked her brain. The gator, whose head was above the water's surface and its body below, moved slightly, sloshing the water.

The reptile opened his massive jaws and seemed to move toward Lynn, but it turned out to be a feint. Lynn flinched anyway and felt her gastrointestinal tract cramp. She decided the alligator's next move would be the real thing.

She made a decision. She tried to remain as still as possible while she unbuttoned her shirt, but her shaking hands made this difficult. When she freed the last button, she slowly peeled off the shirt. Meanwhile the gator opened and closed his huge trap several times.

Lynn knew that the alligator's jaws could crush any part of a human body with ease. But she also knew that the creature's jaws had almost no strength if they were held closed. With a hand on each sleeve, Lynn slowly spread her shirt apart. She had to pick her moment and move at the speed of a strobe light.

In one sudden motion, she threw her shirt over the gator's head and took a big step with her right foot, placing it astride the reptile's body. In the next motion, she pivoted 180 degrees and mounted the gator, simultaneously sitting on its back and sliding her hands up the animal's head and holding its jaws shut, her shirt between her hands and the leathery skin of the six foot reptile.

The gator thrashed violently, taking its mount—Lynn—on several 360-degree rotations within the confines of the pit. Lynn held on. After this initial burst of fury the animal seemed to calm and then became still.

Meanwhile, Lynn held the jaws as though her life depended on it because she knew it did. She figured if she released her grip she wouldn't last longer than a Chanel pocketbook at a half-price sale. With jaws free, the gator would likely go for one of Lynn's legs. There was enough water in the pit for the reptile to follow its genetic proclivities and lie horizontal in the water while putting its torso into a furious and repetitive spin to try to rip the limb from Lynn's body.

Lynn held on to the creature's jaws and began to think. Damn. She'd left her cell phone on the boat, the new one she'd obtained after Aubrey Lowe had played Roger Clemens with her old one. Her flashlight, too, so there was no way to signal. If she yelled, the only people who might hear her were the perpetrators of the diabolical gator-pit scheme. If they learned their trap had worked, they would likely do Lynn in quicker than the gator.

Rolf knew where she was, but she'd told him she'd be home very late and they'd decided they would sleep at their respective homes. She had told Whitman Jenkins that she was going to follow Aubrey Lowe for one night, not two, so the admiral wouldn't miss her either. Rolf was her best bet, but that meant she'd have to hang on until morning when he might phone then perhaps come to her house, let himself in, and find that her bed had not been slept in.

All night holding this six-foot alligator by the jaws wearing nothing but her shorts, panties underneath, and her sports bra. What a picture that would make, she thought. Her two main worries were falling asleep, and having the bad guys whose voices she'd heard decide to check on their trap.

She began to ponder who the bad guys might be. Aubrey Lowe could not be one of the voices she had heard near the light because Lynn had just left him out in Turtle Bay setting his illegal gill nets. Jack Espinosa. He had to be the prime suspect, if for no other reason because he was "Mr. Alligator," having hunted them for years, both legally and otherwise, running guide trips for others to hunt them, and, of course, doing jail time for his fraudulent gator-permit scheme. And there was obviously some relationship between the back-bay murders of Millard Savage and Sammy Osceola and the activity Lynn had detected on the deserted mangrove island. She wasn't writing off Aubrey Lowe, but Jack Espinosa would get renewed attention if she ever survived this gator pit. Maybe Johnnie Osceola's instincts were right about her father's killer.

Lynn held on to the alligator's jaws. The minutes became hours. Twice more the gator took Lynn on a 360-degree ride around the pit in an effort to loosen Lynn's grip on its jaws. Between these episodes the animal was still. Lynn's hands were cramping and she was unable to swat the mosquitoes which found the water at the bottom of the pit. She heard nothing further from the area of activity on the island. Fatigue and sleep deprivation began to stalk her.

She semi-dozed, but that was harshly interrupted as the gator moved again. She was able to look at her watch: 4:30 a.m. She thought of Charles Lindbergh and his flight across the Atlantic. Every time Lynn read the story or saw a documentary about it she marveled at Lindbergh's feat of staying awake so long at the controls of his little plane. Succumbing would have meant sure death from a plunge into the Atlantic. Lynn figured that if she surrendered to sleep it would mean grisly dismemberment and a slow agonizing death for her.

TWENTY-EIGHT

LYNN BEGAN TO SENSE what she had been waiting for. Her tip-off was that, looking down, her eye could begin to make out the half dollar-sized raised rectangular ridges which comprised the craggy skin of the gator whose jaws she continued to hold shut. She looked skyward and saw the blackness starting its slow dissolve into the gray which preceded first light. It meant that she was closer to her only hope: Rolf missing her and sending someone to search.

Then she heard it. Something in the brush above the pit. A constant sound. A raccoon? An iguana? As the sound came closer it became unmistakable. Footsteps. They sounded very much like those of an animal. The two-legged variety.

The footsteps drew very close, then stopped. Lynn, in a near stupor from exhaustion and sleep deprivation, suddenly became alert and tightened her grip on the gator's jaws. She wondered whether, if she ever got out of this, she would be able to move her cramped hands again. She heard two more steps. Someone was moving right to the edge of the pit.

She was about to look up when suddenly the entire pit was bathed in bright light. When she did look up all she saw was the white-out blindness which comes with looking directly into the beam of a powerful flashlight. Involuntarily, she looked back down.

"Hey, Woo," called a man's voice from above.

The light bathing the pit dimmed as the man swung the flashlight away from being pointed directly at Lynn. Slowly, Lynn lifted her head. There at the top of the pit stood Aubrey Lowe, a flashlight in one hand and his .357 Magnum in the other. The flashlight was no longer pointed at Lynn, but the gun was. Lowe stood there in his standard commercial mullet-fishing uniform: the suspendered bottoms of his yellow slicker, T-shirt underneath and an old green hat with an inscrutable logo on the front.

Lynn was instantly struck by the perfection of it from Lowe's standpoint. All Lowe had to do was squeeze off one round with the Magnum pointed at Lynn's head and then the gator would dispose of the evidence for him. Lynn's mind quickly took a perverse path of wondering how a medical examiner would perform an autopsy on her body when it was in various mangled pieces and inside the gullet of a six-foot alligator. Embarrassment or modesty over Aubrey Lowe seeing her in her bra never registered. She was too exhausted and frightened for that. Lynn braced herself for the shot. As exhausted as she was, death would almost be a relief.

But instead of firing, Aubrey Lowe spoke. "Listen to me, Woo," he said. "At the count of three, I want you to let go of that gator and jump back as far as you can. We're fixin' to have us a dead gator. You follow?"

It took Lynn several moments to respond because she had been steeling herself, physically and spiritually, for the fate that Aubrey Lowe was now saying belonged to Lynn's companion for the night.

"Hey, woman!" Lowe yelled. "You with me?"

Lynn snapped out of it. "Yeah...yeah, I'm with you. The count of three, right?"

"Right. Now hang on a minute," Lowe said.

Suddenly the pit went dark again. Lynn could sense that the light was being used somewhere above her. After several moments, the light flooded the pit again. Aubrey Lowe had found a piece of mangrove wood on which to prop the flashlight, aiming it so it illuminated the pit without blinding Lynn. Aubrey Lowe was now standing with both hands gripping the pistol, aiming it at the alligator's head.

"Okay, Woo, you ready?"

"Yeah, ready."

"Okay. One...two...three!"

At "Three!" Lynn sprang backwards from the gator, releasing her grip on the creature's jaws, and plastered herself against the wall of the pit furthest from the gator. She did not think to cover her ears against the thunderous report of the Magnum which reverberated through the pit. Lowe pumped three bullets into the head of the gator. After some initial lurching and writhing, the creature lay still. Lynn tried to hold her hands to her ears but found she could not straighten her fingers. They were severely cramped in the configuration they had assumed around the alligator's head all night.

"You all right?" Aubrey Lowe called.

"Yeah...yeah, I'm fine," said Lynn.

"Just hang on there, I'll be back in a minute," Lowe said, and disappeared.

Lynn sank to her knees in the water, leaned back against the wall of the pit, and tried to straighten her fingers. They were starting to come around, but nausea, exhaustion, and relief all flooded over her. On her knees anyway, she said a silent prayer. She tried to wring the water out of her shirt, then she put it on.

In a few minutes Aubrey Lowe and the light re-appeared. There was now enough light for the two to see each other without the flashlight. Lowe had two mooring lines from his boat. He tied them together and threw one end down to Lynn. The other he took to the nearest tree and, using it as a capstan, pulled Lynn out of the pit.

Out of the pit, Lynn was shaky and not very steady on her feet. She looked at Aubrey Lowe, not saying anything.

Lowe spoke first. "Excuse me, lady, but you look like shit," he said to the mud-caked Lynn.

Lynn managed a thin smile. "That's the nicest thing you've ever said to me, Aubrey."

"Believe I'd just throw them clothes away," Lowe said, looking Lynn up and down.

Lynn nodded, then said, "Aubrey, I thought you were going to shoot me instead of the gator."

"Why the hell you think that?"

"Well, you almost did the other night."

"Shit. I wouldn't of shot your ass. But then you wouldn't of turned me in for gill nettin' neither. Least I didn't think so."

"You saved my life. I owe you."

"Ain't no big deal. Maybe you'll stay off my ass for good now about any gill nettin' I might want to do."

Lynn smiled again. "The way I feel right now I'd probably look the other way if I saw you robbing a bank."

As Lynn flexed her fingers, trying to get some feeling back, she looked at the muted mauve color of the pre-dawn eastern sky. She knew it would soon be brick-dust pink on its way to the big orange ball peeking its way over the horizon. Last night she had wondered if it was a sight she'd ever see again.

"Mind if I ask you a stupid question?" Aubrey Lowe said.

"Fire away."

"Not important really. Just kinda wondering what in hell you're doin' out here in the middle of the damn night in a hole in the ground with a big-ass alligator."

"It's a new form of transcendental meditation."

"What?"

"Just kidding," Lynn said. Then she looked Lowe straight in the eye. "The truth is I came out here the last two nights to follow you. After our little encounter on the water the other day I figured you might have something to do with the murder of Millard Savage."

"That's that ol' boy they found out here strung up on a tree, right?" said Lowe.

Lynn nodded. "I figured maybe you and Millard surprised each other out here and he got the worst of it." Lynn shrugged. "I was obviously wrong, or you would have left me for the gator. Anyway, you probably have an alibi."

"Nope. Fact is I was out here that night. Didn't see him. Or anybody else for that matter. But I been half expecting Truck Kershaw or somebody to come talk to me about it."

"Truck's boss wasn't interested. I wouldn't worry about it now."

"You still ain't answered my question. What's with the gator and the pit?" asked Lowe.

"Saw some kind of light on shore here. Moseyed over with my trolling motor and noticed four mullet boats beached. Heard some voices near where the light was and headed that way. Then I stepped on some sea grape leaves. Next thing I knew, I was about to be dinner."

"Be goddamned."

"Yep. How'd you find me?"

"I was wrapping things up for the night and saw your boat. Didn't make no sense 'cause you ain't never out here at night. Had to be trouble, that's why I brought Ol' Nellie, here," Lowe said, patting the .357 with his hand affectionately.

Lynn cut a hard glance at the weapon. "I was a lot happier to see Ol' Nellie this time than the other time I saw her," Lynn said.

"Uh, yeah, sorry about that," mumbled Lowe, looking down.

There were several moments of semi-awkward silence. While Lowe examined his rubber boots, Lynn looked again to the east and saw a circle of brassy orange showing just above the horizon, only slightly muted by the pre-dawn gray. A pair of gliding brown pelicans crossed her line of sight, banking and looking for unsuspecting water-bound pinfish, pilchards or threadfin herring. She looked back at Lowe.

"Aubrey, were the mullet boats still beached when you came ashore?"

"Nope, didn't see nothin' but your boat."

"Hmm. Guess the pit blocked out the sound when they left. Or else I'd dozed off. Hey, are you up for doing a few minutes of exploring? That's about all I've got the strength for," Lynn said.

Aubrey Lowe reached in his pocket for three bullets and reloaded Nellie.

"Let's go," he said.

TWENTY-NINE

LYNN AND AUBREY LOWE walked in the general direction that Lynn remembered the light and noise coming from. They came upon one of the taller Indian burial mounds Lynn had ever seen, perhaps fifteen or twenty feet in height. Lynn lingered at the mound, admiring its shell construction, and was about to move on when she stopped short. Something about the mound was wrong. She peered closely at an object she saw poking out of the bottom of the mound.

"Aubrey, what does that look like to you?" she asked Lowe.

Lowe looked at the round, black thing, perhaps four inches in diameter, which seemed to form a hole in the side of the mound and near the ground.

"If I didn't know better, I'd say it's a rubber hose," Lowe said.

Their eyes met as Lynn said, "That's exactly what it is. Let's walk all the way around this way and see what we see."

They walked slowly, looking. On the side of the mound, which was 180 degrees both from the hose and from where Lynn had beached her boat, the shell composition of the mound changed. They saw an area, perhaps four by eight feet, on the side of the mound covered with sea grapes and mangrove branches.

"This looks damn near as out of place as that friggin' hose," Lowe said.

Lynn nodded. "Let's see what's behind this stuff."

They began pulling the pile of brush away. Lowe's efforts were far more zealous than Lynn's. This caused Lynn to say, "Slow down, Aubrey, there might be a booby trap."

Lowe stopped short and looked at Lynn with a new respect and began to exercise care. Lynn wondered if Lowe knew anything of her background. As they finished clearing the sea grapes and mangroves, a wooden bulkhead of fresh yellow pine and a door frame with no door began to emerge.

"We goin' in?" Lowe said.

Lynn whispered, "You have the light?"

Aubrey Lowe held up both hands to show Lynn that the light was in one hand and the Magnum in the other.

Lynn's lips cracked in a crooked grin as she said, "Follow me, I'm right behind you."

Lowe gave her a look which said he understood both the joke and the fact that the holder of the gun and the light would go in first. Aubrey Lowe turned the light on and walked through the opening which was about the size of a door to a house.

The inside of the Indian burial mound had been excavated and made into a large room with timbers holding up a ceiling which looked to be of a smooth, off-white plastic, stretched tight like those in a modern athletic arena. The excavated shell, including whatever precious bones and artifacts they contained, had been piled on the exterior of the ceiling to make it look original. They immediately saw the rest of the hose they had seen from the outside. It was connected to a portable electric-powered sump pump which was connected to a car battery which was sitting on a small stepladder to keep it dry. The higher portions of the ground were covered in burlap, while the area where the pump was had a few small puddles of water. The only other things in the room were several battery-powered lamps and three dollies like one would see in a warehouse, each with a tarpaulin lying on it.

Lynn was shocked, horrified at the trashing of a precious archaeological site. "This is a crime against history, mankind, and everything else. Let's get out of here," she said.

They left through the opening and carefully replaced the camouflaging they had removed a few minutes earlier. They began looking at the surrounding area and saw what they knew they must: the scattered shell which had been excavated from the mound. As fatigued as she was, Lynn still felt revulsion, fury.

Back at the shore of the island, at their beached boats, Lynn sagged in exhaustion to a sitting position on the bow of the *Boca Broke*.

"So what do you make of that?" Lynn said.

"Somebody's up to no good. Just messin' with them Indian mounds is probably a federal offense. And they messed with 'em bad."

Lynn nodded. "Somebody's using that mound as a clandestine warehouse."

"If that means they're bringing shit in they're not s'posed to, you damn right it's a…whatever you just said."

"What do you think the smuggled merchandise is? You don't need anything like this for drugs, do you?" Lynn said.

"You're asking me?"

Lynn shrugged.

"Nah, I wouldn't think so," Lowe said. "It's something bigger than square groupers."

"Based on what I've just seen, both Millard Savage and Sammy Osceola may have surprised the wrong people at the wrong time and paid for it with their lives," Lynn said. "Look, I saw four mullet boats beached here last night. They were exactly like yours. The bad guys have to be somebody you know. Any ideas?"

"Me? Naw. Hell, they's a bunch of guys out here. They come and they go. I know a lot of them but they's a lot I don't know, too."

"Aubrey, you've already saved my life, but I could use your help with this."

Lowe said nothing for a few moments as he stepped on his boat and laboriously removed the yellow bottoms to his slicker, revealing blue jeans underneath. His slicker bottoms were the type with built-in boots, so he stood in his mullet boat in athletic socks. He then sat on an ancient white Igloo cooler and pulled on a pair of white, rubber, Wellington-style boots preferred by commercial fishermen. When he finished, he looked up at Lynn and said, "How?"

"Just nose around a little bit, ask a few questions, and see what turns up."

"Hmm...don't know about that. Have to be real careful."

"Why?" Lynn asked.

"Some real bad hombres in this game of mine. You think me pullin' a gun on you was bad..."

"Doesn't *anybody* come to mind?" Lynn asked.

"Well, I guess maybe Dearl Lomax."

"You mean Darrel?"

"No, Dearl," Lowe said, pronouncing it *Durl*. "Might have been Darrel at one time, but now it's Dearl."

Lynn did a little double take on that one, trying to let it sink in. "Mullet fisherman?"

"Yep."

"So why do you think he might be involved?"

"'Cause he's a bad ass who don't give a shit. About nothin'. Been in all kind of scrapes with the law."

"You willing to help me on this and do a little snooping? Maybe have a little chat with Mr. Dearl Lomax?" Lynn asked.

Lowe didn't look at Lynn. Instead he was busy stowing his handgun in a small dry bag which he kept under the console of his mullet boat. After that he began stowing the slicker bottoms he had just removed. He was obviously weighing his response to Lynn's question. After finishing his little housekeeping regimen, he put his meaty hands on his hips, looked at Lynn, and spoke.

"I'll see what I can do, but I ain't making no promises. Don't even know why I'm agreeing to do anything 'cept I feel kinda bad about pullin' Ol' Nellie on you, and I'm a little pissed off at somebody trying to get you with that gator."

"Aubrey, I really appreciate that." She looked at him earnestly as it was heartfelt. "Say, do you know Jack Espinosa?" she asked.

"Yeah, not well. Why?"

"You think he might be involved with this?"

"Seems like he's always got some kind of deal cooking, but why would he be?"

Lynn told him what she knew about Jack Espinosa, including his long involvement with the Florida alligator. "Why don't you see how Dearl Lomax and any of his cohorts react to Jack Espinosa's name," Lynn said.

"We'll see what happens," Aubrey Lowe said as he got back out of his mullet boat and, his back to Lynn, began pushing it off the beach.

"Hey, Aubrey," Lynn said.

Lowe stopped and turned to find Lynn's outstretched hand. "You saved my life," Lynn said. "I'll never forget it. I owe you. Big."

THIRTY

ON THE BOAT RIDE FROM Turtle Bay to Boca Grande Lynn ran the *Boca Broke* at a moderate speed and shook her head violently each time she nodded off. Her fatigue and sleep deprivation made her vision blur. She was probably impaired as a boat driver. In fact, if she'd been driving a car, she knew she would have been weaving. She decided she was getting too old to do *anything* all night, much less hold an alligator's jaws shut.

It was seven-thirty a.m. when she tied up at Boatmen's Marina and remembered she and Whitman Jenkins were supposed to go back-bay fishing thirty minutes ago. She groped for her cell phone, called the Jenkins cottage, and made her apologies, saying it had something to do with the murders but she would explain later. Before hanging up she arranged to meet the admiral and Muffy at Squid Row for lunch.

Lynn could not decide whether she was more ravenous or more dehydrated. She went immediately to her refrigerator and filled a large water glass with orange juice. She had some biscuits in the freezer and she popped them in the microwave before letting Mullet out. Not surprisingly, the dog seemed just as anxious to relieve himself as Lynn was to sate her hunger and thirst. Lynn submerged the biscuits in oozing, cloying, almost black Georgia cane syrup. Funny how she almost never ate Chinese cuisine anymore. Maybe she'd seen too much of it in the restaurant. And in Tallahassee she'd acquired a taste for Southern things like biscuits and cane syrup. As a second-generation American, it was perhaps not surprising that her real favorite was now Italian cooking. Still hungry after the biscuits, she remembered some hard-boiled eggs in the fridge and retrieved two of them. She skipped coffee as her mind was consumed by the prospect of the deep sleep which was moments away.

Lynn finished the eggs, let Mullet back in, and was heading for the bedroom when her sleep-deprived brain somehow spun a thought: call Rolf.

He answered on the third ring.

"Hey," he said. "I was just getting ready to call you. What time did you get in? You get any sleep?"

"The answer to your first question is I just got in, and I think that answers your second one."

"You're kidding. What happened?"

"Why don't you meet me for lunch? Squid Row, one o'clock. The admiral and Muffy will be there. I'll tell everybody the story at the same time, okay? Right now I'm about to drop."

THIRTY-ONE

LYNN SLEPT UNTIL NOON, got up, showered, and dressed in her usual island garb. Today she chose navy shorts and a pale yellow shirt with her boat name and *Capt. Lynn Woo* embroidered above the breast pocket. She was hungry again, but lunch was less than an hour away. On the way to Squid Row she stopped at the sheriff's sub-station which was at the site of the old Boca Grande Health Clinic. She wanted to try to catch Truck Kershaw, but when she walked in the lobby she was surprised to see Johnnie Osceola.

Johnnie was dressed in khaki shorts, sandals, a white, long-sleeved fishing shirt, and had a red bandana tied around her neck. Her long black hair was pulled straight back and hung to the middle of her back in a braid with red Seminole Indian beads adorning it. She was sitting in a simple wooden lobby chair reading *Time*. Her long legs, smooth and tanned, were crossed, and she was swinging one of them slowly.

"Johnnie, what are you doing here?" Lynn said.

She didn't look up, just said, "Hello, Lynn. Or should I say Ms. Woo?" The top leg kept swinging like a pendulum at the same deliberate pace.

"Why don't you just tell me what you're doing here?"

"Waiting to see Truck Kershaw," she said, her nose still in the magazine, the leg still swinging.

"What? Why?"

"To see what he's doing about catching Espinosa."

"Now, look, young lady—"

"No, you look, Lynn," she said. She suddenly uncrossed her supple legs and stood up, put her hands on her hips, and looked down at Lynn. Her black eyes were on fire.

"Let's get this straight. I'm *not* a young *lady.* If I'd really wanted to, I'd have had sex with you all night, and if I didn't want to do that, I could whip your ass so bad you'd be in the hospital. And if I hadn't just quit, I could drink you blind. So get off this young lady crap. I just want my father's killer brought to justice, and I'm not leaving this island until that happens. You follow, *Miz* Woo?" She thumped Lynn on the chest for emphasis using the rolled-up edge of the magazine.

Lynn grimaced, trying to decide what she liked least: the thumping on her chest, the things Johnnie had said, or the way she had said them. They stood toe-to-toe, Lynn looking up at the almost-six-foot young woman. Johnnie continued her glare. It was stalwart as she met Lynn's eyes without wavering. Lynn tried to think how she should react. What had she done to deserve *having* to react? How had this twenty-one-year-old feral cat of a woman come into her life?

Finally, she said, "Let's sit down."

They did. Johnnie laid the magazine aside, re-crossed her legs and folded her arms over her small breasts while gazing into space.

"Johnnie, what you need to be concentrating on is your dad's funeral arrangements and tending to his affairs. I can tell you that the sheriff's folks are very competent and I'm sure they're going to solve your father's murder. I'm trying to help. Now you need to be getting back to Tallahassee and attending to things."

The leg swinging started again as she turned to Lynn and spoke. "I've already done all that. Made all the arrangements. My mother even helped. We're having a full Seminole funeral, presided over by both the Chairman of the Tribal Council and my father's Christian minister. The governor may attend. Bobby Bowden is for sure. I've talked to my dad's lawyer, and so has my mother. Everything is fine there. I'll be going to Tallahassee for the funeral. I'm going to stay over for the Green Corn Dance, and then I'll be back here. You can ignore me if you want to, but I'm going to be here and we may as well work together on this instead of separately."

Johnnie's father had once taken Lynn to a Green Corn Dance, a festival including a rugby-like ball game and a ceremonial fire lit by the tribe shaman, who was in charge of the medicine bag.

Just then the door to the waiting room opened and Truck Kershaw walked over to them. They both looked up at him.

"They said Miss Osceola was here, Cap'n Lynn. Didn't figure on seeing you," Truck said.

"Yeah, well, I didn't figure on seeing Johnnie, so that makes us sort of even."

Lynn glanced at her watch. She needed to fill Truck in on the latest developments and still make lunch on time. "Truck, I need a minute with you and then maybe after that you can see what Johnnie has on her mind. I have to be somewhere."

"Sorry, but I can't talk to either one of you right now. Got to go to Ft. Myers."

"To see Symanski?" Lynn asked.

"Nope. Department physical, and I'm already late. Call me later."

Truck retreated through the door, leaving Lynn and Johnnie Osceola alone again. Lynn looked at Johnnie. Her arms were still folded and her eyes, fixed directly on Lynn's, dispatched a killer beam of smoldering rage.

THIRTY-TWO

IT WAS PERHAPS AS early as 1450 B.C. that the Calusa Indians began living along the southwest coast of Florida. The men of the tribe were powerfully built, often four inches taller than their European counterparts, and were accomplished sailors. In fact, their large canoes made of hollowed-out cypress logs took them as far as Cuba, perhaps even Mexico.

The Calusa were hunter-gatherers, and by all accounts, lousy farmers. But they didn't need crops. The waters of the southwest Florida coastal estuaries where they made their homes were stacked tight with delicious fish, shrimp, oysters, crabs, and turtle, and they were experts at harvesting the bounty. Game was also prevalent, and the Calusa regularly enjoyed deer and raccoon.

In addition to food, the mangrove estuaries provided something else: shells, their main building materials. They built entire islands from the shell, sometimes with intricate canal systems. They built mounds to live on as protection against the rising water of hurricanes, and mounds for burying both their dead and their refuse. The latter were called middens.

By the late 1700s, the Calusa had vanished. They were wiped out by diseases to which they had no resistance, like smallpox, brought in by European explorers. Today, all that remains are their shell mounds which are precious artifacts of their history, archeologically significant, and protected from tampering by state and federal law. Which was why Lynn Woo was so horrified at the desecration she saw on the Turtle Bay island the previous evening.

Lynn arrived a little early at Squid Row and secured a good table for four. She ordered a cold Beck's. She wasn't much of a beer drinker, but thought something like a double Absolut that time of day might be bad form. She hadn't taken a Zoloft in several days. In a few minutes she watched Rolf walk in, pushing the front door open with the back of his elbow, thus avoiding contact between his hand and the dreaded germy doorknob. He crossed the dining room, leaned over and kissed her softly on the lips, and sat beside her.

"Glass of wine or something?" she said.

"Well, since you're having a beer, maybe so."

Lynn motioned for the waiter and Rolf ordered a glass of Sonoma-Cutrer chardonnay. One of the things they liked about Squid Row was the selection of wines and the fact that they offered some pretty decent ones by the glass.

"Hope you don't mind my saying so, but you look pretty wiped out," he said.

Lynn looked down at her beer and chuckled, then looked up at him. "Is it that obvious? Well, whatever wiped out looks like, you look just the opposite," she said with a warm smile.

"Sounds like a compliment in there somewhere," he said, beaming back at her.

Squid Row's décor combined art deco with Florida tropical to concoct a sort of off-beat chic which comprised part of the appeal of the place. The floors were black-and-white tile squares. The walls were murals of island scenes painted by local artists, and mounts of tarpon and other game fish peppered the walls. Starched tablecloths and napkins were used at lunch and dinner.

The main dining room had a rectangular floor plan with no foyer or vestibule. So, when someone came through the double entry doors with large glass lights uncovered by curtains, it was usually noticed by the patrons already there.

Such was the case when the admiral and Muffy arrived. Lynn looked up in anticipation when the doors opened and was pleased to see them both. She was not pleased to see the person accompanying them: Robert Tyre. Lynn greeted them, forcing a smile to hide her displeasure at Tyre's presence.

"Hope you don't mind that I brought Robert along," Whitman

Jenkins said, pronouncing Tyre's first name *Robuht* in his Alabama accent.

"Of course not," Lynn lied. "Let's get a larger table."

Jenkins acknowledged Rolf's presence and introduced him to Robert Tyre. "Remember, I want to buy a painting before I leave the island," Jenkins said to Rolf.

"That can be arranged, Admiral," Rolf said with a wide grin.

They sat and ordered lunch. Lynn, Rolf, Whit Jenkins and Muffy Savage chose the house specialty of crab cakes made from fresh, hand-picked jumbo lump. Robert Tyre was the last to order.

"Cheeseburger and fries for me," he said, slapping his menu shut. "The rest of you can eat those crawly critters that came out of some polluted backwater."

All ignored this remark, including Whitman Jenkins who then spoke. "So, Lynn. You stand me up for fishing, then arrange this lunch to explain. I'd have said this wasn't necessary but you said it had something to do with the murders. So, by all means, start explaining." He didn't smile but his tone was good-natured.

Lynn involuntarily cut a glance at Robert Tyre and said, "Actually, Admiral, this may not be the best time or place—"

"Come on, Lynn. Robert and I are partners, and a hundred years ago the three of us used to discuss investigations like this one at length. Please. Go ahead."

Lynn recalled one such investigation. It involved some missing ordnance thought to be sold to the enemy, and a suspicious death. Tyre was one of those people whose vocabulary didn't include the word "we." Lynn did most of work, but Tyre ended up calling it "his investigation," and told the admiral "I did this" and "I did that." Lynn never made an issue of it, but it left an aftertaste worse than Tyre probably expected from the lunch crabs.

Lynn looked at Muffy Savage. Her face showed anticipation. It also showed sadness. A deep, abiding sadness which comes less from the loss of one's mate than from starting to face the cold reality of being alone.

Lynn took a pull on her beer. She looked at Jenkins and decided to begin at the beginning. She reminded the admiral of the session at the Boatmen's Marina bar with Sammy Osceola and Jack Espinosa where Espinosa bragged that his latest "deal" would be his ticket to financial independence. She reviewed Espinosa's references to Charlotte Harbor estuarial mangrove islands being approved for real-estate development and Sammy Osceola's fight against such proposals as a lobbyist in the Florida Legislature. She also reviewed Espinosa's seemingly excessive curiosity about the details of Millard Savage's murder and his background with alligator hunting and poaching, including his felony conviction for fraudulently obtaining permits. And she included the fact that Espinosa was guiding Sammy on his back-bay trip a few hours before the murder.

Revisiting that fact brought waves of guilt over Lynn once again, since she was the one who engaged Espinosa as her own replacement as Sammy's guide.

Then Lynn reminded the admiral of her encounter with Aubrey Lowe at the point of Lowe's gun, and of her plan to follow Lowe.

That update complete, Lynn then began to relate what happened to her on the island in Turtle Bay the previous evening. She got to the part about the alligator pit.

Rolf's mouth and eyes were wide and he had both hands on Lynn's shoulder when he said, "Good God, honey. What did you do? How did you get out?"

Lynn looked at him with a sly grin and said, "Well, I wrestled the gator for a while, then I hypnotized it—"

"Don't do that to me," he said, hitting her playfully on the arm. "Come on. What happened?"

Lynn continued, and when she got to the part about Aubrey Lowe rescuing her, Rolf jumped in again. "Hey, we've got to do something for that guy. Maybe he'd like a painting."

Lynn looked at him and nodded solemnly. "He'd probably

sell it when he found out what they're worth. But we'll do something."

Whitman Jenkins had said little but now asked, "So what happened after Aubrey Lowe shot the gator and pulled you out of the pit?"

Lynn told of the discovery of the excavated Indian mound which had been made into a warehouse. At this, Muffy Savage, a staunch environmentalist like her husband, drew in a ragged breath in the same way as she had when hearing of the alligator.

"That pretty much sums it up, Admiral," Lynn said.

Jenkins looked at Robert Tyre who, engrossed in his cheeseburger, had said nothing. "I have some questions, Robert. How about you?"

Tyre, reaching for one of his last three French fries, said through a mouth full of unconcealed food, "You go ahead, Whit."

Jenkins looked back at Lynn. "First of all, have you told the sheriff about this?"

Lynn shook her head. "Saw Truck Kershaw for a second, but he was late for his physical exam. So, no, they don't know."

"Well, you need to tell them as soon as you can. I'm sure they'll do a complete fingerprint workup on the whole area. I'd suggest they do some research on the things you saw—the dolly, the tarp, the pump, the hose. See if they can figure out where the stuff might have been bought."

"Good idea," Lynn said.

"Any footprints?" asked Tyre between routing his gums with his tongue in search of stray food morsels.

Lynn shook her head. "It looked like the area had been raked. Like a sand trap on a golf course."

Jenkins said, "I'd like to go out there and have a look. What do you say—why don't we go after lunch?"

Lynn shrugged. "Sure."

Muffy spoke. "Daddy, what if those horrible people are still out there, or come back?"

"Sugar, they won't be out there in broad daylight, so don't

you worry." He pronounced it *shugah*. He looked back at Lynn. "Maybe we can round up your deputy friend and he can go with us."

Lynn shrugged again. "We can try. Sometimes those exams can take hours."

The admiral turned to Tyre. "Like to go, Robert?"

Tyre shook his head. "You and I have that conference call at 2:30 on the Peabody deal, then I have to fly to Atlanta to look at the syrup company I was telling you about. That could end up being the best deal I've ever done."

THIRTY-THREE

THREE HOURS LATER, Lynn and Whitman Jenkins were on the island in Turtle Bay standing in the room crafted from the excavated Indian mound.

"So what do you think?" Lynn said.

The admiral stood in the middle of the room. He studied the ground for a few moments before answering. "Is this what one would need as an intermediate warehouse for marijuana?"

"I guess it would work, but this seems a little too involved for smuggling grass."

"Show me where the boats were beached."

They left the mound, carefully replacing the covering over the door, and walked back to the shore of the island where Lynn had beached the *Boca Broke.* Lynn pointed to an area beside her own boat. "They were right here."

"What can you tell me about them?"

"They were just mullet boats. Just like Aubrey Lowe's and all the rest. You know...the bow with the big prow, the outboard mounted in the center of the hull, the flat bottom with no dead rise. Gray like all of them. Cookie cutter."

"What does this mullet fisherman who saved you say about all this?"

"Doesn't have a clue. But I got him to promise to nose around a little bit with the commercial fishing crowd. See what he can dig up."

Jenkins nodded with satisfaction then turned and stood gazing out at Turtle Bay, thinking. Suddenly he whirled to face Lynn. "Tell you what. Why don't we stake this place out tonight? Maybe for several nights. See if they come back." His eyes were lively.

"Why don't we just get Truck Kershaw to do it?" said Lynn. "I'm not sure I'm up for another all nighter."

"Let's get him to join us," Jenkins said, warming to the notion with obvious enthusiasm. "What's the matter, think I'm too old? A little field work. Just like the old days. It'd do us both good. What do you say?"

"I say I had about enough field work last night to last me awhile."

Jenkins went silent and turned back to face the bay. He bent to pick up a small piece of driftwood and skipped it across the water. They both watched an oversized mullet break the water's surface and suspend itself in midair delight and freedom before re-entering Turtle Bay with a solid splash. His back still to Lynn, he said quietly, "Millard. Your Indian friend. Think about it."

Lynn didn't have to.

"What time shall I pick you up, Admiral?"

THIRTY-FOUR

WHEN THE PHONE RANG at ten the next morning Lynn was still asleep. She and Whitman Jenkins had spent the night on the Turtle Bay island and saw nothing. She groped for the receiver, put it to her ear, and answered. When she didn't hear anything, she discovered she had the mouthpiece to her ear. She switched ends and heard Truck Kershaw's voice.

"Am I interrupting something?" Truck said.

"Yeah, sleep," Lynn mumbled.

"What'd you do, fish all night?"

"You might say that. What's up?"

"Can I come over?"

"Sure. Guess I need some coffee anyway. Give me fifteen minutes."

She needed more than coffee. Two all nighters back to back. Her body was silently pleading for mercy. The worst part was that the admiral wanted to do another stakeout tonight. A blessing, albeit mixed because of her finances, was that she didn't have any tours lined up for the next few days.

Lynn pried herself out of bed and shuffled into the kitchen to flip on the coffee maker. Back to her bathroom, she showered quickly, pulled on the day's shorts and shirt—khaki and pink today—and tried to do something with her hair. She wasn't very successful so she decided to skip the lipstick and just be grubby. She headed for the java. The combination of the shower and a few pulls on the coffee mug made a difference, but she knew it wouldn't last. A nap later in the day would be a must. Maybe Rolf would come over and help her get to sleep with some dreamy lovemaking. If that happened it would certainly change her approach to her hair and face.

She stood on her porch waiting for Truck, looking at the day and its effect on the Gulf of Mexico. She breathed the scent of the sea with its exquisite tropical vapors with aromas of salt, rotting seaweed, and tiny critters in their shells. Yet another in a now tiresome series of March cold fronts was approaching from the northwest. The clouds in that direction were the color of lead and seemed to be multiplying ominously. The wind was already freshening, causing the first whitecaps accompanied by the coolness which comes with storm convection.

The oncoming weather always seemed to make the sea birds more active. In front of her house, brown pelicans made repeated, crashing dives into threadfin herrings in schools so large they looked like dark clouds in the surf.

Lynn watched the phenomenon of nature. The herring were simply in the wrong place at the wrong time and would shortly end up as pelican dung and never be heard from again. Their case was not a great deal different from that of Millard Savage and Sammy Osceola, who had been going about their lives in an orderly fashion and tragically ventured into harm's way.

But there was a difference. Pelicans don't prey on each other and neither should people. Lynn steeled herself against her nagging fatigue as she psychologically gathered herself in silent re-commitment to finding the two-legged critter or critters who had taken the lives of those close to her.

Her introspection was interrupted by Truck Kershaw's knock at the door. Lynn opened the thick old pine door of the cottage which had iron straps and hardware almost like one would see in a mountain cabin.

"You all right, Cap'n Lynn?"

"Sure. Come on in."

Without asking, Lynn knew to draw Truck a large mug of coffee, black, and hand it to him. She also knew from Truck's face that something was wrong. Maybe bad wrong.

Lynn motioned to Truck and said, "Let's sit in the living room. Little chilly on the porch with that front coming."

She sank into the sofa and plopped her bare feet on the old

seaman's trunk. Truck took a white wicker love seat across from her, spreading his girth to use most of it.

"Your physical exam must have taken all afternoon and into the night. I tried to reach you," Lynn said.

"Yeah, it did take a long time. And afterwards I had to meet with HR on my pension plan, and after that beat it back for Little League practice. Then this morning's been a nightmare and I need to tell you why, but what were you calling me about?"

"Wanted you to join me on a stakeout."

Truck gave her a look of incredulity after which Lynn launched into a complete recap of the events of the last two nights.

"Why didn't you tell me?" Truck asked.

"I tried to. Why do you think I came by the substation? You threw me over for your doctor."

"Yeah, guess I did."

"The admiral wants to stake out again tonight. Want to come?"

"Yeah, I just might. Have to be on my own, though, because I'm not officially on the case. But the first thing is to tell Symanski about all this so he can do a work up on the whole area. God almighty, wait till the press finds out somebody trashed one of those Indian mounds." Then he paused and his expression changed. "But that's not why I came by."

Truck said it with a grave look with which Lynn was familiar. She didn't know what she was about to hear, she just knew she wasn't going to like it. Lynn gestured to Truck to go ahead and spill it. He seemed to gather himself for a few moments before he spoke.

"It's about your buddy, Aubrey Lowe," he said in one of his deepest growls.

"What?"

Truck took a long sigh. "His wife called last night. Said Lowe hadn't come home for supper before going out fishing like he always does. Early this morning the Coast Guard gets a call from a shrimp boat offshore. They pulled their net and drug up a human head severed at the neck. One of our guys saw it and he's sure it's Aubrey. They're already working on the dental—that'll tell us. Don't know where the rest of him is. Probably some shark's supper. Sorry, Cap'n Lynn."

The sofa Lynn was sitting on suddenly went mushy and seemed to be levitating as the shockwaves washed over her. For a moment she had double vision like on the boat ride coming home from her night with the alligator. This was too much. The admiral's son-in-law, her dear friend, and now the man who had saved her life. All gone. Grief pervaded Lynn's entire being and intensified as she recalled that her actions may have caused two of the murders. If she had taken Sammy Osceola out instead of handing him off to Jack Espinosa, things might have turned out differently. And Aubrey Lowe's murder simply had to be a result of Lynn's request to nose around with the commercial fishing crowd. Lowe must have stuck his nose out a little too far.

All was wrong with the world. Her head pounded. Was she going to faint? Then the guilt became a whirling vortex, feeding on itself. How could she be worrying about her own stress when people close to her were getting murdered? Her gloom became thick and dark like used motor oil, and got worse when Truck spoke.

"When you asked Aubrey to poke around with the mullet fisherman, I guess maybe he took it a little too seriously."

Lynn was now on the edge of the sofa, hands on her knees, staring at the floor. She just nodded, wondering why her dear friend had found it necessary to utter what was blindingly obvious, thus twisting the emotional knife which had, at that moment anyway, lacerated her soul into a scarred and bloody mass of guilt.

"Did Aubrey mention anybody special he was going to talk to?" asked Truck.

Lynn didn't reply, keeping her head down. In a few moments, she looked up and said "No" and looked back down.

In the moment before Lynn had replied she had decided that drawing attention to certain people in these cases had caused nothing but death. So she decided to keep Dearl Lomax's name from her friend for the time being, until she could talk to Lomax first. Particularly since Truck wasn't even officially on the case.

"So you still think Jack Espinosa is our man?" Truck said.

Lynn looked up again and sighed. "Yes. Somehow I think this is all connected and I definitely think Espinosa is our man. I can't tell you any more than that, only that I believe it."

"Wanna know something interesting?"

"What?"

"Espinosa called in a complaint this morning. Says he's being stalked."

"Stalked?

Truck nodded. "Claims somebody moved his boat in the middle of the night and re-tied it in another slip. And says when he left his house this morning, somebody had taken one lug nut off each wheel of his SUV and neatly laid it on the pavement beside the wheel."

THIRTY-FIVE

AFTER TRUCK KERSHAW LEFT, Lynn returned to the porch and sat looking at the frothy gulf, watching the weather come in. Her fatigue and grief enveloped her. How easy it would be to just make the few steps to her bedroom, curl up and take oh, say, a three-day nap, and just forget about everything. But she knew she couldn't. Time to call Dearl Lomax and see what she could learn.

Lynn went on the internet and found that Lomax lived on Pine Island and was in the Bokeelia phone book. If Lomax was either a legitimate commercial fisherman or a thug, there was a good chance of finding him home, because both activities occurred largely at night. Sure enough, on the third ring, someone picked up.

"Yeah, go ahead," the gruff voice said.

"Dearl Lomax?" Lynn said.

"Who's this?" The voice got gruffer.

"Lynn Woo. You know who I am?"

"Some kinda tour guide. Boca Grande?"

"Right. Look, Darrel—"

"Name's Dearl."

"Right. Dearl," replied Lynn. "Look, Dearl, I'd like to come over there and see you, talk to you. Need a small favor. Won't take a few minutes of your time."

There was silence at the other end.

"What do you say, Dearl? Will you give me just a few minutes?"

More silence.

"Dearl...?"

Then Lynn heard a dial tone. Dearl Lomax had hung up on her.

Lynn went back to the directory site on the internet and got an address on Pine Island for Lomax. Then she went to a mapping site and printed out a map with directions to Lomax's home. All that took less than five minutes, the time it took for her phone to ring.

"Captain Lynn Woo," she said into the receiver.

"This here's Lomax."

"Yeah, Dearl, we got cut off."

"Naw, I done hung up on you, but I thought it over, and I'll give you a minute or two if you want to come over this way."

"Yeah, okay. Be quicker if I come in my skiff."

"Yep."

Lynn looked at her watch. Almost eleven and she was hungry anyway. It would be lunchtime when she arrived on Pine Island in her boat.

"How about we meet at the Captain's Table," Lynn said. "I'll treat you to a grouper sandwich."

Lynn had named a waterfront restaurant with a dock on the Boca Grande side of Pine Island, a twenty-minute boat ride. Lomax agreed.

LYNN WENT TO Boatmen's Marina and the *Boca Broke*. She hoped she could get over to Pine Island and back before the front hit with its accompanying storms. The bay was already choppy, but at least going over she would have a following sea. She went ahead and put the top to her rain suit on, figuring the twenty-foot skiff would be taking some waves and spray. Even in this chop, taking the boat was far quicker than taking her SUV, which would have required a one-hour-plus circumnavigation of the harbor by street level roads.

As Lynn pounded through the chop to Pine Island, she thought about Jack Espinosa filing a stalking complaint, claiming that his boat was moved and just one lug nut removed from each wheel of his vehicle.

Lynn knew who it was. It could only have been done by one

person. She even knew what the name for it was: counting coup. No real damage, just sending the message that real damage *could* have been done. Counting coup was a centuries-old Indian ritual. A tribe would enter their adversary's camp in the wee hours of the night and disturb something which was sure to be found the next morning. The message was thus sent that scalps could have been taken if the interlopers had wanted them. The result was demoralization of the foe, and it was effective.

Lynn knew that the demoralization of Jack Espinosa could be the goal of only one person. An Indian whose late father had said she liked to hang with the old guys and talk warrior stuff about things like counting coup. An Indian who was convinced that Jack Espinosa had murdered her father.

Lynn approached the dock of The Captain's Table which was unprotected from the wind and chop coming out of the northwest. There were no slips, just a dock. She idled her skiff around to the side of the dock opposite the wind, carefully nosed up to a piling, and tied a single mooring line to the bow, leaving a good ten feet between the boat and the dock. She used the mooring line to pull the boat momentarily closer, then deftly timed her hop from the vigorously bobbing skiff onto the dock. All very expert.

The waterfront restaurant was small, old, and of white asbestos-shingle construction on concrete piers. Lynn entered through the double screen front doors. With the breeze, they weren't running the air-conditioning. Everything inside was old, but not that old, and of wood, but not fine wood. There was the obligatory attempt at a nautical motif, with a mounted fish here and there, and a landing net hanging, but it didn't really come off. "Rustic" would have been the most charitable characterization of The Captain's Table, and that was a stretch. Only two other tables were occupied. No sign of Dearl Lomax. Lynn sat at a table in back near the kitchen where she could see the door.

She only had to wait ten minutes before a man pushed open the screen doors and began to look around the restaurant. Had to be Lomax.

He was a big one, maybe six-four and two-forty. Pretty good shape, too. Walked like an athlete. He was wearing ratty, faded blue jeans, a khaki short-sleeved shirt, and those white boots which seemed to be the commercial fisherman's standard issue. His green cap had a Cabela's Outfitters logo.

Lynn stood and waved, catching the man's eye. He came to the table.

"Dearl?" Lynn said, making sure it was *Durl* this time.

"Yup," the man said.

"Lynn Woo," she said, extending her hand.

Dearl Lomax saw the hand, but, instead of taking it, looked down at his chair, pulled it out, and sat. Lynn withdrew her hand and sat also, directly across from him.

"What can I do for you, lady?" Lomax said, taking his cap off, laying it on the table, and looking at Lynn.

Lomax was probably mid-forties, but looked older. Mainly because of his weathered skin and graying, crew-cut hair. He had a broken nose and an angular scar on his left cheek which carried perhaps two days' stubble. He spoke with a wheezy, gravelly smoker's voice. Lynn's eyes cut to Lomax's shirt pocket and saw the pack of smokes.

"Well, the first thing is to tell me what you want to eat. I'm going to have a grouper sandwich."

Lomax shook his head. "I done et. Like I said, what can I do for you?"

Lynn looked closer. Lomax's gray eyes peered out through two slits in his puffy face.

"You know Aubrey Lowe?" Lynn asked.

"Yeah, I know him, why?" Lomax said.

"When did you last see him?"

"I dunno. Week ago. Why?"

Lynn watched Lomax's eyes very carefully as she said, "He's dead. Murdered. Found this morning."

Lynn saw the pupils dilate slightly, but no discernable reaction other than that.

"No fuckin' way. How? What?" said Lomax.

"You sure you don't know?" said Lynn.

Lomax bristled. “Skip the fuckin’ insults, lady. Just tell me what happened to ol’ Aubrey.”

“His head sort of fell off his body and somehow ended up in a shrimp net.”

Lynn’s attempt to read Lomax’s reaction was foiled when the commercial fisherman lowered his head and shook it slowly as he put his hand to his crew-cut hair and scratched it vigorously.

“That ain’t good,” Lomax replied as he looked up.

“You sure you don’t know anything about it?” said Lynn.

Lomax’s voice was gruff and hard as he said, “No more’n what you just told me. What do you want from me anyway, lady?”

“I want to know what you know about what’s happening over on the islands in Turtle Bay,” said Lynn.

“I don’t know what you’re talking about.”

“You sure?”

“Look, Miz Loo—”

“Woo.”

“Whatever. This meeting’s gonna end real fast if you keep this shit up. What are you talking about in Turtle Bay?”

Lynn leaned forward, lowered her voice, and bored her eyes into Lomax’s.

“I’m talking about murders, I’m talking about Indian mounds being made into warehouses, I’m talking about gator-pit traps, I’m talking about mullet boats beached in the middle of the night and one of those boats being registered to you.”

Lynn thought the bluff worked, was sure she saw a flicker of alarm in Lomax’s eyes. Then, just at the most inopportune time, a gabby waitress appeared asking for their order. Lynn cursed silently. The interruption gave Lomax a chance to gather his thoughts. Lynn asked Lomax again if he wanted anything to eat. When he said no, Lynn ordered a grouper sandwich and, in an afterthought, decided she’d have a Beck’s beer. The one she’d had yesterday was pretty good. Then she endured seemingly interminable questions from the waitress regarding things like tartar sauce, French fries, whether she wanted any chowder, and whether she thought it was going to rain. Finally the waitress left and Lynn turned back to Lomax.

"I want to know what's going on out there. Drugs? What?"

Lomax bristled again. "I got no fuckin' idea, lady. When are you sayin' somebody seen my boat beached out there?"

Lynn told him.

Lomax shook his head. "Nope, couldn't have been mine unless somebody done borrowed it without my permission. I was home in bed that night. Didn't fish."

"Can you prove that?" Lynn said.

Lomax reached in his shirt pocket and pulled out his pack of cigarettes. They were unfiltered Camels. Lynn didn't even know they were still manufactured. Lomax fished one out and reached in his other shirt pocket for his lighter which he held in his left hand while he tamped the cigarette on it with his right. In a moment a plume of blue smoke rose from the table and wafted toward the adjacent window, pushed by the restaurant's stiff cross-ventilation.

"Florida has a law against smoking indoors," Lynn said.

Lomax picked a piece of tobacco from his tongue using his thumb and forefinger. He ignored Lynn's comment.

"Look, Woo, I don't have to prove nothin' to you. You ain't the cops, you ain't nothin' but some kinda goddamn tour guide."

Lynn tried another tack. "Okay, let's just say for a moment that I was wrong about your boat ID number. Who do you think might know something about this?"

Lomax took a long pull on the smoke and just spread his hands and shrugged as he exhaled in Lynn's face. The message was clear: *The law doesn't apply to me; I do what I want.* Lynn wondered what that included. Illegal netting was surely in there. Was murder?

"Do you know Jack Espinosa?" Lynn asked.

"Not really. He's a guide, ain't he?"

"Okay, let's try this. There were four mullet boats out there. You've got to know those guys, you all know each other. Who should I talk to? Who do you know that might be capable of murder?"

"I reckon we all capable of murder depending on the situation." He pronounced it *sicheeation,* and said it with a wry smile.

"I'm just asking for some names of people I can talk to. I need some help on this," said Lynn.

"Give me one good reason why I should help you on anything," said Lomax.

Lynn thought about that. Good point, since they were strangers. And Lynn felt another stab of guilt as she realized that the last commercial fisherman who helped her ended up headless. She nearly decided to give up on Lomax, but then had a thought. She reached in her shorts pocket, pulled out a crisp hundred-dollar bill, and held it up.

"How about a hundred reasons?" Lynn said.

Lomax glanced at the bill, and rather quickly answered, "I'd need about three times that many reasons."

They eyed each other for several beats. Then Lynn slowly pulled out two more hundreds. She folded the three bills together and tossed them across the table. Lomax gathered them up and stuffed them in his shirt pocket behind the pack of cigarettes.

"Lemme make a call or two. See what I can turn up. I'm gonna be over at Boca Grande this afternoon. Meet me at Boatmen's about seven and I'll tell you what I come up with. Maybe nothin', but I'll try."

With that Lomax abruptly grabbed his cap, jammed it on his head, pushed his chair back with a loud scraping noise, and walked out.

THIRTY-SIX

LYNN HAD A LOT OF time to think about her meeting with Dearl Lomax because her trip back across Charlotte Harbor to Boca Grande was long, arduous, and wet. Not from rain, but from the stout, four-foot chop into which her flats skiff was crashing. She had her slicker on with the hood up, but the waves cascaded over the bow and into her face. She tasted salt on her lips. She tasted something else, too. The grease-laden, deep-fried grouper sandwich had been heavily breaded and it kept offering gastric reminders. Shouldn't have eaten it, she told herself. Could have just saved time and injected some lard into the coronary arteries. A three-mile jog was a must as soon as she got rested.

The meeting bothered her. Why had Dearl Lomax called her back and agreed to it? Why had he agreed to help her for a lousy three hundred bucks? Something didn't pass Lynn's sniff test.

The wind was out of the northwest, and when Lynn made enough headway back west toward Boca Grande's lee shore, the sea in the harbor became more tolerable. When she made the cut into Boatmen's Marina and came down to idle speed, she pulled out her cell phone and dialed Truck Kershaw's number. No answer.

It was pushing two o'clock. After she docked she went by her house to let Mullet out. Not that it was necessary because, although Lynn didn't know how, Mullet could hold it all day while Lynn was out working. While in her house, Lynn's eye caught the inviting door to her bedroom, and her fatigue almost got the better of her. No nap yet, she told herself. Got to keep going. Maybe just turn in real early tonight.

A few minutes later she was in her CR-V on her way to

the admiral's cottage. The rain had just begun and it was now freshening the afternoon's stiff breeze. Lynn's windshield was being strafed with the initial aerial attack of welt-sized drops. Soon they came in sheets and through them she watched the coconut palm fronds billow and whipsaw in response to the wind bursts. It was becoming a full-fledged tropical squall. The tired, brown, dead palm fronds joined the casuarina needles as street debris. Her SUV, taller than a passenger car, allowed her to plow through the deep puddles with no fear of drowning out.

She left her rain gear on the boat, so when she completed her dash to the porch of the admiral's cottage she looked like Mullet after he had retrieved game from a pond. Muffy came to the door. As she approached, Lynn looked over Muffy's shoulder and saw the television on, tuned to what appeared to be a soap opera. She also saw Whitman Jenkins at the wicker desk talking to Robert Tyre, who was sitting across from him.

"Lynn, you're soaked. You poor thing, come in here," Muffy said as she grabbed Lynn's shirt sleeve and pulled her into the screened porch.

"Let me get you a towel," she said, heading back in the house. Then, over her shoulder, "You want one of Daddy's shirts?"

"Just the towel. These outdoors shirts are designed to be quick-dry. Thanks."

In a moment she returned to the porch with a huge dry towel. "I told Daddy you're here. He said to come right in when I got you dry."

Muffy took over the drying process, carefully patting Lynn's face and using her hand to brush Lynn's soaking-wet hair out of her eyes. Muffy's touch was pleasing, delicate, and warm, and Lynn appreciated it. She heard a booming Southern voice at the door to the living room.

"They sell rain suits at Boatmen's, lady," the admiral said with a wide grin.

"Wasn't raining when I left the house, sir," Lynn replied, sheepishly.

"Looks like you could use some coffee," Jenkins said.

"A tall one, if you please," Lynn said.

"You still on that wussy decaf?"

"Yeah, but right now I'll take a cup of double caffeinated."

"Good. A cup of that mud Muffy makes will fix you right up."

Muffy wrinkled her nose at her father and headed for the kitchen. Lynn stood until Muffy returned and handed her a mug of coffee, after which Muffy fetched a new towel to spread on the sofa before Lynn sat. Whitman Jenkins and Robert Tyre had a pile of documents between them which covered the entire surface of the wicker desk. The admiral was dressed in his usual outdoors garb, not at all unlike Lynn. Tyre, on the other hand, had on a Corona beer T-shirt, and jogging shorts which were so short that Lynn was grateful she was not sitting directly across from him. He came bounding up to Lynn and thrust out his hand for an overly rousing handshake. Then he stuck his jaw inches from Lynn's and said with a large, crooked grin, "Back in Michigan we called this a real toad choker."

Lynn looked at him quizzically. "I thought you were from Atlanta. You know...Bobby Jones and all that."

"I am, but my family moved to Michigan."

During this exchange Tyre was steadily backing Lynn across the room with his "close talker" routine accompanied by the foulness of his apparent chronic halitosis.

"So what's up, miss?" Jenkins said.

Lynn cut a glance at Robert Tyre. "Well...there've been some developments on this murder stuff."

The admiral waved his hand. "Lynn, as I told you before, you can speak freely in front of Robert. In fact, he may come up with a helpful idea or two."

With that Jenkins pulled out a bottom drawer of the wicker desk, leaned back in his chair, propped his feet on top of the drawer, and made a steeple out of his hands, waiting for Lynn to begin.

Lynn then told of the shocking news from Truck Kershaw that morning, leaving out the fact that only Aubrey Lowe's decapitated head had been found thus far. Muffy was listening from across the room and Lynn could sense her stiffening. Through one hand held to her mouth she said, "Oh my God, that's the man who saved you from the alligator."

Lynn nodded, and the remorse pervaded her core all over again as the weight of three deaths bore down on her.

Jenkins collapsed his steeple and brought his feet to the floor. His eyes were sad. "Lynn, I'm so sorry. This is a dreadful situation." He looked at Muffy. "This makes me feel like we're a black cloud. We come to this lovely island and lose Millard, then Lynn loses her friend and then the man who saved her life from that gator." He looked absently at the pile of papers on the desk and shook his head slowly from side to side in despair. Then he looked up and said, "Give me the details and tell me what I can do to help."

Muffy slipped into the kitchen. Lynn leaned forward and in a low voice told Jenkins and Tyre everything Truck Kershaw had said about Lowe's murder. Then she reviewed her meeting with Dearl Lomax and the arrangement to meet him at Boatmen's Marina at seven that evening. She shared her concern over Lomax hanging up on her, then calling back, and finally being willing to help for a lousy three hundred bucks.

The admiral listened carefully, hands back in his steeple. When Lynn finished, he was silent for several long moments as he looked up at the ceiling in thought.

Before he spoke, he cut a hard glance at Robert Tyre. "I'm not sure how Robert feels, but I don't like the smell of it. Could very well be a setup."

Lynn said, "I had the same thought, but what could happen at Boatmen's Marina? After all, it's a very public place."

"I'm not sure, but I don't want you to find out. If you decide to go, you need backup. I suggest you call your big sheriff friend and have him and his cohorts hide and watch. Robert?"

Tyre shook his head. "Doesn't smell right to me either."

Lynn looked at her watch. A little over four hours until she was to meet Lomax. She pulled out her cell phone and dialed Truck again. Still no answer. Dialed the Boca Grande substation and found out Truck was off. Despite the weather, they thought he was fishing.

"Looks like Truck's not going to be available. I'm sure as hell not calling Symanski, so if I go it'll be alone," Lynn said.

"No, it won't. Robert and I will go. *We'll* be the ones hiding and watching."

"Admiral, I hate to get you involved in this," Lynn said.

Jenkins looked at Lynn through narrowed eyes and lowered his chin. "Why don't you just come out and say it. You think I'm too old for this sort of thing, don't you?"

"No, I didn't say that, but...well, I just wouldn't want anything to happen to you."

Jenkins dismissed Lynn's concern with a wave of his hand. "What can happen to me just watching? Call me just before you leave for Boatmen's and we'll be there to back you up. Afterwards we can all have dinner here at the Lodge. Why don't you let Rolf know? Say eight o'clock? I'll get Muffy to make the reservation."

THIRTY-SEVEN

WHEN LYNN PULLED INTO Rolf's driveway she saw both his golf cart and his Suburban parked under the house. Good. He was home. She had a key but didn't need it. Rolf was one of the islanders who never locked their homes. In the old days nobody did. But that was back when folks like fishing guides, commercial fishermen, and tradesmen could afford to live on the island. That was when there were just a few gulf-front estates and a smattering of town houses and cluster homes, mostly owned by people from Tampa or Lakeland who drove hard every weekend to get there and back, and fished and played hard while they were there.

Then Boca Grande got discovered by the world at large. The real-estate market exploded and in time buyers from afar paid seven figures for older houses on the north end, then knocked them down to build their beachfront palaces. The bureaucrats at Lee County smelled blood and exploited the new "values" to the hilt causing some of the very wealthy to pay more in property taxes than, say, a bank vice-president earns each year in salary.

Most of the original islanders got squeezed out altogether by the high taxes, sold out, moved off island, and began commuting to whatever work they did on island. The combination of the full upscale build-out of the island and the disappearance of the true locals allowed petty crime to work its way in, filling the void left by the island sons who had pretty much policed themselves. In the old days the locals soon found out who was responsible for what little crime there was, and often dealt with it "internally." A "mysterious boat sinking" was all it took to insure that crimes did not become serial events.

As always, Lynn rang the doorbell as she entered and then called out, "Woman in the hall."

No answer. She called again. Nothing. She walked all around the house including Rolf's bedroom. He wasn't there or in his bathroom. In his studio was a painting which it appeared he had been working on; his palette was where he had laid it. The subject was the 110-year-old lighthouse at the south end of the island which overlooks Boca Grande pass.

She was not alarmed. There was one obvious answer: he was walking on the beach to take a break from painting. She walked out on his porch. The front had pushed through, the rain had stopped and the northwest breeze—already stiff—had become gusty. Whitecaps dominated the seascape. She looked up and down the beach but saw no sign of Rolf.

She stretched out on the most comfortable chair to wait for Rolf and her fatigue rocked her again. She felt herself sinking into the shadowy nowhere of sleep. She dragged herself from the chair and made it to Rolf's bed where she curled up and slipped into an agitated, restless sleep.

It seemed to Lynn she had only slept a few minutes when she awoke. She had to blink her eyes twice to confirm that a smiling Rolf was beside her in bed.

"Mmm...must have dozed off for a minute," she said.

He laughed. "I've been back almost an hour and a half."

She looked at him. Rolf's bedroom had lots of glass on the gulf side and his swept-back, wind-blown, graying hair stood out against the backdrop of the foamy sea. His dark, brooding eyes bored into hers and she could smell him. His manly smell. It reminded her of a pleasingly vaporous blend of expensive leather, hazelnut coffee, and brown sugar. She loved it and could always recall it even when they weren't together. Their kissing began with deliberation but then came heavy breathing, writhing, and then clothes nearly being ripped off.

When their lovemaking had concluded, Lynn lay in his arms, looking up at him. "Thanks, I needed that," she said as she cuddled her face closer to his.

He looked at her and said, "You should see your gorgeous

face now." His tone was one of thankfulness. "No more lines of worry. The more worried you've been looking, the more you've had me worried about you."

"Me, worried? Nah," she said.

He looked at her with mock reproach and said nothing.

"Okay," Lynn said. "The truth is, this murder business is driving me—"

"Fucking crazy?"

"Exactly," she said, then told him about Aubrey Lowe's murder, her meeting with Dearl Lomax, not being able to find Truck, and about the admiral and Robert Tyre going as backup for the meeting with Lomax.

"Come on, Lynn, he's an old man," Rolf said. "And that Robert Tyre looks like a gangster himself. Promise me right now you won't go."

"Got to go, sweetie. You know that."

"All right, then *I'll* go as backup, too," he said.

Lynn took his head in her hands. "My darling, please don't make this any tougher than it is. Anyway, you'll be needing to get ready for something a lot better. Dinner at Boca Grande Lodge. About eight. The admiral's making the reservations."

"Does that mean what's-his-name is going, too?"

"Tyre? Don't know. Maybe we'll get lucky. By the way, how's it going with Muffy?"

"Going fine," he said. "She actually has some talent as a painter."

"What I really meant was how you think *she* is."

"Muffy's like you and I were. Going through hell. But like you and I did, she's coping, and mainly by staying busy. I think the painting lessons are a godsend, but I think the murders are really weighing on her."

"Well, now that we know how Muffy is, how is a person who is much more important to me?"

Rolf looked toward the ceiling and put his finger on his chin in a muse. "Now whoever could that be?"

She went for him again. "I'm not paying very much attention to you these days. I'm sorry, these murders..."

When round two was over Rolf touched her nose with his index finger. "Don't worry about me. I'll be right here when you finish playing Miss Marple."

The sobriquet made her mouth curl in a smile. "By the way, you haven't met Sammy Osceola's daughter, Johnnie, yet, have you?" Lynn said.

"No."

"I wonder if she's interested in painting."

He gave her a quizzical look.

"Never mind," she said.

THIRTY-EIGHT

LYNN DIDN'T KNOW how long her meeting with Dearl Lomax would take, so back at her own house she showered and dressed for dinner in cream-colored pants and a flowered Lilly blazer. She chose her grandmother's jade again, and spent lots of time on her hair and even used a little makeup. The lipstick went on carefully and, at the last second, she decided on a touch of perfume. She fed Mullet but the lab seemed in a foul mood, showing little interest in eating, and mainly just whimpered and licked Lynn. She knew she'd been neglecting the dog and it added to her overall guilt quotient.

She tried Truck again. Still no answer. A few days ago she'd told Truck about some redfish she'd seen one day on a back-bay flat near an island named Cayo Pelau. It was afternoon low water, and on a lee shore behind an island, and therefore out of the wind, probably good fishing. Lynn was willing to bet that's where her friend was on his day off.

At about 6:45 she phoned the admiral. "It's me," she said.

"You leaving?" Jenkins said.

"Yes, sir."

"How about your sheriff's deputy?"

"Still can't reach him."

"Okay, I'm on, but Robert's not. He had to leave town on a deal we're doing. I'm on the way to Boatmen's. I'll be there somewhere. You may or may not see me."

"Aye, aye, sir," Lynn said.

LYNN ARRIVED AT the marina just before seven. The front had pushed all the way through and the rain was over, leaving a stiff northwest wind of perhaps twenty knots. Flags on boats stood straight out in the wind like they were starched, and sailboat rigging made its clanking sound against masts. Not ideal conditions for her freshly coiffed hair.

No sign of Dearl Lomax. Lynn strolled around the docks, looking. As she peered through the window of the small boutique adjacent to the ships store, she saw a man who had just turned away from her glance. He had graying hair, swept straight back. She smiled to herself and shook her head. Rolf. Her self-appointed backup. Her prince had come.

She did not see the admiral anywhere on dock level. That meant he had to be upstairs in the restaurant. Lynn kept strolling, looking.

At ten after seven, an old tarpon guide boat approached the marina docks. It appeared to be an early-model Daniels, perhaps a little over thirty feet, maybe a ten- or eleven-foot beam. The configuration of the boat was what people used to call a "cabin cruiser," with lots of fishing cockpit and a moderate-sized forward cabin. The wheel was on the main deck and the helmsman looked through the windshield over the forward cabin. The hull was white and the cabin was a turquoise of the shade prevalent on Bahamian houses. As Lynn watched the boat approach and come alongside the tee dock she saw that the name on the transom was *Gotabigun*. At the helm was Dearl Lomax.

Lynn walked out to the end of the tee dock, being careful to step on the dock planks with her heels, not the cracks. Lomax was holding the boat on to a piling with one arm. The single diesel engine was idling, making that intoxicating throaty rumbling noise that marine diesels do. As Lynn approached, she watched Lomax watching her, but when Lomax looked away for a moment, Lynn stole a quick look at the restaurant on the second floor. The admiral was looking right at her and gave Lynn a fast thumbs-up.

Lynn reached the end of the dock and dispensed with

pleasantries. "What do you have for me, Dearl?" she asked, remembering to pronounce it *Durl.*

"Hop aboard," Lomax said, with a wave of his hand. "They's a guy down at Cabbage Key says he knows somethin'. Give him maybe half what you gave me and he'll probably talk to you."

Lynn hesitated. She was unarmed, though she had her new cell phone in her blazer pocket. This was definitely a risk. Also, she would probably be late for dinner at the Lodge. But not too late; it was only twenty minutes or so to Cabbage Key, and if she talked to somebody for perhaps fifteen minutes, then she'd be no more than a half hour late. She could phone from Cabbage Key. She turned and looked toward the boutique for Rolf. Couldn't see anything through the windows at this distance. She looked up at the admiral who Lynn figured had to have seen Lomax's motion with his hand for Lynn to board the boat. Jenkins was holding both thumbs down and shaking his head vigorously from side to side. This gave Lynn further pause, but she knew she had to go. She gave Jenkins a quick thumbs-up held against her body so Lomax couldn't see, reached down and slipped her heels off, and with her shoes in one hand, turned and boarded the boat.

Lomax gave a little shove against the piling and the boat began drifting away from the dock. He went to the helm, put the diesel in gear, and began idling out of the yacht basin to the cut leading out to the Harbor. Lynn went near the stern, out of earshot from Lomax, reached for her cell phone and dialed Rolf's number. He answered on the first ring.

"This is Miss Marple calling Inspector Poirot. Come in, Inspector. Over," Lynn said.

"You little twit, that's not funny. Where in *hell* are you going with that guy?"

"Just down to Cabbage Key to see somebody he says has some information. I may be twenty or thirty minutes late for dinner."

"Lynn Woo, you tell that man to turn that boat around right now. You don't know anything about that son-of-a-bitch. He could be dangerous."

"It'll be all right, sweetheart."

"Don't you sweetheart me, you come back here!"

"Gotta go," she said, and flipped the cell phone shut.

THIRTY-NINE

ROLF HAD CONDUCTED his cell phone call with Lynn while standing on the dock just outside the boutique. As he flipped the phone shut, he looked up to see Whitman Jenkins approaching. When they had run into each other twenty minutes earlier, Jenkins had dispatched Rolf to the boutique and himself upstairs to the restaurant.

"We got a problem," Rolf said.

"I was doing this for all I was worth," the admiral said, mimicking the two thumbs down and vigorous head shaking he had used to try to dissuade Lynn from boarding the boat with Dearl Lomax. "That girl always was hardheaded. Were you just talking to her on your cell?"

"Yeah. She said that Lomax guy wanted to take her to Cabbage Key to meet somebody who might have some information. Said she shouldn't be more than thirty minutes late for dinner at the Lodge."

Rolf dropped onto a wooden bench which ran along a wooden railing in front of the boutique and sat, slumped over, looking at the boats in the marina.

"What the hell are we going to do, Whit?" he asked, despair in his voice.

The admiral sat beside him, joining him in staring at the boats for several long moments. Then he straightened.

"I'll tell you exactly what we're going to do," he said in an upbeat voice. "We're going to call the Lodge and change our dinner reservation to 8:30, and we'll wait for Lynn there."

"But we need to call the sheriff... Truck," Rolf said.

"And say what? That Lynn willingly got on a boat with somebody she knows?"

"Well, then, we need to go to Cabbage Key."

"And do what when we get there? Interfere with her meeting and make her mad at us?"

Rolf still had his cell phone in his hand and looked down as he absently open and shut it several times. "Aren't you worried?" he said.

"Of course I'm worried. But there's not a goddamn thing we can do about it." He stood, pulling Rolf up with him by one arm. "Come on. See you at the Lodge in about an hour. Meet us in the bar, okay?"

"Who's coming?"

"You, me, and Muffy. We'll have a drink while we wait for Lynn. Robert had to fly to Atlanta on a deal we're working on."

Rolf said goodbye to Jenkins and went back in the boutique to look at a piece of jewelry that had caught his eye during his surveillance. It was just the sort of thing Lynn liked, but he decided it looked too much like something he'd already given her, so he turned for the door. As he did, his eye caught a glimpse of someone staring at him through the window of the store. The person vanished the instant Rolf looked at the window. Rolf did not recognize the person, but had a clear vision of what he saw: a tall young woman, black hair with a long, braided ponytail held with bright-colored beads.

FORTY

LYNN SNAPPED HER cell phone shut after talking to Rolf, slipped it in her blazer pocket, and walked from the stern of the boat up to the helm and stood beside Dearl Lomax. The boat was still running at idle speed, and when Lynn reached Lomax's side, they were rounding the buoy marking the end of the yacht basin and the beginning of Boatmen's channel. From there it was but a few hundred yards into open Charlotte Harbor.

"This your boat?" Lynn asked.

"Nah, buddy of mine. Does a little tarpon guidin'. Didn't want to take you across the Pass in my mullet boat. Little sloppy out there right now with this wind. Wouldn't want no lady guide gettin' wet. 'Specially all dressed up and smellin' good."

Lynn looked at Charlotte Harbor where they were headed and knew she indeed would not have wanted to be in a flat-bottom mullet boat. Lomax's term "sloppy" may have been an understatement. There was still plenty of twilight left and there were solid whitecaps everywhere she looked. The old guide boat felt sturdy under her feet, and the single diesel felt and sounded strong and reliable.

"So Dearl, who is this guy we're going to see?"

"Don't know his name. Buddy of mine said he might know somethin' and he'd be there around 7:30. Said he'd want a little cash for his trouble."

"Why do we have to go to Cabbage Key to meet him?"

"Don't know that neither. Just what my buddy done said."

"So which buddy is this?" Lynn asked.

Lomax looked over at her, annoyed. "You Perry Mason or somethin'? Jesus, woman, a buddy of mine said this guy might have some information you want. You want to know what I ate for breakfast, too?"

Lynn said nothing. She reached for a teak grab rail on the bulkhead as the boat cleared the channel and entered the choppy bay. Her heels were in a pile by her bare feet. Dearl Lomax was a good helmsman. The boat had a semi-displacement hull and Lomax skillfully adjusted his speed and course to minimize the discomfort from the chop. They rode south toward Cabbage Key in silence for the ten minutes it took to get abreast of Boca Grande Pass.

When Lomax was in the middle of Boca Grande Pass, he suddenly turned the wheel to the right causing the boat to head due west, through the pass, and toward the open Gulf of Mexico.

"Hey! Where the hell are you going?" Lynn exclaimed.

FORTY-ONE

ROLF LEFT BOATMEN'S Marina and went home. He'd planned to stop and change for dinner anyway. The Boca Grande Lodge meant a sport coat, so he went with tan, linen slacks, a striped oxford long-sleeved shirt and navy blazer. He broke out the Gucci loafers and alligator belt. He wanted to look nice for Lynn tonight because of all she was going through. He hoped she'd be able to relax.

Not wanting to be the first one there, he arrived a little late at the Lodge. He walked into the stately old blue-clapboard structure which was almost a hundred years old. He made his way down a wide hall with eighteen-foot ceilings toward the bar. He heard the bar before he saw it—the tinkling of glasses, mixed-company laughter, and soft cocktail piano music reaching his ears.

Rolf walked into the bar, and had to make himself look for the admiral and Muffy instead of yielding to the temptation to just gawk at the fascinating old room. The walls were all dark, aged, pecky cypress. Oriental rugs covered the heart of pine floors which were stained dark to match the cypress walls. The furniture was a potpourri of antique wicker and rattan pieces which all worked together perfectly. Majestic old tarpon mounts graced prominent high open spaces and the rest of the walls reeked with the history of the place.

Rolf never tired of looking at the framed photographs of the island's first anglers who sport fished for tarpon. In those days, anglers fished from large seagoing canoes which were towed to Boca Grande Pass by a small steamship. The guides then rowed the anglers to likely spots and the fishing was on. This was all in the photos which included many lady anglers in long, high-necked dresses standing beside 100-pound-plus tarpon strung up on gallows. This was in pre-conservation days when the fish were routinely slaughtered just for the curiosity associated with weighing them.

Rolf heard the admiral's refined Southern voice call to him.

"Rolf. We're over here." *Weah ovuh heah.*

Rolf spotted him and joined the admiral and Muffy in a little sitting group consisting of a love seat, two chairs and a coffee table. Jenkins had a scotch and water and Muffy was working on what looked like a mint julep.

"What can I get you, Rolf?" asked the admiral.

"Glass of chardonnay?" answered Rolf.

Jenkins signaled for the waiter. While he was giving his order, Rolf glanced around the room. March was still in the "high" season, the other season at the Lodge being "sport" season—a euphemism for tarpon season. The place closed in the summer. The high-season people were there in force. Many of the men were wearing their home yacht-club-crested navy blazers with club ties and something like yellow or seersucker trousers with Gucci loafers and no socks. This included Whitman Jenkins IV, except, being from inland Alabama, his blazer bore no yacht-club crest. The admiral wore a natty bow tie. The women were mostly dressed like Rolf expected Lynn to be, but Muffy had on a simple black dress, a little too city-fied for the island.

Rolf looked at one grouping of three couples and thought he was probably looking at three generations. They all had on "the uniform," and all reeked of old money.

Rolf, Muffy, and the admiral engaged in small talk, trying to avoid looking at their watches. Night had fallen. Finally, Rolf did look at his watch: five before nine. "That's it," he said. "I'm trying her on her cell phone."

Since cell phones were not permitted in the Lodge bar or dining room, he rose and went to a small booth with a table and chair for guests to make calls. He dialed her number and got the recorded message about the cellular customer having turned off his phone or being out of the area. He went back to the table and reported.

They all ordered another drink. At 9:30 Rolf tried Lynn's cell phone again with the same result. He tried her house, too, thinking perhaps she was not feeling well and, uncharacteristically, had forgotten to call. He also checked his own voicemail to see if Lynn had left a message. Nothing.

He dialed Truck Kershaw's home number and got him. Truck confirmed that he had been fishing that day, that he had received Lynn's voicemails, but said Lynn didn't answer any of her phones when he tried to call her back. Rolf told him about Dearl Lomax and the boat named *Gotabigun.* Truck said he'd call Cabbage Key and see if Lomax or Lynn were there. Suggested he call him back in five minutes. Rolf came back and sat down. His hands were unsteady.

"This is not good, people," he said. His voice wasn't steady either.

The admiral put his hand on Rolf's arm and opened his mouth to say something reassuring but nothing came out. Muffy was sitting on the edge of the love seat, wringing a cocktail napkin in her hands. She had said nothing and it seemed to make her feel inadequate.

"Rolf," Muffy spoke up. "What did you say the name of the man's boat was?"

"Gotabigun."

"Oh. Is that some kind of Indian name?"

Muffy had helped without knowing it because it caused Rolf to chuckle and broke the tension momentarily. "No, Muffy, it's *Gotabigun.* You know, like got-a-big-one. As in fish? You're from Alabama, you should have picked up on that."

"Of course. You're right."

After that they sat in silence until Rolf rose again to go call Truck.

He answered on the first ring. "Kershaw."

"Me again. Please tell me she's there," Rolf said.

There was a long silence.

"Truck."

"Nobody at Cabbage Key has seen Lynn or Lomax or a boat named the *Gotabigun*."

FORTY-TWO

"DIDN'T YOU HEAR ME? I said where the hell are you going? Cabbage Key is that way." Lynn pointed southward as she shouted at Dearl Lomax who, sphinx-like, was steering the boat due west through Boca Grande Pass and toward the open Gulf of Mexico.

"You gonna answer me or not?" Lynn demanded to no avail as Lomax remained silent and just steered the boat west.

"Let's put it this way, Lomax. You got five seconds to turn this boat around."

At this, Dearl Lomax cut a glance at Lynn and the corner of his mouth curled in a sinister grin. He emitted a low chuckle, signaling derision for the idea of a small woman being able to physically interrupt what he was doing.

Lynn didn't wait for a five count or pause that Lomax could anticipate. Instead, she moved swiftly, driving her elbow into Lomax's rib cage, which was exposed because his hands were on the boat's wheel. Although his eyes were ahead, Lomax sensed the blow coming, but not soon enough to evade it. It doubled him over, and before Lynn could employ her years of training and deal him a debilitating, if not fatal, blow to the neck, he yelled, "Now! Now!"

Lynn was too intent on aiming her next blow to think about what her adversary just yelled. But in the next instant she did think about it, and just before she started to turn away from Lomax and toward the door to the boat's cabin everything suddenly went white as if she had been thrust into a small room with a thousand strobe lights.

"Make sure she ain't got no gun," Lomax said to one of the

two men who had emerged from the cabin on Lomax's yelled signal. "And fish out her cell phone and give it to me."

The man who had hit Lynn on the back of the head with a miniature aluminum baseball bat, normally used for subduing a frisky fish or shark, stood over her unconscious form. The only thing he took from Lynn's pockets was her cell phone.

"She ain't got no gun, Dearl, but here's her phone," the man said.

Lomax took Lynn's cell phone in his right hand, took a full wind up, and heaved it as far into the choppy sea as he could. "She won't be needin' that where she's a goin'." At that the three men all grinned knowingly at each other.

"Get her in the cabin like we talked about," Lomax said. "We got to get under way again."

"Hey, Dearl," one of the men said.

"What?"

"She's a pretty good lookin' chink. What say we have a little fun before we dump her?"

"Ferget it. We got a job to do. This is business."

The man shrugged in disappointment, but it didn't stop him from some "illegal use of the hands" while transporting the unconscious Lynn to the cabin.

The boat had been drifting with the engine idling since Lomax had pulled the throttle to neutral right after Lynn was hit on the back of the head. Now he put the boat in gear again and continued his westerly course toward the sea.

FORTY-THREE

ROLF RETURNED to the table after his phone conversation with Truck Kershaw. There was no color in his face, and his hands and voice were still shaking.

"Nobody at Cabbage Key has seen Lynn or the boat or that Lomax. I asked Truck to meet us at your cottage, if that's all right. Let's get out of here, shall we?"

"Of course," said the admiral, rising.

It was now pushing ten o'clock. Earlier Rolf had said he was hungry, but now food seemed to be the furthest thing from anyone's mind. They were at the cottage ten minutes before Truck Kershaw showed up. When he came in, Rolf jumped to his feet.

"So what have you done?" he asked, his eyes darting and active.

"Well…I've made some phone calls," Truck said.

"So what's happening? Is the Coast Guard on the way?" His voice was just short of shrill.

"Why don't we sit down," Truck said. They did, both on the very edge of the love seat. "I've called headquarters in Ft. Myers and I did call the Coast Guard. Nobody has seen the *Gotabigun* or had any distress calls that match up with either Lynn, Lomax or the boat."

"So are they searching?" Rolf's voice seemed to go up yet another octave.

Truck hesitated for a long moment, looking at him more earnestly than he ever had. How was he going to tell him this?

"Rolf," he began.

"You're not going to tell me she's dead. No…no, you can't do that," he said, his voice trembling and his eyes getting moist.

"No, I'm not going to tell you that," he spoke as gently as he could. "But I do have to tell you that, as of this moment, nobody is searching for Lynn. She boarded a boat of her own free will and she's only been missing for—what—an hour and a half? The Coast Guard won't go looking. They don't even know where to look. And you can't file a missing persons report for somebody who's less than two hours late for dinner."

Rolf turned away from Truck, and, shaking his head to none of them in particular, said, "No, no, no. This can't be happening." He looked up at Muffy. "This is just the way it was with your husband."

The admiral had been silent, but now he spoke. "Rolf, you've got to calm down. The deputy is right…it's only been a short time—"

"But you saw the guy on that boat."

"Rolf. You must remember that I've also seen Lynn Woo. And I'm talking about under fire in some dangerous—life or death, in fact—situations. Remember? I was her commanding officer. There were some covert missions when she was a lot more overdue than she is now. Trust me, Lynn can take care of herself."

"I know she's a tough woman, but she's not in her twenties anymore. I'm telling you all. She's in trouble. I can feel it." He turned to Truck. "Why can't you get in your boat and look for her? I'll go with you."

"I'd be happy to, but where do I go and what do I look for? It's dark out there and all boats look alike because all you see is a red light on one side of the bow and a green light on the other," Truck said.

FORTY-FOUR

IN THE BOAT'S tiny cabin Lynn regained consciousness. She touched the back of her head and her hand drew back sticky with partially coagulated blood. She moved, and winced with pain. It was because she had moved her head for the first time. It felt like someone had opened it up and poured in a cubic yard of concrete. The sea ran heavy, and near the bow where she sat on a V-berth was the bumpiest place in the boat. Each wave the bow crashed into made the concrete in her head feel like it was cracking and breaking into little pieces. She was disoriented, confused. Where was she? How did she get there? A boat. Whose? It was under way. Where was it and where was it going?

The cabin was small with the V-berth and a small head. No galley. It had a small porthole on each side. Lynn peered out one of them and saw nothing; it was black dark. Suddenly it came to her: Lomax. Cabbage Key. The boat turning out to sea and the fight. The realization that somebody else was on the boat, hiding in the cabin. She could hear voices from the helm area.

She reached for her cell phone. Not there. She looked on the bench in the cabin and saw her small purse and her shoes. Her wallet and everything else was in order. This was no two-bit shakedown; it was clear that their mission was kidnapping at the very least, and more likely, murder.

Lynn went to the cabin door and very gently tested it. It was locked as she'd known it would be. She still heard Lomax and his companion or companions—Lynn didn't know how many—talking, and she pressed her ear to the door so she could make out the words. She only picked up a word here and there. She pressed her ear tighter to the wooden cabin door, strained and picked up the word "chain." Heard it several times.

Suddenly her blood felt like it had turned to ice and her gastrointestinal tract contracted. Chain. She'd had to step over a large pile of it to get to the cabin door. She looked down at it. It was big, heavy chain. Then, to her horror, she saw what was beside the chain: padlocks, some heavy wire, and two concrete blocks.

Lynn listened further. She heard the word "tar" several times and the word "turtle." *Tar.* What could that be about? Turtle was easier. Had to be Turtle Bay, where Millard Savage's and presumably Sammy Osceola's murders had occurred. She listened some more, and heard "tar" again, "chain" again, and "war."

Lynn tried to gather her wits. No more listening, she had to think. Had to try to figure out how to avoid being a human anchor without a rope.

FORTY-FIVE

MIDNIGHT CAME AT Whitman Jenkins' cottage at the Boca Grande Lodge. Muffy had fixed ham-and-cheese omelets for Rolf and her father, and thawed and heated some biscuits which tasted as good as homemade. The admiral took his biscuits, halved them, laid them on a plate and poured thick Alabama cane syrup on them—a product of one of his companies. Then he ate the biscuits with a fork. Rolf barely picked at his omelet but hit the coffee much harder; he was into his third cup.

Rolf had prevailed and, although everyone knew the water was rough, persuaded Truck Kershaw to use the twin-engine sheriff's boat to cruise the harbor and Boca Grande Pass and see if he saw anything. He'd been gone almost two hours.

One look at Truck's face when he walked in the door told Rolf the answer: he'd seen nothing but water and blackness, wind and waves.

After Muffy handed Truck a plate and a mug of coffee, Rolf sat beside him on the love seat where Truck was attacking his omelet with his plate on his knees. Rolf's hands were shaking and all the coffee hadn't helped.

"Okay," he said, touching his temples with his fingertips as he looked at the floor. "She's now almost four hours overdue. It's after midnight. We've got to do *something* besides wait." His voice seemed to climb a musical scale as he said it. It was clear to Truck that Rolf's composure was teetering on the edge.

Truck set his partially eaten omelet down on the coffee table. "You have a phone book?"

When it was brought to him, he looked up Dearl Lomax's phone number in Bokeelia on Pine Island. Dialed the number on his cell phone. When someone answered he apologized for calling so late and asked for Dearl. They all listened intently to Truck's end of the conversation as he asked a series of questions: When will he be back? Do you know what boat he's in? Have you ever heard of a tarpon guide boat named the *Gotabigun?*

Truck said thanks and replaced the receiver. "That was his wife. Said as far as she knows he's fishing in his mullet boat all night. Says she never heard of the *Gotabigun.*"

He picked up the cell phone again and dialed the sheriff's substation. When someone answered, he said "Kershaw," in one of his growls. "We got an overdue powerboat. Put out a bulletin." He gave the details. "What's the number of the Coast Guard station at Ft. Myers Beach?"

He called the number and reported the details of the missing boat and learned that the Coast Guard had no matching distress calls. They promised to feed the description to any planes or boats patrolling near Boca Grande.

"Are there any?" Truck asked.

"I don't have that information," replied the rather officious voice at the Coast Guard station.

Truck broke the connection. "You mean you won't tell me," he said, looking at the now dead phone.

Truck looked at Rolf. Sitting beside him, he seemed small and pathetic as he was consumed by grief and worry. Truck put his arm on his shoulder and said, "You need to keep busy. Keep calling her cell phone and check her house and your messages constantly."

"What else can we do?" Rolf asked.

"Nothing until morning. The Coast Guard will definitely put out a search-and-rescue op then if she hasn't turned up."

Rolf reached for the phone to follow Truck's instructions on the constant calling.

"Wait," Truck said. "Before you do that, let's go over what you saw at the marina again. Was there anything the two of you may have left out?" He looked back and forth between Rolf and the admiral.

Jenkins looked at the floor thoughtfully, then shook his

head. Rolf thought a few moments and said, "Well, there is one thing."

"What?" Truck said.

"After Lynn left in the boat, I went back in the boutique for a minute and as I started to leave I saw someone looking at me, like they were…I don't know, not stalking, but maybe following me. Watching me." He gave Truck the description of the young woman, explaining that she looked like an Indian.

"Sammy Osceola's daughter. Her name's Johnnie and she thinks she's going to nail her daddy's killer."

"Why would she be following me?"

FORTY-SIX

LYNN TENSED HERSELF for every wave the bow of the boat crashed into, knowing that only a few layers of built-up, decades-old fiberglass separated her from the wrath of the heavy sea. She tried to anticipate the waves but, not being able to see, often guessed wrong and was surprised. The results were jarringly painful. Her head was playing sounds reminiscent of a blacksmith's shop and she was having waves of dizziness and nausea. She never got seasick, so she assumed it was a concussion.

Got to think this through, she told herself. But thinking was difficult in the face of the pain in her head. She felt panic start to rise, and started taking long, slow breaths in response, remembering some worse situations years ago. But were they worse? The more she thought about it, she decided that being fitted for a concrete bikini was about as bad as it got.

Got to think. She started opening compartments in the cabin. She found life jackets but no flares. She saw nothing she could use to jimmy open the cabin door. She decided that would be a doomed strategy anyway since there were at least two men, and they were probably armed. They'd simply shoot her and therefore not have to hit her over the head again to subdue her before outfitting her with the chains and the concrete.

She opened more compartments. Mostly fishing tackle. The boat wasn't even legal without flares, she thought. She opened the last compartment. There she saw it. In that last compartment was a small object. She retrieved it and carefully slipped it in a pocket of her blazer along with her wallet.

Lynn directed her attention to the furthest point forward in the bow area and began probing. She removed some cushions which revealed the locker for the anchor rope. The opening from the cabin into the anchor rope locker was small. Lynn eyeballed it carefully to try to assess how small. She took a life jacket and laid it against the opening and marked a spot with her finger to measure the opening. Then she held the life jacket against her torso and compared the rough measurement. She decided it just might work. This was a time when she was grateful for her smallness. But still, it would be tight. She might even get stuck. Maybe that wouldn't be all bad, she thought. If they couldn't get her out, maybe they couldn't drown her. They'd have to figure out another way to kill her.

Lynn began to ease herself into the anchor locker, head first. She didn't go all the way, just enough to test the extent to which she might fit through the opening. She became convinced she would fit. With her head inside the anchor locker, she looked up at the bow hatch and was jubilant to see that it appeared slightly larger than the opening she was currently wedged into. In this position, every crashing wave now caused a crushing blow to her torso, which brought excruciating pain.

She backed her way out of the opening, reached for one of the life jackets, then discarded it as she decided it would prevent her from fitting through the opening. She reached for her blazer and felt the object she had put in her pocket.

Time to make her move. She entered the opening from the cabin to the rope locker again, going in with her back to the bow of the boat, and drew her feet under her so that she was completely in the rope locker crouched in a ball. She then used her head and her hands to ever so slightly push the bow hatch up enough to peer out. Like most bow hatches, it opened from the aft side. This allowed Lynn to look right back through the windshield at the helm. By the dim red glow of the instrument lights, she could see Dearl Lomax at the wheel. Lomax did not appear to be touching the wheel and was not looking forward, but talking to his cohorts, of which Lynn could see two. The boat was obviously running on automatic pilot. "George" was driving, as some mariners liked to say.

Lynn knew she must move fast. She pushed the bow hatch

all the way open, gently laid it back toward the prow of the boat, and then leaned it carefully against the bow rail. Being heard by Lomax was not an issue because of the noise made by the engine and by the hull plowing through the sea. Then she pulled herself up through the bow hatch and crawled onto the deck where she lay prone, lying longitudinally to the boat with her head nearest the stern and feet nearest the bow. She firmly clasped her blazer where the pocket was to make sure the object she had taken from the cabin was secure. She only lay there a moment, waiting for the bottom of the trough of the next wave. When it came she clasped her pocket even tighter, and silently allowed herself to roll off the bow deck, over the side, and into the Gulf of Mexico.

FORTY-SEVEN

AT THE ADMIRAL'S COTTAGE, the vigil continued. Jenkins and Muffy were showering Rolf with attention and concern. Rolf was following Truck's instructions and dialing Lynn's phones every ten minutes or so.

"Truck, how about calling the Coast Guard again. See if they've heard anything," Rolf said.

Truck looked at him with a pained expression. "Rolf, I left them my cell number."

"Goddammit, Truck, just call them. And while you're at it I'd like to know where they'll start searching in the morning."

"Well, if this is related to the murders, the backcountry might be the place to look," Truck said.

"I would agree, Rolf," the admiral said.

"No," Rolf said.

"What?" Truck said.

"I said no. She's not in the backcountry. That boat looked too big for much shallow water. I tell you he's taken her out in the gulf. I know it. I can feel it. Dammit, Truck, she's out there in the water right now. I just know it."

LYNN HAD TAKEN a deep breath just before she rolled off the deck of the *Gotabigun*. When she hit the water she allowed herself to sink. She wanted to minimize the chance that Lomax and his henchmen would see her in the visibility provided to the boat's prop wash by its stern light.

After Lynn was confident that the boat had passed her, she came to the surface and began treading water. She looked at the wake of the boat and saw the white stern light getting smaller and smaller. This was not without difficulty in the sea which

Lynn estimated at five feet. The only time she could see the boat's light was at the top of each wave. She kept watching. No change in course or speed. That meant they didn't see her. She said a silent prayer.

As she treaded water, she looked around her, 360 degrees. No shore lights. Not surprising. She didn't know how long she'd been unconscious in the cabin and how long the boat had run, but it was clear that she was probably at least ten miles offshore.

Survival was her singular goal. She told herself that she, the professional diver, should be suited for this. But she knew her most daunting adversary was hypothermia. The Southwest Florida gulf water temperature in the early spring was usually still in the low seventies, some twenty-five degrees below normal body temperature. Sharks were her other worry, followed by just figuring out how to stay afloat in the five-foot seas while burning the least amount of energy. Her plan had to work and result in a rescue in the next few hours because she knew the Coast Guard would not initiate a search-and-rescue operation until morning. Lynn was experienced enough in sea survival and rescue to know she'd never last that long.

FORTY-EIGHT

IN THE JENKINS COTTAGE, Rolf's composure was hanging by a thread. Truck had called the Coast Guard back. They had nothing, and promised a search of both the gulf and the back bays at dawn. Rolf continued his phone calls.

As he finished another round of unsuccessful phone attempts, he looked at Truck. "Hey. What about that Indian girl…what was her name?"

"Johnnie Osceola," Truck said.

"Yeah. Let's get in touch with her and see if she knows anything about this. Where's she staying?"

"Here at the Lodge, I think," Truck said.

"Well, get her out of bed and get her over here to talk. Let's see what we can find out?"

"Rolf, it's the middle of the night."

"Truck…" was all he said, accompanied by a menacing look.

Truck looked at the admiral. "Can't hurt," said Jenkins. "At her age, she can do without a little sleep."

Twenty minutes later Truck Kershaw returned to the cottage with a furious young Indian woman. Johnnie Osceola had pulled on a pair of shorts and a T-shirt and had not braided her long black hair, which now flowed down her head to her shoulders like a silky waterfall. She was barefoot.

Rolf cleared his throat and decided to take the lead. "You're Johnnie, right?"

Johnnie said nothing, just stood staring at something on the opposite wall known only to her.

Rolf looked down at his shoes, then back up and continued. "Johnnie, I want to apologize for getting you out of bed at this hour. Why don't you sit down? Would you like a cup of coffee?"

Johnnie spoke. "I'd like a lawyer. I thought this was Boca Grande, not fucking Nazi Germany."

At this Rolf said nothing but looked over at Whitman Jenkins and his face said: *You're the Naval Intelligence admiral. You take over.*

The admiral was sitting in his usual spot, behind the wicker desk, the cottage's version of "the bridge." At Rolf's unspoken invitation, he didn't rise, but began speaking from his chair.

"Miss Osceola," he said, "this is not an inquisition or anything of the sort. And my understanding is that you are here of your own free will to try to help us, and, young lady, we could surely use some help."

"I'm not here of my own free will, you old bastard. This big ape dragged me out of bed and forced me over here."

"We're trying to be nice, miss," Jenkins said. "Would you rather the deputy just go ahead and arrest you on a stalking charge?'

"What are you talking about?" said Johnnie.

"Mr. Berglund saw you spying on him at the Boatmen's boutique tonight. What were you doing there?"

"I wasn't there. You're mistaken."

Jenkins shook his head impatiently. "Johnnie, let's stop playing games. I know you know Lynn Woo. She was a good friend of your father's. Lynn is missing. That's why we're all up at this hour. Mr. Berglund saw you at the marina, staring through a window at him, just moments after Lynn was seen for the last time boarding a boat. Now we need to know what you know."

Johnnie Osceola's demeanor changed. Her stiff, defiant posture relaxed. She looked at the floor for several long moments, then spoke. "I was following Lynn, not him," she said, nodding her head toward Rolf. "I know who killed my father. I'm just trying to prove it so he can be arrested. I know Lynn is trying to find out who's behind the murders, too, and I thought she might lead me to something I can use. I saw her get on the boat. I saw you in the restaurant and I saw him in the boutique. I shouldn't have let him see me. That was sloppy."

They all exchanged glances, then the admiral spoke. "So who do you think murdered your father, and do you think the same person murdered my son-in-law?"

Truck Kershaw answered for her. "She thinks it was a fishing guide named Jack Espinosa. I believe Lynn thinks so, too. They might be right."

FORTY-NINE

LYNN WAS FIGHTING for survival. She tried the dead man's float to conserve energy and keep more of her body out of the water to fight hypothermia but with little success. Mostly she just treaded water. She constantly scoured the sea for any piece of flotsam she could cling to and preserve her strength. She saw nothing.

She had plenty of time to think. She wondered if Dearl Lomax could be the brains behind whatever was going on at the Indian mounds in Turtle Bay. She doubted it. Lomax was more likely somebody's functionary. She thought about the words she'd picked up through the cabin door of the boat she'd just escaped from. "Tar" and "war" still baffled her. She'd have to think on that more if she survived. She wondered how Jack Espinosa, her most likely suspect, might be connected with Dearl Lomax.

She was so cold. Why hadn't she looked for a rain jacket or some other clothing to keep her body temperature up a little more? She was so hungry she wasn't hungry. She was numb, weak, and shivering.

Suddenly she felt something. Something in the water rubbing against her leg. Then she saw the dorsal fin next to her. The shark must have been half again longer than she was. Couldn't tell what kind. The big fish circled her once. Then again. Lynn reached in her pocket, took out the object she'd taken from the boat, and got ready. The shark was coming right at her. She hit the creature in the gills as hard as she could with her precious object, praying it was not damaged. Amazingly, the shark turned away. After that, she tried to float again, so her water-treading legs would not entice the huge predator. In a few minutes she no longer saw the shark. She put her object back in her pocket.

Then the strangest thing happened. A silver serving tray came floating toward her. On it was a complete place setting and on the plate was one of her favorite dishes. Not Chinese but her favorite Italian one: Osso Buco. The veal shank was large and lean and the risotto on the plate looked to be just the right consistency. An Austrian crystal wineglass was half-filled with a red wine. She could smell it, and guessed Barolo. The tray came closer. She was suddenly ravenous. She reached out to pick up the fork and the whole thing vanished.

She realized she'd been hallucinating. Hypothermia was getting the upper hand. Her plan had to work, and soon. She tried to occupy her mind to fight the hallucinations and fend off acquiescence to the fatigue and the cold. She was so cold. She was shaking violently, reminding her of the fever she'd had with a flu episode when she'd thought her bed was going to "walk" across the bedroom from her shivering. She was so tired. Felt so weak. If she could just sleep for a few minutes. Maybe if she just lay back in the water for a few minutes, she could sleep floating and wake up refreshed. Yes, maybe just try that for a minute or so… No, she thought. Can't do that. She shook her head vigorously. Got to stay awake. Anything else is a decision to die right then. And, she decided, she wasn't quite ready to do that. Got to keep paddling and floating. Got to keep thinking.

But her thinking got the best of her. Suddenly she wasn't in the Gulf of Mexico but in a blue cave south of Tallahassee with full dive gear. She was low on air and all her dive lights had failed. She pulled on the guideline. My God, where was Dave? She began to weep uncontrollably.

Then she saw something. Good God, it was a boat. A flats skiff like hers. It was idling up to where she was. Her best island friend was at the helm—Truck Kershaw. "Hey, Lynn, there are some tailing redfish up in Bull Bay, and I found some bald eagles are nesting. Hop aboard and we'll run up there and…

She snapped out of it. More hallucinations. She cursed

herself. Got to make her mind work on *real* things, she told herself.

She reached in her pocket for the object she had taken from the cabin of the boat. It was an EPIRB, an acronym for Emergency Position Indicating Radio Beacon. She looked at the cylindrical device in her hand and saw the small green light steadily flashing, indicating that it was continuing to put out its signal.

EPIRBs emit a signal which is picked up by satellites. Lynn knew that the efficiency of the technology could be catch-as-catch-can. She knew of cases of satellites having to make multiple passes before picking up a signal. Tragic delays in getting the Coast Guard to launch a search-and-rescue operation had occurred. She watched the little flashing green light on the EPIRB and said a silent prayer.

Lynn felt even weaker. Colder. She tried to make her brain work. She went back to the murders. Sorted everything out all over again. She kept coming back to Jack Espinosa. Everything pointed to him. Dearl Lomax must somehow be working for him. But what could "tar" and "war" mean?

Well, come to think of it, she did know what war meant. The cold war at least. Suddenly she was back there. She was in a full wet suit doing a clandestine dive, planting an electronic device on the hull of a Russian ship. God, she wished for that wet suit now. The cold. She was so sleepy. She was no longer sure if she was sleeping or not. Maybe that few moments of sleep wasn't such a bad idea after all. Maybe she'd just try it for a few seconds...

FIFTY

IT WAS ALMOST THREE A.M. when Truck Kershaw's cell phone rang. He had it on ring mode, and everyone in the cottage had been dozing except for Rolf, who had just finished making his ritual series of calls to Lynn's cell phone, her house, and his voicemail. They jumped at the sound.

"Kershaw," he growled curtly into the phone.

Rolf had to endure a seemingly endless series of "yeahs" on Truck's end of the conversation. Other than that, Truck said nothing else except thanks at the end. He flipped the phone shut and looked at Rolf.

"That was the Coast Guard. They've picked up a signal from an EPIRB about eighteen miles out in the gulf."

"What's that?" Rolf said.

"It's a little gizmo people keep on small boats. If the boat goes down and they go in the water, they take it with them and it puts out a signal that satellites pick up."

"Thank God," he said.

"Don't thank him yet. They've scrambled a search-and-rescue op, but EPIRB's aren't as accurate as something like GPS. It's pretty old technology. They still have to find her—if it's her—in the middle of the damn Gulf of Mexico. And the other thing is..."

"What?"

"She has to be alive when they get there. If it *is* Lynn, she may have been in the water for many hours and it's pretty cold this time of year. You're familiar with hypothermia."

Rolf nodded, then looked at Whitman Jenkins. "Whit, I *know* it's Lynn. I guess we're going to find out if she's as tough as you think she is."

FIFTY-ONE

LYNN OPENED HER EYES. It was excruciatingly bright so she closed them again. Then she tried opening them again, just squinting this time. She was desperately trying to tread water, but she realized her hands weren't moving. Legs either. She tried harder; she didn't want to drown after surviving this long. But nothing would move. She got more used to the light and opened her eyes wider. She must have made it through the night, but the sky looked odd, it was stark white and very close to her. Something wasn't right here. Then it occurred to her that the explanation was simple: she had drowned. That's why her arms and legs would not tread water any more. Everything was so bright and white. Was she in heaven?

She looked closer at the white sky. She realized that her vision had been initially blurred but now it got sharper and she wasn't looking at the sky at all but at the ceiling of a room. She looked down at her arm and saw an IV in her vein, a sheet over her legs. Good God, she was in the hospital! She heard someone in the room scrape a chair on the floor, rise, and come to her bed.

She looked up into Rolf's intense, dark eyes. He bent over and kissed her on the forehead then stroked it.

Still very weak, she smiled thinly and in a small voice said, "Have we met?"

He smiled back. "Once or twice. So who do think you are, anyway, Esther Williams?"

She grimaced. "At least you could have said somebody closer to my age."

Lynn had no recollection of the Coast Guard swimmer in the water with her, or the basket, or the tops of the waves being whipped frothy by the turbulence from the helicopter blades. No recollection of her basket swinging in the wind on the way up to the white Coast Guard helicopter with the large, red, diagonal stripe on its side. The swimmer had told Truck Kershaw that he figured they were too late, that he didn't know if Lynn would make it. When Truck told that to Rolf he replied that the swimmer should have talked to the admiral, that then he'd have known how tough Lynn was.

"How do you feel?" Rolf asked.

"Oh, just peachy," she said, trying to lift her head off the pillow but finding it too laborious and abandoning the attempt.

"We almost lost you. It took forever to get your body temp up."

"When I was out there, I promised myself I'd never be cold again. When I get out of here I'm going out and buying about twenty sweaters. Might just wear them all summer."

He laughed. "They've been feeding you intravenously, but guess what? I understand some Jell-O is on the way." He said it brightly, making a happy face like an elementary school teacher.

His happy face dissolved. "Time to get serious for a minute. Let me tell you who all is out there waiting to see you. First of all, the press."

"Screw the press," she said.

"That's what I figured," he said. "I talked to your doc and he won't let them in right now anyway. The admiral and Muffy want to see you. They've been amazing. Stayed up with me all night. So did Truck. He's here, too, with some of his people. They want to talk to you and I imagine you want to talk to them, too."

She nodded.

"That's about it except for the Indian girl."

"Johnnie?"

"She's really something, that one."

"That's putting it mildly."

At Lynn's instruction, Rolf brought the admiral, Muffy, and Johnnie in for a few minutes just to visit and so Lynn could thank the admiral. She wanted to keep it short because she knew her strength was low and she wanted to use it for talking to Truck about what happened, and about Dearl Lomax. When the admiral and company left, Rolf brought in Truck. He had somebody with him. Lt. Stan Symanski.

Lynn didn't see the diminutive Symanski at first because as they walked into the room he was in Truck Kershaw's wake. Lynn's eyes were fixed on her friend as he approached the bed. Had they both been standing, the circumstances would have resulted in an embrace. But it wasn't physically possible, and their greeting amounted to Truck tenderly enveloping Lynn's small hands in his huge ones until she saw Truck's dark eyes get watery.

"So what's next, Cap'n Lynn, the English Channel?" Truck's almost obligatory zinger helped him past his teary moment.

"Very funny. You know if..." Lynn was in the midst of a rejoinder when she spotted Symanski behind Truck. "Oh, hello, Lieutenant. When I was treading water all night, you're not exactly the person I was dreaming about seeing first. Although you might have come in handy singing *God Bless America* as I was going down for the last time."

"I can understand why you feel that way, Ms. Woo. I appreciate you seeing me. I'd certainly be grateful if you could answer some questions for us. That is, if you feel up to it right now."

"Oh? Well, let me tell you what *I'd* be grateful for. I'd be grateful if you would tell me that you've tracked down one Mr. Dearl Lomax and thrown his ass in jail."

"I'm afraid I basically can't tell you that," said Symanski, with a tug at the knot of his solid white necktie.

"Why the hell not? What are you doing?" Lynn got her head off the pillow a few inches as she said it, but then let it go back.

"Easy, Cap'n Lynn," said Truck. "How about telling us what happened with Lomax."

Lynn started with the meeting at the Captain's Table on Pine Island, and took it to when she rolled off the *Gotabigun* into the sea.

Truck nodded all the way, and when Lynn finished, he said, "That's about what we figured. Well, here's the deal. We already picked up Lomax."

"Good. So he is in jail."

Truck shook his head. "'Fraid not. He says he had an appointment with you. That you came to meet him of your own accord. That you got on the boat with him of your own free will. That he was responding to your request for help."

"All that's true, of course," said Lynn impatiently.

"Then he claims that you asked to go out into Boca Grande Pass because you thought you saw a suspicious boat. Out past the sea buoy, he said you suddenly and inexplicably leaped overboard. He claimed he smelled alcohol on your breath when you got on board, and that you were staggering around the deck drunk. Claims he was worried you were going to fall off sooner."

Lynn had picked up on where this was going. "Go ahead," she said, irritation in her voice.

"He says he tried to save you immediately, but with the onset of darkness and the fast currents, he couldn't find you."

"So why didn't they call the Coast Guard or put out a mayday?" Lynn asked it with disgust because she knew what the answer would be.

"Said he wanted to, but he'd forgotten his cell phone and his marine radio was on the blink. Said he figured his best chance to save you was to stay in the area and search. Says he did that for several hours, and then gave up and called our headquarters in Ft. Myers as soon as he got in. He *did* make the call."

"Why am I not surprised to hear all this? I guess that's what I would have said if I'd been hired to kill somebody and whiffed."

"We're tailing him 24/7, Cap'n Lynn."

"Great..." Lynn mumbled as the futility of it all seemed to tax her strength. Her eyes closed and Rolf stepped up and gently nudged Symanski and Truck toward the door.

FIFTY-TWO

TWO DAYS LATER Lynn was eating square meals and walking the halls of the little hospital in Englewood. Her concussion was mild. She had a small bald spot on the back of her head where her stitches were, but she was able to comb her hair over it. She was ready to go home.

Rolf and Muffy came to collect her. They were both decked out in colorful island wear, almost like they were on their way to a party. Lynn basked in the nurturing attention and joked that she might consider going for another swim if this was what being rescued was like.

When they arrived at Lynn's cottage, Johnnie Osceola was sitting on the front steps, waiting. Lynn was surprised to see her because Rolf had said she was in Tallahassee at her father's full Seminole Indian funeral. Lynn had planned on attending before her unscheduled aquatic event intervened.

"Hi, Johnnie. Sorry I missed the funeral," Lynn said.

Johnnie Osceola didn't move, didn't look at Lynn, but instead watched an iguana over a foot long scurry into the hibiscus hedge next to Lynn's cottage.

"My dad would have loved it... Maybe he did love it," Johnnie said. "Would have been better if you'd been there because you were supposed to be a eulogist. Was in my dad's will."

"Like I said, I'm sorry—"

"Hey, you kind of had a prior engagement for a swim party," she said with the corner of her mouth curled. "Forget it."

Lynn nodded. "Well, don't just sit there on the steps or I'll have to get you a stick to whittle. Come on in."

They all went inside where Lynn had her reunion with Mullet, who almost knocked her down, and nearly swept the coffee table clear with his wagging tail. She petted him vigorously, scratching him thoroughly behind his one ear, then resumed her conversation with Johnnie.

"So Johnnie, the funeral's over, what are you doing back down here? You haven't graduated from the university yet, have you?" she asked.

Johnnie had flopped down on Lynn's sofa and crossed her arms and her long legs, swinging her foot like she had at the sheriff's substation that day.

"We've had this conversation once, *Miz* Woo. Maybe your concussion was worse than they thought. Let me play it back for you. I'm not leaving this island until Jack Espinosa, or whoever is my father's killer, is found, arrested, or dead. Is it coming back now?" she said while looking across the room into space and swinging her leg even more vigorously.

Lynn glanced at Rolf before saying quietly, "Yeah, I remember the conversation. But do you remember the part where I said I don't agree with you? You need to go back to school, young lady."

Johnnie turned her head to look at her sharply and Lynn remembered what Johnnie said the last time she called her "young lady." She appeared ready to explode again, but then seemed to think better of it. She looked back into space and said, "I can finish the one term I have left of school anytime. I only had one father."

Lynn shrugged in resignation, then turned to Muffy. "What's the admiral doing this morning?"

"Staying close, hoping you'll come by to see him."

"I want to. Soon as I make some phone calls. Need to cancel the few charters I have until I can get back in my groove."

Thirty minutes later they all walked into the Jenkins' cottage at the Lodge. Lynn and Whitman Jenkins embraced, and Lynn thought the admiral was as close to showing emotion as she'd ever seen in the years she'd known him. They spent some time discussing Lynn's physical condition and touched again on a few details of her ordeal at sea. Then the conversation turned to the murders.

"Well, I called Truck Kershaw a while ago," Jenkins said.

"And?"

"They've got a full-time tail on Dearl Lomax."

"I knew that."

"He tried to get a wiretap authorization but came up blank. Not enough probable cause. Your word against Lomax."

Lynn shook her head in disgust. "What about checking the boat for fingerprints? There was at least one other person with Lomax."

"You probably think I'm too over the hill to have thought of that, but I did. Same answer. Civil liberties stand in the way."

Lynn shook her head again. "Well, as revolting as that is, let's face it—Lomax is a pawn on the board. Somebody else is pulling his strings. Somebody like Jack Espinosa. That's where I plan to put my attention."

She glanced over at Johnnie Osceola and saw her perk up.

"What do you propose to do and how can I help?" said Jenkins.

"Well, the first thing I want to do is talk to Truck."

"Figured that. I've arranged for us to have lunch at Boatmen's Marina." He looked at his watch. "In about fifteen minutes."

Johnnie Osceola spoke up. "Good. What are we going to talk about?"

Lynn looked sharply at her. "You're not going to talk about anything, because you're not going," she said. "I can't make you go back to Tallahassee like you ought to, but I'm not going to let you get involved where you shouldn't."

Lynn could see the rage in Johnnie's black eyes. The eruption almost made it to the surface before she controlled it and simply stood and walked briskly out of the cottage without a word.

Lynn shrugged again. It occurred to her that shrugging was a frequent reaction of hers to things Johnnie Osceola did and said. She remembered what Truck had told her about Espinosa's boat being moved, and SUV wheel lug nuts being removed—the Indian-style counting coup incident which had to have been perpetrated by Johnnie. She'd meant to talk to her about that.

Tell her to cease and desist. She was going to have to get really tough with that girl sooner or later, probably sooner. For her own safety. And for the sake of not mucking up the chance of bagging the murderer.

FIFTY-THREE

LYNN DROVE DOWN Banyan Street on her way to lunch at Boatmen's Marina. After what she had been through, checking on her favorite street was almost like checking on Mullet. The high sun was filtering through the canopy the banyan trees made and making little fingers of light on the gnarly, root-laden trunks. She went slowly down the short street and took it all in.

Truck Kershaw was waiting for Lynn and Jenkins at a table at Boatmen's upstairs restaurant. The table was on the water side and looked right down at the moored boats, the yacht basin, and open Charlotte Harbor beyond. The front which had caused the heavy sea during Lynn's ordeal had long since given way to calm, sunny high pressure. Lynn looked longingly at the blue-green water, but then looked back at the admiral and remembered Millard, Sammy and the man who'd saved her from the gator—Aubrey Lowe. Time to buckle down, she thought. She needed to come up with something.

Lynn and the admiral ordered the flounder special while Truck went with his usual—two grouper sandwiches. Lynn resisted the urge for a vodka on the rocks, or at least a Beck's.

"So what's up with the tail on Dearl Lomax?" Lynn asked.

"Nothing. All he's doing is catching mullet legally with a cast net. Knows he's being watched."

"Did you find out who owns the *Gotabigun?*"

"Nope. It's not a documented boat. Most of them that small—thirty-some foot or whatever it was—aren't. Must be a Ft. Myers boat, because nobody around here has ever heard of it."

"Hmm," Lynn said. "All right, here's something I haven't

"I know, sir. And you've already done a lot. I'm going to ırt by trying to find out more about Mr. Espinosa. When I ›, I'll bounce it off you and see what you think."

told you about my little swim." She related the eavesd st
she did with her ear against the cabin door, hearing the st
"tar" and "war." "That mean anything to either one of d
she asked.

Jenkins and Truck looked at each other and shook t
heads.

"Doesn't to me either," Lynn said. "But I'm going to ke
thinking about it. There's something in those words, I just don
know what. Okay. What do we do about Jack Espinosa?"

Truck shrugged. "Nothing much we can do except watch him. Got a tail on him, too. But he could be doing whatever he's doing by phone because we can't get a wiretap authorization—"

"Yeah, the admiral told me that."

"—plus, he's kind of got us on the defensive at the moment."

"How's that?"

"He's filed another stalking complaint. Somebody was in his house last night while he slept."

"How did he know?" asked Jenkins.

"They put his coffee maker inside his refrigerator and inside the coffee pot was an arrowhead."

Lynn groaned silently and looked past her two companions and out to the water of the harbor. Johnnie counting coup again. Not even subtle this time, using an arrowhead. She couldn't tell Truck she knew who it was because Johnnie would end up in jail. Got to get this corrected alone. Got to get tough with that girl.

Lynn looked back at Truck. "Well, time to dig in on Espinosa."

"You dig," said Truck. "I'm pretending I'm not hearing any of this, but I'll do what I can off duty. Maybe a little bit on duty, too."

Lynn looked at the admiral, who said, "Lynn, you know I'll do whatever you want me to."

FIFTY-FOUR

LYNN AND ROLF had decided to have a special get-out-of-the-hospital dinner at Squid Row that night. He facetiously made her promise not to go on any stupid boat rides or swimming trips and stand him up again.

Rolf was off island that afternoon and suggested Lynn wait for him at his house in case the traffic was bad. She went inside his always-unlocked house and waited. Turned on his television. Stock market down again. If this kept up she was going to have to book more charters, try to raise her rates, or get into something else. She flipped to the Discovery Channel. There was a piece about cave diving. She quickly switched to the House and Garden channel.

She was watching a show about a surprise house remodeling while the owners were away when the kitchen door suddenly opened. Rolf rushed into the house, carrying a shopping bag.

"Hey, sorry," he called as he threw the bag on the kitchen counter. "Had to go to Sarasota to get some special paint I needed, and there was a bad accident. I-75 was a parking lot. I'll grab a shower and be ready in a flash. Soon as I get rid of all these art store germs." He conducted two vigorous hand washes at the kitchen sink then headed for his bedroom.

"Relax, honey, and take your time. I'm just watching the boob tube."

Lynn switched to ESPN. She was one of those women who liked baseball. Spring training had started. The Rangers trained within thirty minutes of Boca Grande; she'd grab Truck one day and take in a game. Maybe when the Braves came—

A bloodcurdling scream from Rolf's bedroom shattered her

thought. She sprang from her chair and sprinted toward his room. The screams continued, "Lynn! Stay out there!"

She continued to run toward him. In Rolf's bathroom she found him, totally nude. He had somehow climbed up on top of a large baker's rack in his bathroom.

"I told you to stay out there."

"What in the world...?"

"Just carefully crack the door to the room where the shower is, then close it fast."

Rolf's bathroom was more like a suite of rooms, with separate compartments for shower, toilet, and bathtub. Lynn began to open the door to where the shower was.

"Be careful," he said.

Lynn slowly opened the door and looked in. There in Rolf's shower was a live alligator of somewhere between four and five feet in length. Lynn quickly shut the door.

Their special dinner ended up being a pizza delivery because, after Lynn called Truck, they had to wait for the local man the state hires to dispose of wayward alligators. When the hired ex-poacher had done his thing and the subdued gator's jaws were wrapped tightly shut with duct tape, the man showed Lynn and Rolf a tag which was wired to the creature's leg. In a Sharpie pen someone had written: *Tell Woo to back off. It gets worse.*

FIFTY-FIVE

THE NEXT MORNING Lynn went to Boatmen's Marina. After walking to her slip and checking on her boat, she went to the marina office and found the manager, Jason Headley.

"Cup of coffee?" Lynn said, nodding her head and eyes toward the ceiling and the restaurant above it.

Headley looked at his watch. "Got a tackle salesman coming, but yeah, I got time, what's up?"

Lynn didn't reply but started walking to the restaurant. Real or perceived, Lynn was still sporting a food-intake deficit after her night in the water and her time on hospital food. Once upstairs, even though she'd had breakfast, she ordered an English muffin with her coffee.

After the waitress left the table, Lynn said, "Jason, tell me about Jack Espinosa."

"Jack? Like what?"

"Like everything you know about him. Start with his business. He keeps his boat here, how often does he charter?"

"Funny you should ask that. I don't know how he makes it as a guide. Most of the good ones get, what, 200 days a year or more? Bet Jack doesn't get half that. Why are you asking?"

"You know of anything else he does to generate income?"

Headley chuckled. "I don't know how well you know Jack, but he's always talking big. How he's going to be able to buy the marina any day now, and I'll be working for him. Been going on ever since I've known him, but he never gets specific."

Lynn paused while her English muffin was placed before her by a waitress she hadn't seen before—a weathered girl with a smoker's cough and pruny skin from either the sun, the smokes, or both.

"Who does he hang with?"

"Well, he...uh, Lynn, you didn't say why you were asking all these questions."

"Jason, I can't tell you. All I can say is that it's important and I really need your help."

Headley mulled that for three or four beats while he studied Lynn's face, then he continued. "Okay. He mostly hangs out with women he meets at the bar in there." He motioned over his shoulder. "I think some of them are pretty and poor, and others are ugly and rich."

"Jack the Gigolo?"

"Maybe. Lynn, I don't know him *that* well."

"He ever talk about his past?"

"Mainly his time pitching for the Pirates before his arm got hurt. Says he'd be in the Hall of Fame by now. Obviously, he never mentions his conviction on the gator stuff."

"Was he ever married?"

"Yep. Divorced."

"You know her?"

"Met her, that's all."

"She still around?"

"I think so. Think she remarried and lives over in Englewood some place."

"Know her new name?" Lynn asked.

Headley shook his head. "Tell you who might, though. You know a mullet fisherman named Dearl Lomax?"

Lynn felt like she'd stuck her finger in a lamp socket. "Matter of fact, I do."

"Well, he's Jack's ex-wife's brother. Why don't you ask him?"

FIFTY-SIX

LYNN WASN'T GOING TO phone Dearl Lomax and get hung up on, and she wasn't up on the investigative techniques necessary to trace people by various married names, so she decided to take a short cut. She called Truck Kershaw.

"You promised some off-duty or on-duty help. Not sure which this is, but I need some," Lynn said.

"Fire away."

Lynn told him about her conversation with the marina manager. Truck said he'd get back to her. In two hours, he did.

"Her name's Judy Hemphill now. Here's her address and telephone number. Lives in Englewood."

"You're a great American," Lynn said gratefully. "By the way, anything on that little love note that was wired to the leg of Rolf's pet gator?"

"Back off, Woo? Forensics worked it over pretty good. Nothing. A Sharpie pen is a Sharpie pen. The label and wire are commodities. No DNA, they must have used sterile gloves. We may be dealing with some pretty smart people."

LYNN DIALED Judy Hemphill's number Truck had given her. Mr. Hemphill answered.

"She ain't here, she's at work," the man said. Lynn could hear a television game show blaring in the background.

"And where might that be, sir?" Lynn asked.

"Who wants to know?" His tone was bellicose.

"Oh, sorry," Lynn said. "This is Joan Ridley at the bank? We're processing checks and just couldn't make out the amount on one of them. I just need to call her and verify it."

Lynn prayed that the woman had a bank account

somewhere—many people do not—and that the man she was talking to did not realize that banks don't do what Lynn was pretending to be doing. They simply didn't have time.

"Oh," Mr. Hemphill said. "She's the church secretary over at Beach Baptist. You want the number?"

Lynn didn't call her. Didn't want to get turned down and didn't want to have to come up with another charade to make sure she wouldn't.

The Beach Baptist Church was nowhere near the beach; it was on 776 right in Englewood. It was a small, contemporary A-frame affair, built right on a concrete slab. Probably a sixties or seventies vintage building. Lynn was in luck; she found Judy Hemphill in her own office, alone. She tapped gently on her open door right under the sign bearing her name.

"May I come in?" Lynn said with a big smile.

Judy Hemphill was quite pretty, well dressed, and appeared refined if not sophisticated. How could she be Dearl Lomax's sister? Something just didn't fit.

"How can I help you?" she said.

Those words and the ones which followed resolved the disconnect between her and Lomax. Her dialect clearly revealed her West Virginia mountain upbringing. She talked more like a hillbilly than Jed Clampett. Lynn had to steel herself to avoid smiling with amusement. "How can I help you?" had come out *how kin I hep ya?*

Still smiling, Lynn said, "May I sit down for a minute?"

"Sure," she said. *(Shore.)* Lynn wondered absently why she left the *nuff* off the *shore.*

The office was not a large room, and her desk was one of those wraparound affairs with bookshelves, cubbyholes, and work space everywhere. Papers and files rose high in neat piles. An empty plastic take-out salad container with a fork on the edge was on her desk, evidence of an early lunch just finished. It made Lynn hungry again. Lynn guessed Judy Hemphill was a one-woman administrative department for the whole church, and suspected she was overworked. Lynn took the only other chair in the room. It was directly across from Judy Hemphill.

"I'm Lynn Woo."

"Judy Hemphill," she answered, offering Lynn her hand.

"Yes, I know. I'd like to talk to you about your brother and your ex-husband. I just want to ask a few questions about them."

Her pretty face had been shining with warmth and perhaps anticipation over what this congenial, pretty, Chinese-looking woman might want with her. Now it sagged with gloom. "Are you from the police? *(PO-lice.)* Are they in trouble?"

"I'm not from the police, but they could be in trouble, I'm not sure yet. If you could just tell me a few things, I might be able to help them stay out of trouble."

Judy Hemphill's countenance said that Lynn had taken a perfectly lovely day and turned it into hell. "What kind of things *(thangs)* do you want to know?" she asked.

"Well, you could start by telling me how long you were married to Jack Espinosa?"

"A little over twelve years."

"Whose idea was the divorce?" Lynn asked.

She hesitated a moment or two, then rose and walked to the door, closing it. When she returned to her desk chair she said, "My idea. I led a different life then. Jack done got into some bad things. Drugs, too much alcohol, and I got caught up into it. I knew we was both headed for trouble. He was usin' and even dealin' some, and I didn't want to go to prison. Then I met some people from this church and they helped me find the Lord. It done turned my life around. I tried to get Jack to come to church with me, but he didn't want no part of it. We drifted further apart, and I done filed for a divorce."

Lynn couldn't believe she actually pronounced it *DIEvorce.* "How did Jack and your brother Dearl Lomax get along?

"Good. Too good, really. They was dealin' drugs and alligator skins together. Jack ended up takin' the rap, though. Dearl's always been so slippery. Still don't know how he got out of doin' time. Say, would you like a cup of coffee?"

"No, thanks, but you go ahead," Lynn said.

She smiled and shook her head. "It's what I overdose on

these days, and I done had too much today already." Her smile faded, and she put her elbows on her desk. "I ain't told you nothin' that lots of folks don't already know. I s'pose at some point, you're gon' tell me who you are and why you're asking these questions, Miz...Woo?"

"Please call me Lynn."

She smiled again. "And I'm Judy."

"Judy, I'm from Boca Grande, and there've been some strange things going on there. I'm just trying to learn more about it. One of my best friends is the sheriff's deputy and I think he may have an interest in your ex-husband and your brother. If you can tell me more, I may be able to dissuade him from... wanting to talk to them."

She mulled that for a few moments while studying Lynn's face. "All right, go ahead," she said.

"Are you in contact with Jack now?"

"No. 'Bout once a year I'll see him at Publix. When that happens we go to opposite sides of the store. We never had no children, you know."

"Jack's boat seems to be at the dock a lot of the time, not many charters. You know of any other income he has?"

She shook her head.

"Ever hear him talk about some big real-estate deal?"

"Always. But nothin' ever comes of 'em."

"How about your brother. In contact with him?"

"Yes, but only when he's broke and needs me to—quote unquote—tide him over."

"How about Jack and Dearl, they still hanging together?"

"I think so. Some, anyway," she said, looking troubled again.

"Do you think they're involved in something together? Something they shouldn't be?"

Her hands were on the desk now, and she looked down at them, appearing to carefully examine one of her bright red fingernails. When she looked up she said, "I pray not. My brother and I don't get along that well, but I don't want to have to visit him in prison."

"Any idea what he might be into?" Lynn asked.

She could see her waging a mighty battle with whether to answer this one.

"I overheard Dearl talking about guns," she said.

"Guns?"

"Some new kind of gun from overseas somewhere. Shoots gazillions of bullets a second. I don't know nothin' 'bout guns so it didn't mean much to me, but it seemed like a pretty big secret. He didn't know I done heard him talking about it."

FIFTY-SEVEN

DESPITE HER POST-BREAKFAST booster of English muffins when she was talking to the marina manager about Jack Espinosa, Lynn was starving again. On her way back to the island from Englewood, she called Rolf.

"Hungry?" she said when he answered.

"Well, I'm just before getting cranky, let's put it that way."

"I'll take that as a yes," she said.

"A big yes. There's this commissioned piece I'm late on. Got up at the crack and skipped breakfast."

"Pelicans on a Pole, say twenty minutes?"

"Book it."

"Would you mind calling the admiral and Muffy, too? I want to talk a little murder stuff."

"Are you ever going back to running tours, *Captain* Lynn?" he asked.

"Yeah, if I could get some charters. Twenty minutes. See ya." She broke the connection.

Pelicans on a Pole was located right in the village of Boca Grande—a fancy way of saying downtown. It was décor-challenged with tile floors and white drywall. The only thing that saved it was the wonderful art on the walls, all of it for sale. Rolf had one painting there, easily the highest-priced work in the place. The custom-made lunch sandwiches were legendary, rivaling New York delis in size. It was one of Truck Kershaw's favorite places. Lynn chose the rosemary ham on rye with whole-grain mustard and a Martinelli's apple juice to wash it down. Rolf and Jenkins had the stacked turkey. Their waitress had an idle cough and Rolf said, "Do you have a cold?"

"Just getting over one," the waitress said.

Rolf smiled politely but grimaced when she left.

"I suppose you're going to eat your sandwich with a knife and fork?" Lynn said, rolling her eyes.

He spread his hands and said, "She touched my water glass then I touched it afterwards, what else can I do?" Then he paused a couple of beats. "This, I guess." And he pulled a tiny bottle of Purell out and used it vigorously.

Rolf was successful in getting Whitman Jenkins there, but not his daughter.

"Muffy couldn't make it?" Lynn said.

"Having a bad day," said Jenkins. "Lynn, I don't know what she would have done without you and Rolf. She's not ready to go back to work at the company yet, and she's already written all her thank-you notes for the flowers and the memorial contributions. Rolf, I swear, if it weren't for you and those art classes..." Jenkins just shook his head from side to side.

After that there was silence as the three of them dug into their mammoth sandwiches. Their conversation came between bites.

Jenkins looked at Lynn and said, "So what's the latest?"

Lynn did her best to reply through a mouthful of rosemary ham. "Well, the big news is that there's a connection between Jack Espinosa and Dearl Lomax."

"Really? What?" Rolf said.

"How about used to be brothers-in-law. How about used to run drugs and alligator hides together."

"Fascinating. Tell us more," Jenkins said.

Lynn did. She reviewed her meetings with the marina manager and with Judy Hemphill, ending with the part about the guns. "What do you make of that, sir?" Lynn asked the admiral.

"Not sure," Jenkins said. "Haven't heard of any gunrunning in years. But then it's been years since I've been in a position to hear about it."

"What about some new kind of gun that fires, as she says, a gazillion rounds a second?" Lynn asked.

"Hmm. I understand our government is working on a couple of different things like that, and then there's a really sexy new concept weapon out of New Zealand. Called the Brent, I think. Don't know any more than that. Whether it's in production or anything. But, in any case, I think you're on the right track with this Espinosa fellow. If I were you, I'd get Truck on him."

"Admiral, Truck's not even on the case, and I wouldn't trust Symanski to investigate a jaywalking."

"Suit yourself. But I think whoever investigates should pursue that real-estate angle with Espinosa. Could be a vein to mine there."

Rolf had been listening but now spoke up. "That makes sense to me, too, but, Lynn, get Truck or somebody else to do it. I mean, what will they try next, throwing you out of an airplane? You need to go back to running tours and diving. That's why you came down here. Don't you think you've done enough?"

He made a lot of sense. What *was* she doing continuing to play detective? Why not just tell Symanski everything she knew and then go back to trying to make her business work? This was costing her money. Money she needed.

But she knew she couldn't stop. She had more guilt than she could deal with already. If she didn't get to the bottom of these murders, it would just get heavier. The worst thing was having to explain it to Rolf. She wasn't sure she knew how.

"Rolf," she said as she put her hand over his and looked in his eyes. "I agree with everything you said. But I still have to do this."

He met her eyes, finished chewing, wiped his mouth with his napkin, and replied, "I know. And I knew that's what you'd say. Just please, for God's sake, be careful this time."

As she looked at Rolf, she felt love and appreciation for this wonderful man wash over her. What was the matter with her? Why couldn't she make a deeper commitment to him? She nodded to Rolf, and, as she brushed a tear away, looked back at the admiral. "I'm going to look up Mr. Espinosa," she said.

"Excellent," Jenkins said. "Would you like some company?"

"I'd be honored," Lynn said.

FIFTY-EIGHT

AFTER LUNCH, Lynn bade the admiral goodbye and said she'd call him when she figured out where Espinosa was. She lingered with Rolf on the sidewalk in front of the restaurant, and he held her for a moment.

When they separated she said, "If you weren't so protective of me, maybe I wouldn't love you as much as I do."

He smiled, bent slightly and kissed her on the forehead, then turned and left.

Lynn went home and let Mullet out. The Lab seemed out of sorts. Lynn thought she knew why. Mullet liked to go on the boat with her, and it had been a long time. The dog looked up at Lynn, his tail wagging, his one ear sticking up, whimpering softly. It occurred to Lynn that Mullet's eyes were expressive, too, and wondered if the dog, in its own way, was imparting the same message to her that Rolf had. Rolf had taken care of Mullet while Lynn was in the hospital, and he said the dog seemed heartbroken. Whimpered constantly.

She turned her attention to where Jack Espinosa was. On the off chance that he might be out on a fishing charter, Lynn phoned Boatmen's Marina. Sure enough, he was. Lynn found out what time Espinosa usually came in, then called the admiral. She picked Jenkins up and they drove to Boatmen's Marina to wait for Espinosa. When they arrived and began their wait, once again Lynn looked longingly at the water. She was really starting to miss it.

There was no breeze, and it was unusually hot for late March, just the way Lynn liked it. So hot, in fact, that they made sure they waited on a covered bench out of the sun. Jenkins picked up a discarded newspaper and fanned himself. They were there a little over forty minutes when Espinosa idled his skiff into the marina.

Nobody could say Jack Espinosa was not a good fisherman. In fact, he was the consummate outdoorsman—field, stream, or sea. Some people said he *thought* like a fish. Or a duck, or a deer, or a gator, and so it went. He proved it again on this late March day in Boca Grande, as he came in with his limit of snook, the prized game fish of the area.

Espinosa took his catch of two large snook, two redfish and several sea trout to the fish-cleaning table. His clients, a middle-aged couple resplendent in flats fishing clothes, followed to watch the proceedings.

Lynn nodded to the admiral and they walked over to Espinosa. In front of the clients, Lynn put on as much congeniality as she could muster, engaging Espinosa in conversation about the day's fishing, and being highly complimentary of his catch. As a seeming afterthought, she asked if, by the way, she could have a quick word with him when he was done. Lynn did not introduce the admiral.

Espinosa expertly cleaned the fish, placed the filets in baggies, then placed the baggies into larger bags with ice. All very efficient and thoughtful of his clients who would take the fish. Lynn and the admiral had to wait while the clients paid, and while Espinosa hosed off the fish-cleaning table and his skiff.

Finally, he swaggered toward them with his usual gregarious grin. "Goddamn, it's hottter'n a pair of black panties at an Elvis concert, ain't it?"

Lynn thought the admiral might have said something like "Indeed it is, and unseasonably so." But while she and Jenkins gave the crack an obligatory smile, neither said a word.

"I'm all done, so what's up?" said Espinosa.

"Jack, meet Admiral Whitman Jenkins. Dear old friend of mine."

"A real admiral, huh?" said Espinosa with a grin as he shook hands with Jenkins.

"How about a beer? We're buying," said Lynn.

"Have to be a quickie, I got plans," Espinosa said.

They went upstairs to the marina's bar which already had some customers. Lynn led them to a remote table in the restaurant area. In a few minutes, the table was graced by three cold beers and a shallow bowl of bar peanuts. Espinosa scooped up what seemed like half the bowl of nuts and hurled them into his mouth. While chewing, he said, "So what's up? Why do I think it might have something to do with what you came to my house about?"

"You're smart, Jack," Lynn said.

"If you want to talk about that again, then why is he here?" Espinosa said, motioning to Jenkins and taking a big quaff of his beer.

"My commanding officer. Visiting on the island."

"Oh."

"One other thing. The victim of the first murder was his son-in-law."

Still chewing nuts, he said, "Oh. Sorry, Admiral."

Jenkins nodded in acknowledgement.

"Jack, when did you last see your ex-brother-in-law, Dearl Lomax?" Lynn said.

"Hell, I don't know. Why?"

"Just answer the question," Lynn said.

He laughed derisively. "Lynn, I don't have to answer any fucking questions from you. Who you think you are, Inspector Clouseau or something? You still thinking I had something to do with your Indian friend's murder? Look, we went through all that the last time. Like, this is where I came in, ma'am, and I—"

"Listen, Jack, I just…"

"No, you listen. Let me tell you what I'm concerned about. I ain't sure somebody's not figuring on murdering *me*."

Lynn and the admiral looked at each other. "What are you talking about?" Lynn said.

"Somebody's stalking me. It's like they're sizing me up before they kill me, just to let me know they can do it whenever they want. They come in my house while I'm sleeping. Don't know how they get in but last night was new. They actually came in my own bedroom. Brought my butcher knife in from the kitchen and stabbed the pillow next to me and just left it there. Scared the livin' shit out of me when I woke up the next morning. I told Truck Kershaw about the other stuff they've done but he ain't doing shit about it."

"Well, I don't know anything about that," Lynn lied. "But I'm sorry. When I see Truck, I'll remind him and tell him to call you about the latest incident."

Espinosa waved his hand in the kind of disgust designed to imply that he wasn't planning on holding his breath waiting for Lynn to do something. Then he took a big pull on his beer and dove in for some more peanuts.

Lynn looked intently at Espinosa before she asked the next question. She focused on his pupils, looking for a reaction. "Tell me about the guns," Lynn said.

Either this guy is good or the guns angle is a dead end, Lynn thought, because nothing registered other than genuine puzzlement.

Espinosa did a put-on double take. "Guns? What are you talking about now?"

"Oh, just your new deal like you were talking about. That's going to allow you to give up guiding where you can just hire me to take you on the water. Distributing the new illegal guns that fire a gazillion rounds a minute—" Lynn was improvising "—through makeshift warehouses made from the Indian mounds on the Turtle Bay islands. Too bad a little murder had to make things untidy, eh?"

Jack Espinosa just stared at Lynn for a long time with a look of incredulity, shaking his head from side to side. He seemed to be deciding whether or not to be angry. He seemed to be counting to ten. Then twenty. Finally, he took a long pull on his beer, cleared some nuts from his mouth with his tongue, and spoke.

"Look, Lynn, I, uh...heard about your...incident on the water." He licked some peanut salt off his lip. "Sorry that happened to you. Only thing I can figure about all these things you're saying is that you must have hit your head when you jumped off that boat. Now, I'm sorry this man's son-in-law was killed and sorry about your buddy, but I had nothing to do with it. Yeah, I got a new deal all right, but it's nothing to do with guns, drugs, gators, or anything illegal. Just between us, the state's putting a new interchange in on I-75 over in Charlotte County. I sort of found out about and sort of got an option on the property. If it happens, I'll make a pile of money. So there, now you know." Then he glanced at his watch. "Hey, gotta go. Thanks for the beer. Nice meeting you, Admiral." And he was gone.

Lynn and Jenkins looked at each other.

"That was rather spectacularly unproductive," said the admiral.

Lynn just nodded, looking down at the table. Then she said, "Let's get out of here."

As they walked down the steps to the dock level of the marina, Lynn bolted into a run, startling Whitman Jenkins. Lynn had seen the shadow of a familiar figure duck around the corner of the marina building. She hustled after the person, and when she rounded the corner, saw nothing. Whoever it was had given her the slip. She was certain it was Johnnie Osceola.

FIFTY-NINE

LYNN DROPPED THE ADMIRAL off at his cottage and then went home. She sat on her porch looking at the Gulf of Mexico with the tail-wagging Mullet's head in her lap. Lynn scratched the dog's single ear slowly and consistently. Mullet loved that. The water was glassy calm and it was still hot. Perhaps only six more weeks until she could sit in the same chair and see huge, rolling tarpon, their silver scales flashing in the morning sun. She looked down at Mullet, scratched behind his ear more vigorously, and said, "All this'll be over soon, boy, and we'll be back on the boat. Don't worry."

The phone rang. It was Rolf.

"How'd it go with Espinosa?" he said.

"If your golf cart's charged, I'll tell you in person."

"Is there an invitation in there somewhere?" he said.

"You bet. You feel like a steak? I just feel like a steak. Still kind of hungry."

"Want me to pick them up?" he asked.

"If you'll do that, I'll stand up, oh, say an '89 St. Emilion?"

"Now you're talking. Give me thirty or forty minutes."

Lynn hung up and went to her little wine cellar. She picked out one of her few Bordeaux left over from when she could buy at wholesale through the restaurant. It was a 1989 Chateau Pavie and she stood it up so the sediment would find the bottom of the bottle. Later, she would open and decant it. That done, she caught a shower and changed.

As she emerged from her bedroom, the doorbell rang. Rolf? Couldn't be—he would have just walked in. She opened the door. To her astonishment, there stood Truck Kershaw, dressed not in his sheriff's deputy uniform but in something which looked exactly like a spacesuit. His hands were behind his back.

When Lynn collected herself, she looked the deputy over and said, "Well, you're obviously off duty. Only thing I can come up with is you're going to a costume party dressed as John Glenn."

"John Glenn's white, Cap'n Lynn. You got to do better than that if you want what's behind my back."

"What's behind your back?"

Truck put one big paw in Lynn's view. In it was a large mason jar filled with something golden in color. "Wanted you to see what I had to go through to be able to give you this jar of fresh honey," he said.

"Good God, you're a beekeeper now?"

"This is my first jar, you tell me."

"Come on in here, you need a beer."

"I can live with that. Hotter'n hell under this hood," Truck said as he lumbered into the house.

Truck stripped off his beekeeper's suit and on Lynn's porch they enjoyed the view. Truck had a cold Bud Lite, Lynn her Absolut on ice. After about two swallows, Rolf showed up, put the steaks in the kitchen, and joined them with a glass of chardonnay. Lynn had the Beatles on, and the ballad *Here, There and Everywhere* played in the background. After a "honey tasting," Lynn and Rolf lavished rave reviews on Truck.

"So Truck, whatever possessed you to start keeping bees?" Lynn asked.

Truck took a pull on his beer. "Stupid, huh? I don't know, my mom, I guess. She was always after me to do something besides watch TV. And she always *loved* honey." He took another pull.

"Truck, I think that's super," Rolf said with a smile.

"So what's the latest from the super sleuth?" Truck said, trying to change the subject, seeming to be uncomfortable with the attention he was receiving.

Lynn updated them both on the meeting with Jack Espinosa

and updated Truck on her meeting with the ex-wife, now Judy Hemphill.

"Everything's looking like a dead end right now," Lynn said. "What's going on with Dearl Lomax?"

"Nothing," Truck said. "He's no dummy. Knows he being watched. Next he'll be going to bible study."

"What's Symanski doing? Anything?" Lynn asked.

"All hell's broken loose on the Indian mound thing. The Feds and the FDLE are in on it. Messing with those things broke all kind of laws. Anyway, just about the whole backcountry out there by Bull and Turtle Bay has been staked out every night, and they've done air and satellite infrared surveillance. All indications are that no more of these warehouses have been set up. With all the heat, they may have moved to some other location. Maybe they don't even need Lomax anymore."

"So who's Symanski's top suspect?" Rolf asked.

Truck drained the Bud Lite. "Far as I know, he ain't got one. If you'll excuse the expression, I don't think he knows whether to shit or wind his watch."

"He's not interested in Jack Espinosa?" Lynn asked.

"Nope."

"I'm beginning to wonder if I should be either," Lynn mused, studying her glass which was almost empty. She continued to study the glass, then she thought of something.

"Johnnie Osceola's still staying at the Lodge, isn't she?"

Rolf and Truck both shrugged. Lynn went into the living room and dialed the Lodge. Johnnie was still registered and answered the phone on the second ring.

"Johnnie, it's Lynn Woo. We were just having a drink here at the house and something's come up about your dad. I know you're on the wagon, but how about coming over for a glass of cranberry juice or something? Come as you are."

When Johnnie showed up ten minutes later, she had on the Boca Grande uniform of shorts and a flats fishing shirt. Lynn noticed with displeasure that Johnnie's long, silky legs caught Rolf's eye. Lynn had used the cranberry juice offer as a metaphor, but that's exactly what Johnnie asked for. She seemed distant, if not sullen.

"So how's it going, being on the wagon?" Lynn asked. "Tougher than you thought or not?"

Her tone was flat as she answered. "Doesn't matter whether it's tough or not. When I decide to do something, I do it."

It occurred to Lynn that she had certainly found that to be true. Then she got to the reason she had asked her over.

"Johnnie, we've been talking about the murders, and I was just updating Truck on a meeting I had today with Jack Espinosa. I guess you didn't know I had a meeting with Espinosa today, did you?"

The question told her she'd been spotted at the marina. She didn't answer, just gave a long sigh and crossed both her arms and legs and started doing her vigorous leg swing while looking out at the gulf.

"Well, anyway," Lynn continued, "I was just about to tell Truck and Rolf about Espinosa's complaints about being stalked. Truck, Espinosa has a new stalking…says somebody entered his house last night and stabbed the pillow beside him with his butcher knife while he slept. Scared the crap out of him when he saw it the next morning. I told him I'd tell you about it." Lynn avoided any reference to the Indian rite of counting coup.

"Huh," said Truck. "Things have escalated and they're not stopping. Guess we'll have to get serious."

"What does that mean?" Lynn asked.

"Stakeouts, fingerprints, interviews to determine likely suspects. Stuff like that."

"If you were to catch this person, what sort of sentence would they be facing if convicted?" Lynn was looking directly at Johnnie.

"Hell, I'm not sure, Cap'n Lynn. I want to say the last one I can remember was…" Lynn was sitting between Johnnie and Truck, and, hidden from Johnnie's vision, she gave Truck a thumbs-up sign indicating she wanted a high number. "…oh, five to seven hard, I think." Truck now knew exactly what was behind the conversation.

"Seven years hard time, eh?" said Lynn, nodding. "Well now, Truck, if you got a bona fide tip on a likely suspect, what would you do?" Lynn was still looking at Johnnie.

"Twenty-four-hour tail, print-matching, maybe DNA. A tip on a suspect would be a big help. You have one, Cap'n Lynn?"

Lynn looked at Johnnie for a several long moments while Johnnie, looking even more sullen, continued to stare at the water, and her leg-swinging became even more pronounced. A momentary tension hung over the porch. Finally, Lynn looked back at her friend and answered. "No. Of course I don't have a suspect. I thought I might at one time. But I'm sure I was mistaken. If the person I was thinking of was ever involved in anything like that, I'm sure they won't be again."

"WHAT WAS *that* all about?" Rolf said when it was just the two of them. "I think I know, but you tell me."

"Either Johnnie Osceola's coup counting days are over, or I'm turning her in. Simple as that."

SIXTY

LYNN WOKE THE NEXT morning in her own bed, but she was not alone. Rolf was curled beside her and Mullet was on the floor where Rolf liked the dog instead of in the laundry room—Mullet's usual room. The filets had been perfect—Lynn always liked to top them with a little gorgonzola—and the St. Emilion was superb. She awoke refreshed, not a hint of a headache. Rolf always said that good red wine does not give one a headache.

Rolf was still asleep and she watched him for a few moments. I do love this man, she thought. Lynn slipped out of bed, let Mullet out, and pulled on a long T-shirt Rolf had given her. Twenty minutes later, she was back, carrying a tray with a poached egg, a croissant, and some of Truck's honey. A small glass of fresh orange juice and a cup of the Cuban coffee Rolf liked completed the tray.

"Good morning, sir," she said gently, as she leaned over and kissed him on the forehead. Then she squeezed herself into a sitting position beside him on the bed.

"Ohh," he snuffled in a sleepy voice with a smile as he awoke at the kiss. He scooted up to a sitting position and the sheet fell away from his naked body. He drew the sheet back just enough to cover his crotch.

Lynn broke out in a grin. "Sir, it's not often that we room-service waitresses get to see what I just saw."

He broke out in a wide grin. "It's not often that the waitresses are as cute as you are."

"Hmm. Are you sure you're hungry yet?" she said, beginning to slowly pull the sheet away again.

He immediately yanked it back up and said, "Yes, waitress,

I'm *very* hungry. But after I have my breakfast, I'm not sure *what* I'll do with all the energy I'll have."

Lynn felt a stir of sexual anticipation. She felt good. As good as she could feel with people killing her friends, destroying precious artifacts, smuggling guns or whatever, and apparently getting away with it. It troubled her that Truck wasn't even on the case, that Symanski was clueless and apparently spending his time dealing with the federal and state law-enforcement bureaucracy, and that Lynn's prime suspect, Jack Espinosa, was inscrutable. She figured she must be overlooking something. Perhaps something obvious. She needed to know more about Dearl Lomax's mention of some new kind of gun, and she still hadn't figured out what "tar" and "war" meant.

She went back to the kitchen and got one of the croissants which had come from the marvelous island bakery. When she returned to the bedroom, Rolf had just slipped back into bed having come from the bathroom. She sat in the chair by the bed and slathered her croissant with Truck's honey. But she didn't eat it. Rolf didn't give her a chance. Her T-shirt came off, and Rolf fulfilled his promise to burn some of the energy his breakfast had provided. Afterwards, they lay in each other's arms again and her mind went back to Lomax, the guns, "tar," and "war."

"I'm going to call Judy Hemphill again," she announced to Rolf.

She got up, dressed for the day, went out to the phone in the living room, and got her at the church office.

"Do you have somebody with you or can you talk?" Lynn asked.

"No, I'm fine. In fact, the pastor done walked out a second ago," Judy Hemphill said.

"Look, Judy, I want to thank you for giving me the time you did yesterday. You were very helpful," Lynn said.

"That's all right." In her hillbilly dialect it was more like *das aw rat.*

"I keep thinking about your brother, Dearl. Do you all *ever* talk?"

"Well, not very often," she said.

"I was just hoping you could speak to him and ask about those guns you overheard him talking about."

Lynn heard nothing but silence.

"Judy?"

"I'm here. I'm sorry, but I can't do that," she said.

"Judy, I need your help."

"What if he's involved in somethin' illegal?"

"All the more reason because then *he'll* need your help, too."

More silence.

"How about it, Judy?"

"I don't know, I'll think about it. But right now I have to go. I have a bad tire I have to get fixed," she said.

"A what?" Lynn said, having trouble with her Jed Clampett accent.

"A tire. It's got a slow leak and I've got an appointment at the tire store to get it patched. Call me in a day or so. Bye..." And she hung up.

Lynn was stunned. Judy Hemphill's mountaineer pronunciation of 'tire' was *tar.* Have to go to the *tar* store to get her *tar* fixed. Lynn furiously dialed the church's number again and caught her before she left.

"Judy, just one quick question. And I know this may sound crazy, but please just bear with me. What are coat hangers made from?"

"What?"

"I know it's crazy but just please answer me, what are coat hangers made from?"

"Wire, I guess." Sure enough, she pronounced it *war.*

"Thanks, Judy. Now just one quick question. Have you ever heard your brother talk about a man named Robert Tyre?"

She hesitated. "I'm not sure, I don't think so."

Lynn thought she hesitated too long. She thought she had indeed heard Dearl Lomax mention Robert Tyre. And now Lynn knew that she, too, had heard Lomax mention Robert Tyre's name. She overheard it through the cabin door when she was kidnapped on the boat. The word *tar* was Tyre and the word *war* was wire. Lomax and his henchmen were talking about Robert Tyre and talking about the wire they were going to use to tie Lynn's hands and to help secure the chain to her body before they drowned her.

Finally a breakthrough. She had to quickly warn the admiral that he might have a gun-smuggling murderer for an investment banker.

"By the way," said Judy Hemphill, still on the line. "I had someone else call me up and ask questions. Said she was from the police *(PO-lice)*, but she sounded very young and inexperienced. Didn't tell her as much as I done told you."

The ubiquitous Johnnie Osceola, Lynn thought.

SIXTY-ONE

AS SOON AS LYNN BROKE the connection with Judy Hemphill, she tried the admiral's cottage. No answer. He and Muffy liked to go over to the Lodge's beach club about this time of day and do lap swimming.

Rolf had dressed and was sitting on the porch with his coffee. Lynn joined him. Another gorgeous day. Clear. Light winds. She saw numerous walkers and shellers in swimsuits, and one angler patrolling the surf with a fly rod looking for snook. Schools of small baitfish had begun showing up along the beaches and the brown pelicans were having their way with them. Lynn was always fascinated by the birds' acrobatic dives, each one culminating in a slashing explosion at the water's surface and the certain violent death of a small baitfish.

"Did you get her?" Rolf asked before a long pull on his Cuban coffee.

"Boy, did I," she said, and told how she finally learned what "tar" and "war" meant.

"I told you I never liked that Tyre guy," he said. "What about Whit?"

"Tried to call him to warn him about Tyre. He and Muffy are probably swimming. I'll just go over there and wait if I have to."

She sat and thought about the new information and what it meant. Yes, she must warn the admiral. But she kept coming back to the guns. She was convinced that there was something to that. She had an idea, but she had to concentrate very hard to remember a phone number from many years ago.

She stood. "Got to make another phone call," she said.

"Oh? Who's this one to?"

"Can't tell you."

He looked up with one eyebrow raised, thinking it was banter, but he saw that her face was stone serious.

SIXTY-TWO

THE NUMBER HAD a Virginia area code. Lynn remembered the digits but thought she may have had two of them transposed. She tried it one way and guessed wrong. The other way it worked.

"Yes?" a voice said.

"Do you have any tickets to Sunday's game?" Lynn said.

"I'm sorry, you have the wrong number," the voice said.

"Wait!" Lynn said, racking her brain. Got to remember this, she told herself. It came to her. "What I meant to say was…are the bass biting in the lake?"

There was a long pause, then, "Just a moment."

She was on hold so long she almost hung up. Finally a different voice came on the line. "Would you like to order some flowers?"

"Blue gardenias," Lynn said.

"Do you have an order number?"

Lynn gave him a numeric code.

"We'll call you back to confirm your order," the voice said, and the line went dead.

Suddenly Lynn was panic-stricken. How would they know where to call her? Then she felt foolish. Of course, any housewife had caller ID, and the people she had just called had a lot more than that.

Now Lynn had a problem. She had no idea how long it would be before the callback came, and she had to keep trying the admiral. Her cell phone was the solution. She fetched it and dialed the cottage again. Still no answer. They must still be swimming. Or maybe grocery shopping. They liked to go to the off-island Publix. It bothered Lynn that she could not get in touch with Whitman Jenkins but when she thought about it she decided that the admiral was probably not in danger. Not yet anyway.

She waited. Lunchtime came. Rolf had left midmorning to get busy on his painting, so she ate some yogurt, then waited some more.

Just after two the phone rang.

"Capt. Lynn Woo," Lynn said.

"You still want the flowers?" the gruff male voice on the line said.

"Yes," she said.

"What kind were they?"

"Blue gardenias?"

"This better be good," the voice said.

Lynn hesitated. It was a familiar voice. From many years ago. "It's you, isn't it?" Lynn said.

"Yeah, it's me. I'm still in. Unless you have a bug, this is a secure line, but don't say or ask anything you don't feel like you have to. This is highly irregular, and, like I say, it better be good."

"It's good to hear your voice."

"Yeah."

"I, uh, need some information."

"No shit."

"Yeah….uh, say, is there any buzz about some new kind of gun? Probably an illegal one? One that, as somebody put it to me, fires a gazillion rounds per second?"

"That it?"

"Uh, no. There's something else," Lynn said.

"I'm waiting."

"You remember Robert Tyre?"

"How could I forget?"

"I need the latest on him. Actually, I sort of have the latest. He's an investment banker. Working closely with the admiral—"

"Jenkins?"

"Right. Brokering acquisitions of small food companies all

over the country to add to the admiral's product lines. But what Tyre was up to before that is what I need," Lynn said.

"Anything else?"

"No."

"You want what I get when I get it or all at once?"

"When you get it, okay?" Lynn said.

"Sure."

"When will I hear from you?"

"When I get it."

"Oh. Yeah, okay. Hey, good to hear your voice."

"I'll call you from home sometime and we'll catch up."

"Yeah, that'd be great," Lynn said and then realized that the connection had been broken.

Now what to do. She was pinned down to the phone at her house, not knowing whether her answers would come in an hour, a day or a week. She called the cottage again on the cell phone. Still no answer. She dialed Truck and got him.

"How are your tars?" Lynn asked Truck.

"What?"

"I said how are your tars?"

"You know, Cap'n Lynn, there ain't nothin' worse than a white man or a Chinese woman tryin' to talk like a black man and can't."

Lynn couldn't suppress a chuckle. "Well, let me ask you this, do you have any war?"

"Now I get it. You and Rolf started your cocktail hour early."

Lynn then took her friend out of his misery and explained, reminding him of the overheard "tar" and "war" words on the boat and then telling of her conversation with Dearl Lomax's sister, both of whom used the same West Virginia mountain patois.

"So you have Robert Tyre in the crosshairs now?" Truck said.

"Yes, and I've been trying to get in touch with the admiral to warn him, but I can't get an answer. Should we get Symanski in on this?"

"I'll call him if you want, but let's face it, you really don't have anything."

"Right now."

"What do you mean?" Truck asked.

"All I can tell you is that I expect to know more soon."

SIXTY-THREE

LYNN DECIDED SHE WAS going to wear out the send button on her cell phone because every twenty or thirty minutes she dialed the admiral's cottage. Finally, a little after six, Muffy answered.

She didn't want to alarm her, so she just said, "Well, ya'll are home."

"Not ya'll, just me," Muffy said.

Lynn perked up. "Oh? Where's your dad?"

"Naples. One of his friends from Birmingham has a winter home down there and Daddy went down to play golf with him. He was going to stay for dinner and spend the night."

"Oh, I see," said Lynn, trying to sound casual. "When's he coming back?"

"Tomorrow morning sometime. You want me to have him call you?"

"Did Robert go with him?"

"No, but he'll be here late tomorrow afternoon. Do you want me to have Daddy call you?"

"Yes. Yes, I do. I figured you two were swimming today."

"I did this morning. Then I went to Sarasota shopping. Last time I'll do that this time of year. St. Armand's was a zoo."

"I'll probably see you sometime tomorrow, Muffy," Lynn said. "You all right? Anything I can do for you?"

There was silence before her reply. In a small voice, she said, "I'm all right. At least for somebody who's pretty much sad all day and all night. I don't know what I'd have done without you and Rolf."

Lynn didn't know what to say to that, so she said nothing except goodbye. She felt better. If the schedule Muffy outlined was accurate, she would have plenty of time to warn the admiral tomorrow before Robert Tyre arrived. And with luck she'd have some valuable data on Tyre which might explain some things. She'd have to carefully and tactfully review with the admiral whatever she learned because she knew Whitman Jenkins was very high on Robert Tyre. She must let the admiral down easy. But the admiral would know where Lynn got her information and would therefore trust it. After that they could discuss things thoroughly. Just like the old days. Together, she knew they'd get to the bottom of it. She was ready for that to happen. Ready to get back to promoting her business and her pleasurable island life.

SIXTY-FOUR

ROLF WAS STILL FIGHTING his deadline on the commissioned painting, so he stayed at his own house that evening. Lynn picked up one of those scrumptious rotisserie chickens from Gibson's, the island grocery store with the landmark old pink gas pump out front, and enjoyed it with some roasted potatoes which were left over from the steak dinner with Rolf. She ate while watching the travel channel and a show on English castles. She turned in early.

When the phone woke her from a deep sleep, her vision raked across the digital clock that told her that whoever was calling was doing so at almost one a.m. Must be a wrong number.

"Lynn Woo," she mumbled into the receiver.

"I got something," the voice said.

"What?" said a groggy Lynn.

"Don't have all night, you want it or not?"

Now she recognized the voice. She forced alertness on herself, sat up in bed and grabbed a pad and pen from the bedside table.

"Yes," she said. "I'm here. Go ahead."

"Okay, regarding guns of the type you were asking about. There's a new electronic one out of New Zealand called the Brent. It's named after the inventor and founder of the company. Guy named Brent Ashcroft. Kiwi guy, I guess. What you heard is true. It can stack bullets and fire a half a million rounds a minute."

"Impossible."

"Nope. Remarkable technology, really. The next bullet is on the way before the first one leaves the barrel."

"This really works?" Lynn said.

"Believe it."

"So is it considered legal? Does the military want it? What?"

"That's where it gets interesting. This Ashcroft is really struggling to get the U.S. government to deal with him because they want to work with U.S. companies. The Pentagon is waiting on Raytheon to improve their Phalanx model, and they also like the smart gun that Alliant Technosystems is developing."

All this was like so much mumbo jumbo to Lynn. Been out of the loop too long, she thought.

"Well, it sounds like this Ashcroft fellow is going to have to be patient," Lynn said.

"Exactly. Except he's got one little problem."

"What?"

"He's out of money. Actually it could be a big problem. Our assets in New Zealand tell us the Brent is now in production. But the rub is that nobody can seem to find out who the customers are. Can't trace the shipments except for some that went to Cuba."

"No way."

"Way. Oh, there were some other shipments, too. South Africa, for example. Could be legal, but the fear is that because he's had trouble raising new capital, he may have, shall we say, not been fussy about who the buyers were."

"Scary stuff," Lynn said.

"Yep. That's all I've got now, but we're working it some more. Call you again when I have something new."

"Wait, don't hang up," Lynn said, remembering how her first conversation ended so abruptly and not knowing which of them would be initiating any future calls.

"What?" the voice said.

"Two things," Lynn said. "One is, what about Robert Tyre?"

"You said you wanted what I got when I got it."

"Right. I was just wondering when you might have something on Tyre."

"Same answer as last time," the voice said.

"Yeah, I know—when you get it. Here's why I'm asking. I think Tyre's turned. Not in the way we used to mean, but toward crime. I think he may be illegally involved in this Brent gun trade, and I'm worried about the admiral's safety."

"What does this have to do with me?"

"Well, I need for you to bend the rules a little bit," Lynn said, knowing that she had no clue what the rules were anymore. "See, the admiral's coming back here to Boca Grande tomorrow morning sometime and Tyre's supposed to arrive later in the day, maybe late afternoon. I need to get over there and warn the admiral, to talk to him about all of this, particularly Robert Tyre."

"So what's the rule-bending?"

"If you call me after I leave to go over there, I need for you to call me there. And if you can't get me, I need for you to call my...my gentleman friend."

"We talking live-in?"

"Depends on the day."

"I got to call on this line," he said.

"I'll have him here if I'm not," Lynn said.

There was a long pause, then, "Okay."

SIXTY-FIVE

LYNN TRIED TO SLEEP after the phone call but it didn't work. She stayed in bed and tried, but all she did was think. The business about the new gun technology from New Zealand was fascinating and Lynn was convinced there was a tie-in to the murders, and that Robert Tyre must be behind the whole thing. In her mind's eye she could see crates of the new high-tech guns stacked up inside the Indian mounds made into warehouses, ready for shipping.

When dawn came she rose and after she let Mullet out and back in, as was her custom, she reviewed everything with the dog to see if she was overlooking anything. Her review was greeted by the usual whimpering, tail wagging, and perking of his single ear. Lynn had some orange juice and oatmeal, followed by two cups of strong coffee. It was still before eight, but she dialed Rolf anyway.

"Hi, it's me," she said.

"Why are you calling me in the middle of the night?" Rolf said, his voice scratchy and his tone cranky.

"Almost eight, my dear," she said cheerily.

There was silence on the other end. Lynn wondered if he was going back to sleep. Couldn't let that happen. "Rolf," she said. "You there?"

"Unfortunately, yes," came the furry-voiced reply.

Then she explained her problem. That she needed him to babysit her telephone while she was at the admiral's cottage.

"How am I supposed to finish this commissioned painting?" His voice was now clear and wide awake.

"Rolf, I… We're talking life or death here."

"Why is everything you do always more important?"

She said nothing. Neither did he for a few moments.

"I'm sorry," he said. "Why do I say those things? Of course I'll be there. What time?"

"Soon as the admiral calls saying he's back on the island."

It was after lunch before that call came. Lynn heard Whitman Jenkins' authoritative voice on the line. "Lynn, Muffy said to call you."

"Yes, sir. I just need to come over and talk about a couple of things."

"I need to talk to you, too. I shot 78 yesterday and I need to tell you about every hole."

Lynn smiled to herself. "Admiral, why don't you just write me a letter about that. Maybe email me."

"So you can delete it? No, indeed. I can't wait to tell you."

"I'll be there in twenty minutes or so."

She called Rolf. In ten minutes he arrived to cover her phone, and shortly after that she was in front of the Jenkins cottage.

SIXTY-SIX

MUFFY SAVAGE MET LYNN at the door to the cottage and they exchanged a hug. Lynn thought about Muffy's appreciative comments about the support she had received from Lynn and Rolf, but she knew she really hadn't done anything. Rolf was the one who had spent the time. Rolf was the one who told Muffy how it was for him when he became a widower. But Lynn knew that if she and Muffy's father could get to the bottom of these murders, then she would have done her part.

When Lynn made it to the living room of the cottage, the admiral was standing in the middle of it in a slight crouch with his hands in front of him. He was clutching an imaginary golf club.

"Okay, now look at this," Jenkins said. "Here was my old swing." He made a phantom golf swing. "And here's the new one." He made another swing. "See the difference?"

Lynn was reminded of the comedy film about the famous male model who had different facial "looks" which, when he assumed them, seemed to be identical to each other. The two practice golf swings Whitman Jenkins had made looked absolutely identical to Lynn.

"Yes, I see what you mean," Lynn lied. "I assume you used that new one to shoot the 78."

Jenkins gave her a sly look. "Funny girl. Yes, I did. Are you sure you don't want a hole-by-hole?"

"Oh, yes, sir, I really do. Could we set that up for, say, your next trip to Boca Grande?"

The admiral laughed appreciatively. "Touché." Then, in an instant, his face went cold serious as he sat behind the wicker desk and waved Lynn toward the love seat. "What's up?"

"Well…"

"Daddy, aren't you going to offer Lynn anything?"

"Of course, forgive me, Lynn. Coffee or something?"

After spending most of the previous night examining her ceiling, Lynn's morning coffee inoculation needed a booster shot. Besides, this was going to be an important meeting. She accepted and when Muffy had brought the steaming mug with the leaping tarpon on it, she took a deep gulp and cleared her throat.

"Admiral, I need to talk to you about Robert Tyre."

"What about him?"

"How well do you really know him?"

Jenkins frowned as he studied Lynn's face, looking hard into her eyes. "What kind of question is that, miss? You and I both served with him, and I've worked with him in business for several years now. He's a little obstreperous, talks with his face right in yours, and…well, he was always kind of out there on the edge. But I think he's a good man. Where are you going with this?"

"Well, sir…I…"

"Spit it out, miss."

"Well…I think he may be our murderer."

Lynn watched Jenkins continue to stare at her with no change in expression. Lynn met his gaze toe-to-toe because she wanted him to know of her conviction. The staring went on for several more very long moments. Then Jenkins abruptly stood and walked across the room to where his putter was leaning against the wall. A single golf ball was beside it. Saying nothing, he picked up the putter and made several practice putts on the area rug. Then he picked up the golf ball and replaced the putter against the wall. He sat down behind the wicker desk again, and held the golf ball between his fingers as he looked back at Lynn.

"Ordinarily, I might throw you out of here for making an accusation like that. But I have too much respect and affection for you not to hear you out," Jenkins said. He continued to stare at Lynn.

He was waiting for Lynn to speak, so she did. "You remember the words 'tar' and 'war' I heard from Lomax on my little boat ride with him?" Lynn said.

Jenkins nodded.

Lynn then told him about Lomax's sister, Judy Hemphill, and their identical West Virginia hillbilly dialects and how Lomax and his henchmen must have been talking about Robert Tyre.

"What do you have, other than that, which links Robert to the murders?"

"Nothing, but—"

"Nothing?"

"Well, not yet, but—"

"Hold on a minute. You're telling me that based on Lomax's saying a word which sounded to you like 'tar,' that you have concluded that Robert Tyre murdered my son-in-law, and some other people as well?"

Lynn was now shaken by doubt. She felt like she had so many times when she was under this man's command—inadequate, unsure. The admiral had a way of doing that. The maddening thing was that he was almost always right.

"Sir, there's more," Lynn said, feeling like a lowly, stuttering ensign.

Jenkins said nothing, just waved his hand, signaling for Lynn to continue.

"I played a card I never have before." And she told him about her phone calls to the Virginia area code. Told him what she had learned about the guns, and that she hoped to learn more about Robert Tyre.

Lynn continued. "My main purpose in coming here to talk to you about this is to warn you in case there is something to it. You might be in danger. And the other reason is to do what we're doing now. To talk it through and try to figure it out."

Jenkins nodded, then said, "Who did you talk to on the inside?"

Lynn told him.

"Not exactly an unimpeachable source," Jenkins said.

Lynn was incredulous. "What did you say?"

"You heard me," Jenkins said. "Our intelligence resources are like movies and popular songs. They ain't what they used to be. Nothing like when you and I were in it. After Iraq, how can you believe anything those people say now?"

"But, Admiral. You and I used to be those people."

"My point exactly. The Church commission crippled the entire intelligence community and it's never recovered. Assets in New Zealand? Jesus, girl, I'll bet we don't have any human intelligence on the ground there at all. I'd take anything you get from our friend with a shaker of salt if I were you."

Lynn could not believe what she was hearing. What was going on here? Why wasn't the admiral with her on this?

"Lynn, I can see why you thought Robert might be somebody to think about. And I really appreciate your concern for my safety. But I can assure you, Robert's been too busy to have *time* to fit in any murders. He's a good man, and I'm sure there's another answer to all this."

Muffy Savage had listened in silence up to this point, but now she spoke. She bore a troubled look. "Daddy, I wish you'd listen to Lynn. There's just something about Robert that's always bothered me."

"Oh? What's that, darlin'?" Jenkins said.

"I don't know, he's just..."

"Female intuition?" Jenkins asked.

"Yes, I suppose you could call it that."

Jenkins turned to face his daughter who was in a rattan chair a few paces from Lynn's love seat. "Honey, I have the utmost respect for women's intuition, but I have to tell you that I never used it when I was serving my country."

"Well, what if told you something that wasn't intuition?" Muffy said.

Lynn and the admiral both perked up.

"And what would that be, honey?" Jenkins asked gently.

She looked down at her lap where her hands were engaged in a wrestling match with each other. "Well, I..."

"Go ahead, Muffy," Jenkins said, this time not so gently.

"I feel terrible about this...but, I was sort of looking in Robert's briefcase the other day."

"What? Muffy, how could you?" her father said.

"He left it open on the kitchen table for a few minutes. I wasn't snooping, I just glanced at it, but I couldn't help but see this plane ticket. Daddy, it was from Air New Zealand."

SIXTY-SEVEN

THE WORDS "AIR NEW ZEALAND" rolled gently off Muffy Savage's tongue, but they landed in the room like a pallet of concrete blocks falling off a forklift truck. Lynn suddenly felt like she'd had a transfusion. She said nothing, just looked at the admiral with anticipation. So did Muffy.

Jenkins looked back and forth between the two of them, seeming to realize that they both expected him to say something.

"So you both have it figured that an Air New Zealand plane ticket makes Robert the murderer, eh? Muffy, you shouldn't have been looking in someone else's briefcase, but I must compliment you on your powers of observation. Now as far as Robert and Air New Zealand are concerned, I was aware that he had a New Zealand trip planned."

"You were?" Muffy asked, a little wide-eyed.

"Of course I was," the admiral said. "He's been invited down there to fly-fish for those big ol' brown trout they have. Wanted me to go, too, but I told him one of us needs to be a little closer to home with all these acquisitions we've got cooking. That make you feel better, honey?"

"I suppose so," Muffy said, looking at her hands again. "There's still something about him..."

Lynn suddenly felt as if she were trying to swim in a lap pool filled with molasses. She hadn't the strength to move any muscle in her body. She wasn't sure if she could talk. Tyre *had* to be somehow dirty. But everything that came up in support of that notion was summarily blown away by the admiral like a laggard duck being plugged by a blind full of hunters. This was not going as she had planned or expected. She didn't know what to do or say next. She wished her phone call would come.

In pursuit of a little time to think, and to provide some more stimulus, she asked Muffy for more coffee.

At the very moment Muffy placed a fresh mug in her hand, the phone rang. She answered. "It's for you," she said, looking at Lynn.

Lynn's emotional roller coaster hit bottom and began to soar again. Could this be the call? It must be. Lynn was still sitting on the love seat and Muffy handed her the portable phone. The admiral was still behind the wicker desk, looking at her.

"Lynn Woo," she said into the handset.

It was the voice. "Can you talk?"

"I thought you could only call me on my phone."

"Your gentleman friend gave me this number. You need to hear this."

"I'm listening," Lynn said.

And she did. All the while looking right at Whitman Jenkins, who now averted his gaze and studied the golf ball he was turning over and over with his fingers.

The voice said, "I don't know who you're with right now, but maybe all you *should* do at the moment is listen. Robert Tyre hasn't been an investment banker in over two years. He did handle a number of acquisitions for Whitman Jenkins, but many of them were losers, and the admiral is broke. His lawyers are currently preparing a bankruptcy filing. But he and Tyre have been working on something. Nobody knows exactly what. Tyre has made multiple trips to New Zealand and the admiral has been tapping a lot of his old contacts to follow the situation on the new gun systems the Pentagon is evaluating. Says he's representing some lobbying interests. Looks like too much smoke for there not to be a fire. I'm trying to get more, but I figured you could use this as soon as I got it. I talked to your gentleman friend and told him to warn you if I couldn't get you. I don't know whether this is good news or bad—probably bad."

Lynn gave her caller the same treatment she had received during their first conversation: she simply broke the connection without saying goodbye. She did it while not taking her eyes off

Whitman Jenkins, who continued to fiddle with the golf ball, seeming to be carefully examining its dimples.

Lynn let the portable phone slide to the cushion of the love seat while she continued to stare at Jenkins. The air in the cottage was pregnant with a pent-up explosive charge which was about to detonate. The silence became elongated as Lynn continued her stare and Jenkins' eyes did not leave the golf ball. Finally, it was broken.

"It's you."

When Lynn said it, she hissed it out through tight, barely open lips, making it scarcely audible. The admiral looked up from the golf ball and his eyes met Lynn's.

"I beg your pardon?" Jenkins said evenly, calmly.

"I said it's you. You and Tyre." The words were quietly and methodically ejected from Lynn's lips, one by one, like tickets from a dispensing machine. At this, Muffy's cupped hand flew to her mouth.

"Lynn, whatever are you talking about? You need to leave this detective stuff to the hired hands and get back to your shelling and diving," Jenkins said.

"I never wanted to leave it. Wouldn't have except for you and Tyre and your gun smuggling—"

"Now just a moment, young lady—"

"Shut up, Admiral! Your gun smuggling with a little friendly murder thrown in. Your son-in-law, my friend, Sammy Osceola. Just kind of a family affair, right? Not to mention a decent man who saved my life." Lynn's voice was rising. "Who are you selling the Brent guns to? Third world dictators? Druggies? The Mafia? Terrorists?"

"You're crazy, woman. I don't need to get involved in some two-bit gunrunning scheme, I've got a large food company to run—"

"You're broke, Admiral, and Robert Tyre hasn't done a deal in over two years. All he's done is travel to New Zealand, and *not* to fly-fish. It's over."

Muffy was sobbing. "Daddy?" she said in a small voice.

Jenkins put the golf ball on the desk and his chest heaved

in a huge sigh. He leaned over and put his hand in his large satchel-style briefcase at his feet by the desk. "Muffy, let me get you something from my briefcase here which will explain everything."

"Stop!" Lynn said.

It was too late. Jenkins' hand emerged from the satchel with a .45 automatic pistol which he pointed directly at Lynn.

SIXTY-EIGHT

"DADDY!" SHRIEKED MUFFY when she saw the gun.

"Muffy," Jenkins said, his voice now unsteady for the first time. "You've got to be with me on this. I'm your father. Now that Millard's gone, you and I have to stick together. I've never needed you more than now."

Muffy buried her face in her hands and continued her sobbing. "Oh, Daddy, how could you?" she said through her weeping.

"How could I, you say?" Jenkins kept the .45 aimed at Lynn. "How could I not? It was all for you, anyway. I couldn't let it all go down the drain after those bastards who bought my daddy's company just up and terminated me like some...employee." He said the word "employee" with an expression that made him look like he smelled something bad. "I had to put together the food-manufacturing conglomerate I'd worked on. I had to save the family name, our fortune. All for you, Muffy. Hell, my life's over anyway. And the company's so close. All we need is the shot in the arm of capital this little gun deal can give us, and we'll be fine. Avoid bankruptcy and everything. You'll see, Muffy. It'll all work out great. I just need your help."

"That's all bullshit, Whit," Lynn said, her deference to the admiral over with. "The truth is you sold the family business and you could have been set for life. But no, when you didn't get along with the buyer, you had to go and gamble the family fortune on some risky roll-up scheme so you could *show 'em*. It was an ego thing—it wasn't saving the family name and fortune. You'd already done that. Then when it didn't work out, it became a game of financial survival. That's when murder became acceptable. Tell it like it really is!"

"Don't let her talk to me that way, Muffy, I'm your father," he said, looking at Muffy but still keeping the gun pointed at Lynn.

Muffy's head was still buried in her hands.

"So how did you get in the gun business?" Lynn said. "Robert Tyre couldn't find any more peanut-butter companies to buy?"

"Most of the companies Robert found for us to acquire turned out to be duds. And the good ones, well, we couldn't seem to properly integrate them into our business. Things went from bad to worse. We ran out of cash. Then, through one of his old contacts in the Pentagon, Robert heard about the Brent and how they were about to fold because they were out of money and didn't have anybody to ship to. It took me a while to come to grips with the fact that terrorists and criminals might have this gun. But I finally decided that since they'd get them from somebody else anyway, it may as well be us, and I may as well save my company with the money we'd make.

"Robert found Dearl Lomax and set everything up. Robert did all the work, really, including the trips to New Zealand to meet with Brent Ashcroft. He was in it for the fee I'm supposed to pay him. A big one, I might add.

"The one thing we never dreamed we'd get involved in was…Millard…and…" He choked up. "I still can't believe he stumbled onto Lomax and his crew building that warehouse out in the back bay. Muffy, I'm so sorry…"

Jenkins let out a few sobs of his own as his emotions merged with the reality of his responsibility for his son-in-law's murder. Sagging in grief, he held his non-gun hand to his eyes and momentarily lowered the gun. Lynn moved instantly toward him, but Jenkins sensed it, straightened, and pointed the gun at Lynn again. Lynn sat back down.

"As bad as I feel about what happened, the worst one will be you, Lynn. I always thought of you as another daughter. I tried to stop this. You saw me signaling to you at the marina not to get on that boat with Lomax. But now you've given me no choice." He put his other hand on the gun and began to aim it at Lynn's head.

Muffy suddenly screamed, jumped from her chair and threw herself in front of Lynn, half sitting on her lap.

"So what did you always think of *me* as, Daddy? Why don't you tell me now, because you'll have to kill me first. May as well, then things would be neat as a pin, right? No witnesses, nobody to rat on you."

"Get out of the way, Muffy!" Jenkins yelled.

"No! Put down the gun, Daddy!" she yelled back.

Jenkins cocked the automatic and put both hands on the stock again, taking aim. It had never occurred to Lynn until this moment that her former commanding officer would shoot anybody, much less her *and* his own daughter. Her mouth went dusty dry. She didn't know for certain whether the gun was aimed at her head or Muffy's—they were so close together. Her mind started to try to assess options and she couldn't think of even one. Got to do something. Can't just sit here and let this man shoot us.

Just then Lynn's peripheral vision picked up something. Something near the kitchen. Then she realized it was a figure which had slid seamlessly into the room in total silence. It was a familiar figure, tall and slim. It held what appeared to be a small .22 pistol. Johnnie Osceola quickly and efficiently shot Whitman Jenkins three times in the forehead, causing him to slump over in instant death, the .45 automatic dropping to his lap.

Muffy screamed an agonizing scream. Lynn looked back at Johnnie. The .22 had disappeared and she now held the biggest, longest knife Lynn had ever seen. Johnnie was a blur as she moved to Jenkins' body and was instantly on top of him with the knife. Lynn realized with horror that she was about to witness a scalping. Muffy continued to scream as Lynn reacted. She threw Muffy off her lap, sprang to her feet, and pulled Johnnie off the dead Jenkins only to find the point of the huge knife resting against her own throat. Their eyes were inches apart, and Lynn was chilled with terror by what she saw in Johnnie's. They were blacker than usual, and burning with a primal rage. She'd seen it in men and had to deal with it, but never in another woman. And this was a woman, no girl.

"He killed my father, Lynn," she hissed. "The only way you can keep me from my rightful destiny is to give up your own life."

Lynn tried not to gulp but she did anyway. She did not doubt her for a moment. "Johnnie," she said, "if you stop now, you can save your own life, and stay out of prison."

The black eyes bored into her, not changing.

She tried again. "Your dad would not want you to do this," Lynn managed to choke out.

She snarled. "My dad was a nice man. But he was too nice. He was more like a white man than a real Indian. Your choice, *Miz* Woo. I need your answer."

More long moments of intense contact with those hard black eyes. What was she going to do, actually let her scalp Jenkins right in front of his daughter? But she had no doubt that Johnnie would run her through with the knife.

For the second time within a few moments, there was a startling surprise. A deafening explosion rocked the cottage. The three people still alive started to hit the deck. Lynn's immediate thought was of a bomb. Then she looked up and saw the front door had been taken out, glass panes splintering, and that Truck Kershaw was barreling into the room, service revolver drawn. Rolf was right behind him.

"Drop the knife, miss, it's over!" yelled Truck, his gun aimed at Johnnie, held by both of his baseball-mitt-sized hands.

The tense air could have been cut with Johnnie's big knife in the long moments that followed. Johnnie spent those long moments looking back and forth between Truck and Lynn, waging a moral battle influenced by her perception of centuries of culture. Her knife hand trembled.

"Johnnie," Lynn said gently. "Drop the knife. Your father's killer is dead and you killed him. I'm sure we can keep you out of prison because you saved Muffy and me."

The trembling intensified as she came to her decision. She dropped the knife and collapsed into sobs. Lynn held her, and Rolf went to Muffy and did the same.

SIXTY-NINE

WHEN ROLF HAD FIELDED the call from Lynn's contact with the information about Robert Tyre and the admiral, he immediately tracked down Truck Kershaw. He had sensed from what the voice on the phone had said, and the way it was said, that some kind of trouble was in store.

At the cottage, yellow tape was everywhere as were crime scene personnel, including the white-necktied Lieutenant Symanski. Lynn, Rolf, Muffy, and Johnnie all gave their statements. There were other details, too, like packing some things for Muffy to stay at Lynn's since she was not permitted to spend the night at the crime scene. Not that she'd ever want to spend another night in that cottage. Muffy was, of course, the biggest loser. Her husband, her father. Lynn knew she and Rolf would have to pitch in trying to help Muffy rebuild her life. Rolf thought Muffy had real talent as a painter. Maybe that would be her salvation.

In her statement, Lynn told about the guns, but not how she knew, attributing the knowledge to an anonymous tip from someone identifying himself as an old Navy buddy. Symanski was waiting for the feds to arrive.

Lynn was able to get Jack Espinosa on the phone and apologize to him. She also told him she was sure his days of being stalked were over. Lynn made a mental note to tell the manager at Boatmen's to pick up a nice dinner tab for Espinosa and put it on the *Boca Broke* account.

Symanski gave the order to pick up Dearl Lomax. But there was one detail to resolve. Truck Kershaw beckoned for Lynn and Symanski and, in a huddle outside the cottage, they agreed on a plan.

THE CAUSEWAY WHICH LINKS Boca Grande and Gasparilla Island to the mainland has a toll booth staffed 24/7 to collect the four dollars it costs to get on the island. Night had fallen by the time the rented white Lincoln pulled into the toll booth, its driver fumbling for the ones.

Robert Tyre reached through the rolled-down window of the Lincoln to hand the money over. He didn't look at the attendant he was giving the money to because he was trying to refasten his seatbelt. When the attendant took the money and said "Thank you, sir," Tyre jerked his head around in obvious horror to look straight at the source of the words. He saw Lynn Woo staring at him.

Tyre looked straight ahead and saw a sheriff's cruiser had pulled in front of him, blocking his path to the bridge. This had happened on a signal from Lynn, the only person on the island, other than Rolf and Muffy, who could have immediately identified Robert Tyre. Tyre slammed the Lincoln in reverse, quickly rotating his head only to see that another cruiser had boxed him in from the rear. Tyre glanced back at Lynn who was standing in the toll booth, casually leaning against a counter with arms folded in front of her, coldly staring back at him.

Tyre threw open the car door, jumped out, and started running. He saw other sheriff cruisers on the road leading back to the mainland, so he headed through some sea grapes and began sprinting down a path leading away from the toll booth. The path was lined with exquisite pink bougainvillea. Not well trimmed, its blossoms invaded the path and its jaggy thorns scraped at Tyre's white dress shirt as he ran. The path made a sharp right turn after about thirty yards, and, at full sprint, Tyre made an Emmitt Smith–like cut around the corner and accelerated. A mistake. Abruptly, his face became aware of the path's abrasive, oyster-shell surface. But he couldn't move his face because it was being mashed against the path by Truck Kershaw's boot. He could, however, see the shell becoming two-tone as blood seeped from his mouth. The forearm shiver Truck Kershaw delivered while Tyre was at full sprint would have made anybody's football highlight film.

AFTER ROBERT TYRE'S ARREST, Lynn went back to the cottage. Johnnie was still there, and when Symanski was through with her, Lynn walked her back to her room at the Lodge across the street. She only went as far as the lobby of the grand old place and stopped to say goodbye. She looked directly at Johnnie.

"So what's next for you?" Lynn asked.

She shrugged. "Finish school, I guess."

"What about becoming a Seminole warrior?"

She shook her head. "At this point I've kind of been there, done that."

"Understand. Hey, got to ask you. What's the answer?"

"What's the question?" she said.

"Would you have?"

"Would I have what?"

"You know what I'm talking about," Lynn said.

"Killed you? I don't think so."

"Why not?"

She looked at her moccasins for a moment and when she looked up, her mouth curled in a saucy smirk. "Because I still think you're kind of hot, *Miz* Woo."

In spite of herself, a broad grin spread over Lynn's face. "Have a good life, *Miz* Osceola."